2050

ATLANTICA

Pittsburgh

Nuevo York

Fallingwater

Washington

COLUMBIA

2050

A novel by

Dave Borland

RED ANVIL PRESS

OAKLAND, OREGON

This is a work of fiction. Any resemblance of the characters to persons living or
dead is purely coincidental.

RED ANVIL PRESS
1393 Old Homestead Drive, Second floor
Oakland, Oregon 97462—9506.
E MAIL: editor@elderberrypress. com
TEL/FAX: 541. 459. 6043
www. elderberrypress. com

RED ANVIL books are available from your favorite bookstore, amazon. com,
or from our 24 hour order line: 1. 800. 431. 1579

Library of Congress Control Number: 2007927091
Publisher's Catalog—in—Publication Data
2050 / Dave Borland
ISBN-13: 978-1-932762-72-3
ISBN-10: 1932762728
1. Science—Fiction.
2. Futuristic—Fiction.
3. Speculative—Fiction.
4. Politics—Fiction.
5. America—Fiction.
I. Title

This book was written, printed and bound in the United States of America.

DEDICATED TO:

My wife Charlotte and our family for their love, patience and support,

ACKNOWLEGEMENTS:

David St. John, my publisher for his faith in my creation and the advice and guidance he provided me over the past year. Also to Raven OKeefe for her creativity in designing the cover and to Jenny Magar for her excellent editing. Also I want to thank my friends, Walter Barker, Deborah Haase and Louise Riley for reading and commenting on my manuscript and to Abby Dalton for her initial editing assistance.

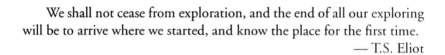

We shall not cease from exploration, and the end of all our exploring will be to arrive where we started, and know the place for the first time.

— T.S. Eliot

prologue

n the late 20th Century, unprecedented immigration changed completely the cultural foundations of the United States. As new majorities took over, a counter migration began as Americans moved back to ancestral countries. By 2038 the country had a new demographic makeup, which caused Congress to empower a Constitutional Convention to decide the future composition of the country. Some states chose annexation into Canada, Mexico, or Caribe, while others combined into new countries. In 2040 the United States was dissolved by Congress.

Another event of the time was climate change that caused most of the United States to be draught stricken except the Northern Appalachians where the United States constructed a huge artificial aquifer. By 2050, Atlantica, a new country, controlled the aquifer and unexpectedly decided to use this water resource to gain concessions from its neighboring countries. This act violated UN mandates and threatened hemispheric peace.

This is the scenario for Kurt Sloan, who decides to escape Atlantica by hiking a long-forgotten trail. His journey, filled with unexpected events and people, is woven with these natural and human changes in the world of 2050.

chapter one

is mind was made up. He was leaving tonight. Kurt Sloan now knew how he would get to the small village of his ancestors in Scotland. Up to this point, the problem had been the execution of his plan. The time that he'd spent delving into the Sloan family history had ironically provided him the ways and means to leave his beloved homeland in the year 2050.

Kurt worked for the government of Alleghenia, which was the western-most state in the new country of Atlantica. His job site was in the Castro Library in the University Center section of Pittsburgh. As he thought of his station at work, he chuckled to himself. Most of his associates were either Latino or Africano, and the joke was that he was the token Anglo. In truth, he was. Kurt graduated from the University of Pittsburgh receiving both a master's and doctorate in Historical Research prior to the fall of the U.S. Kurt had then been hired by Alleghenia to work as a historical research associate for Dr. William Alexander. As the years went on, even with constant assurances by Dr. Alexander that conditions for Anglos would improve, Kurt realized he did not fit in with the new country. Kurt was an outsider in his homeland, and his condition had become intolerable. After toying with the idea for months, he made up his mind to leave Alleghenia and go to Scotland. This had been a strange time in his life, and he thought about how things had finally worked out.

For an Anglo in an administration job it was extremely difficult to get a visa. Security was tight and he would never be permitted to take any data with him, family history or not. He had decided to handle the problem of leaving after he found all the information he needed.

Kurt lived a quiet social life. In the past year he spent much of his off time in the basement of the library, where the historical records of the defunct Carnegie Library were kept. On his off-days he searched for Sloan family records. He found numerous references to his family in the archives.

Recently he concentrated on searching for data concerning the Pittsburgh Aquifer System, where his father had been chief project engineer. He wanted this to be part of the Sloan history that he took with him. He could locate nothing definitive, just newspaper articles on the building of the Aquifer, until two weekends ago, when not only did he find data on the Aquifer, but the solution of how he was going to leave Atlantica.

Late on that Saturday, while continuing his research at the library, he took a break and began walking through the dark halls. He noticed a sign over one of the rooms that said PLANNING DEPARTMENT. This meant nothing to him, however it aroused his interest. He entered and switched on the light which exposed a room full of metal cabinets. He browsed around and noticed one of the cabinets had a nameplate that read, PLANNING SCHEMATICS, PITTSBURGH AQUIFER SYSTEM, 2022-2042. He was overwhelmed with his discovery.

He decided to scan all the materials into his datafile, not spending any time to digest the contents. He was concerned Security monitoring would pick up his heat imprint or notice the download activity. The next day he returned to the library and his good fortune continued. While returning files to the archive room he saw, propped up against the corner wall, a very colorful advertisement which he had never noticed before. It read, THE GREAT ALLEGHENY PASSAGE GRAND OPENING, MAY 1, 2008. He looked closely at the smaller print. It described the opening of a new trail that would go from Pittsburgh to Washington, DC. He remembered another cabinet he had seen that was labeled ALLEGHENY PASSAGE. He found it along a side wall. Kurt opened the top drawer and discovered maps and mileage descriptions of the trail through the Allegheny and Laurel mountains into the Potomac River valley of Maryland. Its final destination was still Washington; however, this was now the capital of the new country of Columbia. He could not believe what he was looking at.

His plan would be to leave as soon as possible. He knew once he left, Security would become aware of his absence. At that point they would download his work and personal data activity looking for clues as to why he left and where he was going. Normal travel routes would be impossible for him to use. The trail was his escape route and the Aquifer data that he previously retrieved could possibly be used to barter in Columbia for passage to Europe. He was aware that Columbia had been trying, unsuccessfully, to gain water access from Atlantica when the Aquifer opened early next year. Kurt would begin his hike on the old trail to Columbia. He thought of the journey ahead and the irony that the trail, opened in 2008, designed to go from Pittsburgh to Washington, DC, would be his escape route in the year 2050. He knew his decision was dangerous, but absolutely necessary for him to achieve his goal of freedom.

Kurt was leaving the library for the last time. He walked

down the wide, marbled steps rolling in his hand the silver capsule that contained his family history and the Aquifer data. He hoped that its contents would be sufficient to convince Columbian authorities to grant him air passage. He hadn't studied the data in detail, but one thing struck him as he remembered his first sighting of the documents. On the last page was his father's signature as chief engineer and the notation that "This System Is For All The People of Our Hemisphere."

The underground water system had been built by the United States government with the capacity to collect, deliver, and recycle water to most of the landmass of the United States. Because of a combination of factors: global warming, solar activities, and natural hemispheric changes in wind currents, the precipitation zones in North America had drastically changed over the last fifty years. Beginning early in the century, the Northern Appalachian mountains began to unexpectedly receive more precipitation than any other region in the Northern Hemisphere. The United States recognized this drastic change. Concurrently other areas of the country were becoming drought ridden. A massive project to create the world's largest man-made aquifer system was designed and construction began in 2022. This system would capture and retain water from the various rivers and streams in the Appalachian area; six new retention lakes would be developed; a huge underground storage capacity would be constructed combining newly discovered caverns and lined abandoned coal mines; and a reverse conduit system would return water to be recycled. It was the largest government project in world history. It was close to being completed when the United States ceased to exist and the country of Atlantica, within whose borders the Aquifer System was located, gained control of this state-of-the-art system.

Leaving the library, he looked across the empty street and could make out against the fading light, the ghostly outline of the gothic Cathedral of Learning, once the centerpiece of the University of Pittsburgh. It looked like a forty-four-story castle in the sky. Kurt knew the story of its building and that funding was assisted with pennies donated by the children of Pittsburgh over one hundred twenty years ago. Tonight, it rose straight into the darkness. To Kurt it looked as if it came from the days of medieval England, instead of the days of the First Depression Era in the United States. A few lights were sprinkled about its base, but from there, all the way to the top, it was dark. He recalled as a young boy how the building would be a blaze in white light. In recent years, it had sadly reminded him of an abandoned cathedral in disrepair.

Five years ago, the Alleghenia Administration moved the University System to a new campus along the Monongahela River. Most of the buildings in this area were now government facilities like the library where he worked. The cathedral remained, too huge to move and too beautiful to destroy. To the old-timers that remained it was a symbol of a city and an area that had created the industrial power of the defunct United States. The Administration had decided to use the cathedral as a repository for its records. Kurt was saddened by that news, but at least the cathedral would remain standing, as it had for so much of the history of this area. Its darkened shadow was next to the other ominous-looking structure in the old school campus, the Heinz Chapel.

The beautiful chapel seen this cool evening gave Kurt chills, as he remembered meditative visits where he sat amongst its magnificent stained glass windows. In some ways, the chapel symbolized what had become of Kurt's state of mind. What had been, was no more.

Kurt turned away from the cathedral and Heinz Chapel

and began walking briskly toward Panther Hollow. He passed in front of another relic of a long-ago time, the shuttered Frick Museum. This area was where he had matured and learned about the world. Now, as he was leaving, it sadly seemed just a collection of antiquated buildings.

The walk was depressing, especially since it was probably the last time he would be on this sidewalk he knew so well. Shortly, he reached the weathered Panther Hollow Bridge, which now only had two walking lanes, vehicular traffic having been banned for the last few years. He picked up his pace, letting his long legs stretch free from their daily confinement in his office space.

He was born and raised in a secure old Scotch-Irish Pittsburgh family. Even as a child he had an avid curiosity as to how things worked. Early on, it was puzzles. Later in school, it was geometry; then engineering; then physics; and finally, any type operational system. Oddly with all his mathematical and logical interests, his first love became history, concentrating especially on how political and social systems developed. This passionate interest evolved into his professional work, now with the Historical Commission of Atlantica. The position gave him the authority to do personal research, which was, ironically, what enabled him to recently do his family research.

The history of his native homeland became his passion. As a young man, he was an idealist and sympathetic to the demands of the new influx of Latino immigrants that had begun early in the century. Slowly, then in a tidal wave, the Latino culture began to dominate many parts of the United States, including this area. When the U.S. was dismantled and Atlantica formed, the reality of the new culture gradually began to overwhelm him. By that time, a great majority of U.S. citizens had either emigrated overseas or to one of the new countries. The emigration decisions made by citizens during this time were primarily based on their cultural, religious, and ethnic similarities.

Kurt stayed on, but increasingly it became more difficult for him. He had to learn Spanish as a work requirement because it was the language of government and business. Few people spoke English. Six months ago, life became worse. The Administration tightened travel for Anglos who worked in sensitive positions. For reasons he could not understand, his position was included in this classification. From that point, Kurt experienced a confinement he hadn't felt before and realized he could no longer remain.

Kurt looked ahead. The bridge was empty, except for a light fog coming up from the valley below.

chapter two

urt began to work for the new government
after the breakup of the U.S. in 2040. He had graduated from
his master's program and written his thesis: "Two American
Revolutions." It compared the time of the 1770s to the 2030s
and the forces that created both the beginning and end of
the United States. The work was extremely well received by
academia in Atlantica.

He was approached by Atlantica to work in their new
Historical Review Commission. The work was recognized in
Paris by the UN who was actively attempting to coordinate the
collection of historical records of the U.S. Actually he found
out afterward that it was the pressure from the UN Historical
Commission and Dr. William Alexander that almost forced
Atlantica to offer him the position. At first he refused to
consider the new country's work offer, thinking he may go
to Europe like most of his friends had done. Some associates
with whom he had become close while at the University of
Pittsburgh and who were advocates of the new country urged
him to sign on with Atlantica. It was the "wave of the future,"
as one of them had said to him. This plus his idealism and
the practicality of working in historical research about his
homeland convinced him to accept the offer. So he joined

the Historical Commission and began his work with Dr. Alexander. Kurt found out in his first year working with the commission, Anglo history was not a priority with Atlantica.

Kurt lived sparsely with only the basic necessities. He kept his prized personal possessions secure in his leather carrying case, which he had with him at all times. It was a sense of everything being temporary that Kurt felt. He remembered his father always had their most vital records and a set of emergency equipment, rations, and tools available in the cellar of their home. He said to Kurt that you should always have an emergency plan in place in case of any disaster, natural or man-made. He never forgot this, and the leather case contained his personal items, including his datafile with his complete ID required by all governments and the UN.

Citizen IDs contained DNA, photos, voice scans, and a life profile. He also had a few personal keepsakes such as a gold piece from his mother and personal discs with long-ago special events spent with his family, including several video scans with his father before he died. Also, in his leather portfolio was his hand-written history of the times in which he was living. He began this project when he started working with Dr. Alexander. The work picked up from where his master's treatise left off.

His parents always said his mind was his strongest personal possession. They constantly kidded him about living in his own world because so many times when they were talking to him, he seemed to be somewhere else. His mind was always working on some new idea which he would write into his notebook. He preferred the old-fashioned way of recording: writing. It always felt more direct from brain to paper. Eventually, his thoughts, ideas, and life experiences were written in his portfolio.

On the bridge, Kurt felt cool air hit his face as the temperature dipped unseasonably low. He would need to dress warmer tonight when he began his journey. He stopped as he approached the center of the bridge. There were only two low-density light scans at either end, and at the center it was dark. He thought of the old movies of London as he looked ahead through the foggy scene.

Kurt walked to the railing and looked down through the floating light at the abandoned roof of the skating arena, which had been built after the turn of the century. Beside the darkened arena were the yellow rail lights of the Tram system. According to an article he read in the defunct Pittsburgh Post-Gazette, this was the most heavily used line of the old mono-rail system. That system went about thirty miles in six directions from the Golden Triangle, the center of the city. Now there were three Tram lines which intersected in Center City where the three rivers met.

Kurt was suddenly aware of the sound of shuffling feet. He looked through the mist and could see a man walking toward him. He leaned over the bridge once again, as if unconcerned, then turned and began to walk toward the man. The shape ahead came into view as they both reached the center of the bridge. He was a large man with sloping shoulders. Kurt could hear his heavy breathing, as if the man was having physical problems. "Who are you, Mister?" came a deep, gruff voice.

"A worker, that's all," Kurt replied softly.

"Where are you from?"

"Greenfield," Kurt quickly answered. "Why do you ask?"

"I'm just checking. Couple hooligans ran this way after trying to ransack a house over by the old CMU campus. The System picked them up, but they must have sensed the signal. Anyway I'm looking for them. Got ID?" he groused.

Kurt reached into his datafile, pulled out his ID card, and gave it to the man. He looked at the picture, read the description, looked at Kurt, and then gave it back to him.

"Looks okay. Have you seen anybody in a hurry on the bridge?"

"Nobody, haven't seen a soul since I left work." He waited for a response. The man looked at him and didn't say anything.

"Can I pass?" Kurt said quietly, trying not to rekindle any anxiety in the stranger.

"Sure, get on with yah. I see a couple more coming across up ahead there. I'll find those bastards."

Kurt walked passed the man. He was a Publican, whose duties were like the beat patrolmen of many years ago. Most of them were Anglo ex-policeman from the U.S. time. Even though most of the Anglo population had left the area, some older workers with basic skills remained and were hired by the new government. As Kurt passed the man, he could make out the uniform he was wearing. It was blue with several red diamond-shaped patches signifying External Security. This force had been highly successful in keeping the streets and businesses safe in the major cities of Atlantica, especially Pittsburgh.

"Keep your eyes open for those hooligans," he called back to him. Kurt picked up his pace as he crossed to the end of the bridge and headed toward his boarding house.

Kurt pounded up the narrow street with little light coming from antiquated solar street lamps. He knew this street brick by brick. As he reflected about his past and his upcoming departure, he thought of his best friend Raoul and Dr. Alexander, his mentor and supervisor. He blurted out, "My God, Raoul and Dr. Alexander. I haven't told them. Raoul will understand my leaving, but Dr. Alexander will not. I have to say my goodbyes to them. They're the only two people I have to see," he continued.

Dr. Alexander, his eighty-year-old Anglo mentor, taught Kurt everything there was to know about historical research. Dr. Alexander was his boss, and Kurt knew he would be upset at his leaving. He was a fascinating man, who had fought in the Terror Wars of 1991 and 2003 in Iraq. As a professor at NYU in New York, he was almost killed in the 9/11 Terror Attack of 2001 in lower Manhattan. It changed his life. He reenlisted at age thirty-three after 9/11 and went back to Iraq where he was wounded. After returning, he resumed his teaching career and was still going strong at eighty. He had been a patriot of the U.S. and as a teacher believed in the yearnings throughout history of the human struggle for freedom. As he mellowed, he believed strongly that negotiation and compromise were preferred over the killing of innocents for any reason by anyone. Dr. Alexander's wife was dead, and his only daughter had left for England years ago with his grandchildren. It was shortly after his wife died that he hired Kurt as his research assistant. In the ensuing years they had become close, both in their work pursuits and as friends. In the workplace, the doctor researched historical events and their meaning, while Kurt supported him, especially in the data and analysis work.

Dr. Alexander was the only Anglo to head a department for the Administration. He was a world-renowned historian and had been recommended for the position by the United Nations. His primary focus was to create a historical database on the new country and to develop a preservation program for the area's history. This is the section where Kurt worked which allowed him to work late and on weekends without any apparent increased Security monitoring. Kurt realized that telling Dr. Alexander would be difficult, and he would probably not want him to go. He had already said it on many occasions.

Raoul was a different story, knowing him he might

want to throw a party. Raoul Lopez-Hernandez was a "life-liver," as Kurt always called him. Raoul came from a humble background in Puerto Rico. He came to Pittsburgh and was hired by Atlantica because he was a Latino with strong satellite communications skills. That was a positive aspect of the revolution when it elevated a man of Raoul's caliber to a top-level position. Kurt understood and appreciated Raoul getting this major professional break because he deserved all he ever received.

Raoul, his wife Luisa, and his youngest sister, Carla, lived in Squirrel Hill, not far from Kurt's boardinghouse. Dr. Alexander lived on top of Browns Hill Road, also a short distance from his house. Kurt would be able to stop by their homes before he began his journey. Raoul's other sister, Maria, with whom Kurt had an intense romantic relationship last year, was now pursuing her career in France. Maria had been a highlight of his last years in Pittsburgh, but was a woman on a mission that did not include Kurt. His friendship with Raoul had endured, and their relationship had actually become stronger. Raoul's basic decency, honesty, and great sense of humor, endeared him to Kurt. For some reason, even coming from completely different backgrounds, they had hit it off. Not to have that friendship would be painful.

Ironically, Kurt felt as strong in his bond with Dr. Alexander, who had become not only a father figure, but a life figure, someone whose life and ethics he wanted to emulate. To be as vital as Dr. Alexander at his age was what Kurt wanted with his own life at any age. It was going to be tough not to have these two men in his life in the years ahead.

Kurt's mind wandered from Raoul and Dr. Alexander to a sudden tightness in his gut. He wondered if he was doing the right thing by leaving his home and this country. A smile spread slowly across his face as he realized how various levels of one's thinking converged creating difficult choices for how one was to lead their life. He was confident of his decision to leave and how he was going to do it. It was rational, realistic, and probably more dangerous than he had anticipated.

Suddenly, light blossomed brilliantly as the full moon was freed from a quickly moving dark cloud mass overhead, a reminder to Kurt that no matter what humans do on this earth, nature just keeps rolling along. "Well, old man," as he looked at the outline of the same face he imagined he'd seen on the moon since he was a small boy, "I know I'll see you no matter where I go." He would be in his room in a few minutes, and he walked even faster through the now dead black night as the skittish moon disappeared once more.

chapter three

Kurt reached the bottom of the hill and looked up at the boardinghouse that sat astride a bluff above a curve in the Monongahela River. He knew the history of the house. It had been owned by the Bolena family, who had gone back to Bari, Italy, where the family had come from in the 1880s. They had deserted it seven years earlier. Last year Kurt found a few pictures of family members in a small attic room. Faces of great-grandfathers taken in Italy, then grandfathers, fathers, and their grandsons. The whole family was gone now, either dead or back in the old country. The house was now owned by the Administration, who docked Kurt's pay each month to cover his rent and power charges.

Kurt entered the house walking over the creaking wooden front porch and sliding his card into the security lock. He climbed the stairs and at the landing listened to hear for the only other person living in the house, Martin McDonald from Jamaica, a student at the university. McDonald told Kurt his objective was to get to Paris and earn a master's degree in Material Delivery Systems. In the past ten years, Paris had become the educational center of the world. "Special Graduates" sponsored by their countries went to the World Specialist Centers for Master's Degrees. Paris had become in many respects, the world's de facto capital. Kurt realized that

McDonald must be both extremely bright and ambitious. Kurt had found out that McDonald was also a superpatriot of Atlantica.

Kurt continued up the stairs, walked down the hall past Martin McDonald's room, which was quiet and dark. Kurt quickly entered his room and plopped down on his mattress. He was tired and immediately began to think about his neighbor as he lay there with his eyes closed. During the time Martin and Kurt had shared the weathered frame house they seldom saw each other. Whenever they did, it was usually Martin who did all the talking. He would ramble on incessantly to Kurt about how he wanted to work for "his new country," as he put it, in trade and delivery methods. His goal was to specialize in material deliveries to poor countries in the world. After a few conversations, he began to throw jibes at Kurt for being part of the old, "slave way," a phrase he always managed to slip into the conversation.

Ironically, last night, Kurt had learned much more about Martin McDonald. McDonald had knocked on Kurt's door, shortly after he had returned to his room from work. "Got a minute, Sloan?" he had asked. Kurt opened the door and waved him in. McDonald sat down on the low bench in front of the window. They just stared at each other for a minute. Kurt began to unload his personal items on to his dresser. Finally he turned and asked McDonald what he wanted. The floodgates opened as McDonald went on about the future of Atlantica. How it was so unique in the world and that no doubt remnants of the old culture, referring to Anglos, would do all they could to undermine the country. He went on a preaching tirade that loyalty to the country was above all, the most important value anyone should have. He railed about the past and the greatness of the future. He bragged about his upcoming appointment in Paris. McDonald then switched gears and began talking about how Kurt had an important job with the Administration and he should be proud that they had given him such a position. He mentioned specifically the Historical Commission and the research work he was doing with Director Alexander. This shocked Kurt as to how much McDonald knew about his responsibilities. But McDonald changed subjects again, when he asked Kurt why he was still here in Pittsburgh.

Before he could answer, McDonald again changed subjects by telling Kurt that he had informed the authorities that their house could be torn down because there would only be one tenant when he left for Paris. McDonald explained the housing law required rental houses over hundred years be demolished unless they had a minimum of two residents.

Kurt sat there seething that this man would have taken such action without first advising him. He couldn't figure out why. McDonald lightened up as if trying to help Kurt by adding that there were many great old houses across the valley in Squirrel Hill. He suggested that Kurt move to one of those tenement facilities. Kurt remained silent, but his anger was building inside. A man he hardly knew was telling him where to live? Kurt remembered thinking that this strange man was irrational. He knew McDonald was a fiery patriot of Atlantica's cause, but Kurt couldn't figure out why in the hell McDonald seemed to be so interested in him.

Kurt finally answered by saying that if in fact they decided to tear down the house, he would find a place. His patience had run out, and he slowly asked McDonald why he hadn't told him earlier? But before McDonald could answer, Kurt asked him point blank why he was so interested in him. Kurt saw a half smile creep into McDonald's tanned face. McDonald mumbled something about how every citizen must always be alert at their workplace and home for anything, or anyone, not following the country's guidelines. "We all must look out for the best interests of the community first, then the country," Kurt remembered him saying. Then he had added, "We must follow the 'new rules,'" as he put it.

Kurt had sized up this young, dark, narrow-faced man. He barely knew him. For a few moments, nothing was said, as they both just sat looking at each other. Then McDonald again changed topics and attitude. His face grimaced, the sly smile returned to his face, and he became openly hostile to Kurt. He repeated his earlier comment as to why an Anglo would still be here. "You don't seem to have any friends here, so why remain in this new country?" he asked. He then went one step further as if to goad Kurt by directly questioning Kurt's loyalty to the new country, referring to Kurt as a WASP, which was an even more derogatory slam than the usual Anglo.

At that point, Kurt waved his hand at McDonald and shouted at McDonald, saying that he needed to watch what he was saying and he should get out of his room. As McDonald got up, Kurt sarcastically reminded him of the new constitution, which forbids ethnic slurs like "WASP."

This brought the half smile again to his face. In the back of Kurt's mind was the incredulity that this man was almost reading his mind, especially since he had in his possession the data that would allow him to leave. It was as if McDonald knew what Kurt was going to do. McDonald's most provocative and insightful comment was a short sentence. After Kurt had countered with his racial slur rebuttal, McDonald said, "But remember, anyone in a sensitive job just can't leave, you do know that, don't you?"

Kurt hadn't answered McDonald; Kurt just stared at this man who stood looking at him with piercing eyes. Kurt finally said he was going to bed and McDonald had to leave. Without saying another word, McDonald went to the door. For a few seconds he just stared down at Kurt and then got in a parting shot. "No one," he said, "had better be disloyal to Atlantica." With that, he slammed shut the paneled wooden door. Kurt sat stunned on his bed, feeling the contempt and hatred still permeating from the absent young black man from the islands of the Caribbean.

As Kurt lay there he thought about the past month. How he had found items disturbed in his room when he came back from work. Several times Martin had been at Kurt's door, once as if Martin had just come out of Kurt's room. When he had asked Martin what he was doing at his door, Martin had made a snide comment that he was looking for his cat which they both knew was a lie because there was no cat in the house. From that day on Kurt kept his room secured. He could never figure out why Martin, this guy he hardly knew, would pay so much attention to him.

The whole business of Martin prying into Kurt's business first started a few months earlier when they were talking in the kitchen. It was a general conversation, and for some reason, they had talked about going out for a beer. In the months they had shared this Greenfield house, they had never socialized. A week later Martin came to his door and asked Kurt if he would like to go a 3-D bar in Shadyside, which used to be the chic area of old Pittsburgh. They spent over three hours discussing a variety of topics. What was memorable to Kurt was that it ended in a violent argument. Ever since that night, Kurt had gone over what was said and still couldn't figure out what had sent McDonald into such a rage. He kept thinking about the seething hatred that came to the surface in Martin, after a rather calm start in the evening when he vividly described to Kurt his upbringing.

For the first part of the evening they exchanged stories about their respective pasts. Martin said he was twenty-three and was born in a poor household with no father around. His home was a three-room shack without plumbing on the opposite side of the island from the capital, Kingston. Martin then shared with Kurt how he had been rescued from this poverty by a woman who raised him like a grandson. He talked calmly and wistfully about the area, and the peacefulness of the small village by the sea. Then he stopped quickly, as if programmed and asked Kurt about his upbringing in Pittsburgh. Kurt told Martin that his life was a traditional one for the time. Somewhere in the back and forth conversation he had explained his alienation with what had become of his homeland. Martin, at first, didn't react to this longing for the "old America."

Kurt told Martin how he had been chronicling the history of America in a ledger since graduating from university. At that point, Kurt had picked up his leather-covered ledger and placed it in front of him. He remembered clearly that moment because Martin sat up and stared at the large rough leather portfolio. Kurt went on to explain that it was his personal account of all that happened during the last days of the old country and the beginnings of Atlantica. Martin's interest was obvious, and he wanted to know more about what Kurt had written over the years. Kurt felt an odd sense about his extreme interest in the ledger, so he changed the subject back to Martin's life. Kurt could still see Martin looking at the ledger for a few seconds before replying.

Martin then went on about his schooling and how he got accepted in the Atlantica University System, Alleghenia Campus, three years ago. "It was the true beginning of my life," he'd said forcefully. He emphasized that he was a dedicated believer in the country of Atlantica and the state of Alleghenia.

As the beer worked its ageless process of relaxation, this

young man slowly became openly bitter, angry, and resentful of Kurt and what he represented. He went on about the old majorities, who he said several times had kept people, especially those of color, enslaved for hundreds of years. Kurt would look at him, take a sip, and let him go on. As it turned out Martin never did return to his early days. He spoke only about his future and what he was going to do with his life. Kurt remembered thinking what an admirable trait, but when he would bring up his own interest in history, Martin would become dismissive of anything to do with what had been in this land. He abhorred anything historical about the United States. As the night wore on, Kurt was getting tired physically and of this abusive, cocky young man. At one point as their obvious differences of viewpoint came to a head, they began to shout at each other.

"Why are you hanging around my city if you're so goddamn nostalgic for the slave days, WASP?" he'd shouted.

At that comment Kurt got up to leave, but then sat down, looked Martin right in the eyes and in a quiet, forceful tone, said, "You ungrateful bastard. You got a perfect community. You took over everything that was already in place: schools, transportation, water supply, food distribution centers, everything, and in eight years, this place is barely functioning. Maybe it's perfect for you and your fellow visionaries, or whatever you call yourselves, but it's not for those who for four hundred years built a society unique in the history of man," Kurt bellowed in retort. "You've driven out the people that created all that you have today. I thought there would be some type of blending between us. Nothing old is valued," he shouted.

A minute passed. Kurt rose and said, "I must go. I'm glad we met tonight. You know, McDonald, over the past five years, I've really tried to contribute something to this new country.

I'm an idealist at heart. I wanted this new country, this new world, for that matter, to succeed even while regretting the loss of my own country, but the hatred and suspicion of the past, my past, makes living here impossible. The peoples of the world have retreated to enclaves of their own kind because they fear domination by those different than themselves. I guess you could say they are trying to avoid what you folks have endured for centuries. Isn't it an interesting phenomena we are living through?" he concluded wanting to continue.

Before he could continue, McDonald said tersely, "The oppressor fears oppression. What a laugh! What a joke on the history of this world. And you, the great white hope are scared and can't handle what we have lived with for generations. Sorry, Anglo, it's our turn, our rules. We lead, you follow. Get it!" he loudly screamed in Kurt's face.

Kurt jumped up, looked down, and retorted. "Do whatever you want. It's your country now," he thundered at Martin, who stared up at Kurt. A frozen grimace of hatred in Martin's piercing black eyes glistened and reflected back at Kurt. Kurt couldn't help seeing Martin's half snarling smile that quivered vaguely at the corners of his mouth.

Martin kept that look at Kurt for what seemed like minutes. Finally he'd replied slowly saying that his government was now a country and a system for those who once were outsiders. "Now you are the outsider," he'd said emphatically. He'd looked up at Kurt with burning contempt, got up, and walked past him without saying another word. Until last night, they had hardly spoken since that explosive evening, but McDonald's unusual attention to Kurt and his room made him wary of the young man.

As Kurt lay there now with his eyes wide open, he could picture McDonald looking at him with that sneer on his face. Since their row, he'd thought of him quite a bit and what a perfect recruit he was for this new government. Committed, and volatile, this was a man in the right place, at the right time. Kurt could still see his penetrating look of hatred, as if he embodied all the oppression minorities had endured from whites over the past centuries. Conjecture, maybe, but that grim, tight drawn face with a hint of a smile at the corners of his mouth, was still in Kurt's mind.

He rose on his elbows and looked out the squared window into the night. He hoped he would not have to deal with his neighbor tonight. Kurt shook the thoughts of Martin from his mind, got up, and began to organize his belongings for his trip. He had a long night ahead of him, and he had to get out of there, now.

chapter four

any years ago, Martin McDonald was found wandering about the island after a horrific hurricane battered Montego Bay. He was found by an elderly English teacher, who had lived in Jamaica her adult life. Constance Louise McDonald had taught at the Christian Seminary in Jamaica for thirty years. She had come from London via Glasgow in 1995, a young girl, abandoned by her only love, a pilot who had suddenly run off with an American girl studying in England. Constance McDonald came to Jamaica to work for the London-based Christian Foundation. She was the director when she found Martin wandering around the twisted, devastated resort town.

This middle-aged, white woman took him in, and since he was too young to communicate his name, she called him Martin after Martin Luther. Martin Luther was her hero; she felt he represented all that was wonderful and possible by man. Over the years she diligently attempted to locate Martin's parents. She eventually learned that his mother, an African woman, had died in the storm. She had been a local teacher, and her father had been a militant leader of his Zulu tribe in Africa. The story was that even after immigrating to Jamaica, he had been a marked man by a code of tribal revenge that still hadn't died. According to locals, he remained a marked man, even in open and free Jamaica. Apparently one day Martin's grandfather was found floating with his throat cut under a Kingston fishing pier.

As far as Martin's father was concerned, rumor in the community was that Martin was born out of wedlock. His father was a British journalist named Thomas who worked for a newspaper in Kingston and locals believed his last name was Sutherland.

As it turned out, the religious Miss McDonald was a literal godsend for this handsome boy. Martin was bright, evident as soon as he entered school. No matter what grade he was in, he was the highest in his class. When he was old enough to understand his background, Miss McDonald shared with him what she had learned about his parents and grandfather.

In his young adulthood, Martin began to realize the inequities of his people. As he grew older, his own experiences began to haunt him. Deep inside he began to resent the treatment by the whites to the underprivileged of his country. To be black or mulatto, which he was, was still, near the middle of the 21st century, to be at the lower end of the social spectrum. He learned early to play the "nice guy" role with the Anglos and the Christian fanatics that he grew up with due to the environment created by Miss McDonald. She was truly a good person, and he vowed she'd never be harmed by anyone because of all that she had done and sacrificed for him. Nevertheless, the more educated he became he realized that she represented all that he resented.

Because of Miss McDonald his life had been a good one. He received an excellent education from the best private schools in Jamaica. Martin was valedictorian from King George Academy and slated for Oxford. He played soccer and rugby. Not a large boy, he was compact, wiry, ran fast, and had excellent coordination. His peripheral vision would astound his teammates and drive his opponents crazy. He could come down the field with the ball and somehow fake to a forward while passing cross field to a streaking left forward without even looking. He was headed for Oxford, but several events occurred that totally changed his life.

Graduation from King George was a highlight for Martin. His speech was received with great acclaim by his fellow students. On graduation day he partied all day and night. Late in the graduation celebration he had finally scored with Patricia Cavendish, a classically beautiful white girl from Kingston, who also attended the co-ed King George. They'd dallied around for two years, friends and study group companions. It was all fun and nothing else until late that celebratory night. In the early morning hours on the North Beach, Martin and Patricia made love. It was his first real sexual experience.

Martin prepared himself as much as possible. Disease was the number one fear of the youth in Jamaica. Babies received shots for AIDS and other known venereal disease. The government had Sexual Establishments which offered clean sex, but what was one to do about the natural, impulsive sexual urges of youth? Martin had thought about Patricia's white body for some time. When he touched her for the first time, precautions were lost in the passion of the moment, like they had been throughout the history of man.

Martin's conquest of her was a memorable moment. He and Patricia made love until the sun came up along the beach. In the early morning he dropped her off a block from her house and drove home. He collapsed into his small, quiet room in the home he had shared with Miss McDonald. In a few minutes he was sound asleep.

As he thought back on that experience with Patricia, he now realized that it had little or no value to his life plan. It was a conquest, an initiation. Now he analyzed it as a power issue.

He appreciated her womanliness, but he loved the control he had over her. A black man controlling a white woman was a victory. In his mind he had won. She was desperately in love with him. One day, however, she was gone. Her father shipped her away as soon as he found out about the relationship. This reaction by her father reinforced his growing awareness of the racial superiority and arrogance of the white race.

When he graduated from King George Academy he had a clear path for himself. His Jamaican government offered him a scholarship to Oxford, which he accepted. After Oxford, his final objective was to be accepted in the World Graduate Program in Paris. That was his plan.

Unexpectedly he received an offer from the new country of Atlantica which he perceived as an exceptional opportunity. They would provide him a scholarship to the University System in Pittsburgh, a government job, and all expenses for three years. He could become a big fish in a seething cauldron of revolution.

Over the years he grew to resent the British sense of superiority, but what was odd, at the same time he'd gained a respect for them because they rallied and saved their way of life. They understood that the movement of populations in the late 20th century and early in this century would spell doom for their way of life. They acted strongly and decisively, expelling millions of immigrants and closing their borders, while the opposite happened in the United States. Another irony of these movements was that over the past twenty years, Great Britain benefited from the masses of professionals leaving the United States when it was clear that, as a country, it was on the decline. The United States lost their vision and their identity while Great Britain rediscovered theirs. Martin became fascinated by all that was happening in this new world, and he vowed to be in the middle of it all.

Something else occurred late summer that profoundly impacted the young man. He had come upon an article from the Atlantica Network in Nuevo York about the death of a world-renown political writer, Thomas Sutherland. Based on the stories told by Miss McDonald about his father and the fact that Kingston, Jamaica was referenced in his obituary, he became convinced that this Thomas Sutherland was his missing father. He immediately began to do further research and started with the Kingston newspapers where he found references to a reporter, Thomas Sutherland. He was a writer who had traveled the world over covering revolutions and was a particular favorite of the new regime in Atlantica. This was extremely unusual for a white writer to be so respected. Martin was overwhelmed and surprisingly felt a sense of pride for the man he believed was his father. The man had never married. This information reinforced Martin's belief in himself and his revolutionary social beliefs. The irony of what he learned from the obituary was that Thomas Sutherland had spent his last years in Pittsburgh covering the development of Alleghenia. Martin had a sense that the offer from Atlantica and Thomas Sutherland's involvement was an omen. He felt his future must begin in Alleghenia—so he accepted their offer to begin college and work for the government in Pittsburgh. He turned down Oxford.

His first week was to be spent, along with other scholarship students, in Nuevo York as a form of indoctrination. What Martin saw was unbelievable for a man of his background. Most of the people he met were either Latino or Africano. The enormous city was operated successfully by this coalition, who at times was historic enemies of the old USA. The mayor, borough council, and police were controlled by these diverse groups.

New York had become a total catastrophe beginning

after 2030. Massive immigrations from Latino countries were coupled with a gradual, then accelerated emigration by the Anglo populace to other states and countries especially to Europe. Advertisements and enticements from European countries seeking skilled workers, entrepreneurs, and business personnel filled the U.S. media. Now in the summer of 2047 Martin walked the streets of Nuevo York in utter disbelief. Gone were the excessively rich. The restaurants served basic, inexpensive foods. There were cafeterias everywhere along with hundreds of restaurants. Open picnic areas flourished. People brought and shared different foods. These were social events where people got to meet one another. Since alcohol was prohibited in public establishments, everything was centered around families and worker-groups. Martin knew then he was on the right path with his life. He recognized that sometime after his master's degree in Paris was obtained he would return to Nuevo York, the capital of Atlantica. Although not as prominent as Paris, Beijing, Tokyo, or even Rio, Nuevo York was the center of the new revolution in North America.

Once he began his schooling, Martin became very much at home in Pittsburgh. Martin felt he was in the best place at this time in his life. It was a place that he'd never heard of until the offer from Atlantica and the reference in the obituary of Thomas Sutherland. It all seemed predestined. Thomas Sutherland became quite an inspiration to Martin whom he thought of many times.

The knowledge gained about Sutherland stoked the fire of genetic interest, and Martin began a search for information on his maternal grandfather. According to Miss McDonald, this man was a Zulu warrior and chief. He was amazed at his genetic mix and was proud of them all. The great irony was that this volatile young man of the revolutionary 21st century had been raised in a Christian moral and ethical environment. According to Miss McDonald, his mother was an extraordinarily beautiful black woman who had been raised a Catholic and if his findings about Thomas Sutherland were correct, he was probably Martin's father. Martin began to sense that his fierce drive and determination came from a combination of a black Zulu chief, tempered by the genes of a white man of progressive intellect and energy. He would soon finish his college in Pittsburgh, pursue his master's in Paris and return to Nuevo York, the center of the Northern Hemisphere with a new position.

chapter five

urt spent an hour packing, adjusting, and repacking his backpack, plus a small duffel bag attached to its side. The hiking gear he had used many times over the past few years would be fully tested over the next days. He stretched his lean body and realized that the last few days had caught up with him. He was tired. He looked at his watch and decided to try to get a little rest before heading out. Kurt lay back on his bed realizing that sleep wouldn't come. All he could think about was his situation as a leftover Anglo, living in Atlantica. He was a duck out of water even at the communal parties arranged by the Administration for the working Anglos. For the most part, this odd group was made up of extreme liberal and Anglo policy thinkers with special backgrounds needed by the Administration. They were complete snobs as they reveled in their new-found prestige. When Kurt talked to them, they couldn't have cared less about the history of the USA where they were born and raised. They were pleased with its destruction and their new-found power. After attending a few parties at the request of Dr. Alexander, Kurt stopped going. These elites had all their basic needs supplied, while the other whites, like the Publican on the bridge, worked at lower-level service and security jobs.

Finally he began to relax. From a slight fog of pending

sleep, he heard a loud noise that sounded like it came from the front door. *Damn it, McDonald's back*, he thought as he got up, turned off the tiny light next to his bed and crept across to his window. The moon shone brightly on the front yard. Two large men in uniform were backing away from the house and looking up at his window with blue-beam lights pointing at the front door and then up to his window. He ducked back behind the aluminum closet door, hoping the metal would stop the penetrating beam of video light. He slid back to the window. Their lights were out, and he saw them turn, walk down to a hovering Skimmer that was in front of the house. They looked again, and one of them sprayed a beam across the windows, and then climbed into the hover craft. They pulled away, stopping once to check the street sign. As they revved up their air-sucking engine, leaves blew up into a swirl. In a few seconds, all that was left of their visit was a vapor trail following down the hill toward the bridge. Kurt watched the now-quiet spot.

He checked his backpack, rearranging it for balance. As he packed he thought ahead to his destination, Columbia. It was highly secured and from what he understood, its border was extremely difficult to penetrate. He hoped that the hiking trail would be simpler. Columbia's Dulles was the closest airport to Pittsburgh with landing rights in England, so it was the logical destination in order to get a flight to London. England had retreated from the mainland of Europe, becoming once again an island nation by closing the Chunnel to France twenty years ago. It even restricted immigration of documented Anglos to only the less populated areas of the island. Since his sister and her family had moved to Scotland before the new restrictions and his parents had been buried there, Kurt had familial rights. He also had his parents' genealogical papers to substantiate their ancestry. All he had needed was something to convince the authorities in Columbia to gain passage. The tiny chip in the cylinder should accomplish his escape.

Kurt did a final check of his backpack, tightened the straps, and set it on the floor. He picked up his leather-bound journal and leafed through some of the pages, then neatly placed it into the backpack next to the zipper backside so he could get to it during the trip. Traveling items, food, maps, and discs were stored in the outside pockets. Inside a tiny, hidden pocket, Kurt put the personal chips that contained his required ID and family history data. When he was done, he sat down on his bed and looked in the mirror. His face was barely visible in the dull light from the solar lamp.

Kurt looked around the room. He had all that he would need. The room was empty. He turned off the lamp and left. He wanted to get to Dr. Alexander's before the ten o'clock curfew.

Kurt knew the old walking trails that wound throughout Schenley Park. Now that he'd made the decision to leave, he thought how absolutely easy it was to actually close the door of his room and walk away. He'd procrastinated for months, been basically packed for a week, became mentally prepared each day up to this moment, but without a definite plan that would work, he couldn't make the final decision to leave. The Pittsburgh Aquifer data and the Allegheny Passage solved this problem while his run-ins with Martin McDonald gave him an added incentive to immediately leave.

He had no accounts to settle; no farewell parties; no valuable merchandise; no family, wife, or children. All he had materially was his family's home in the South of Pittsburgh along the river. A family of the revolution were living in the home and taking excellent care of it based on the visits he had made. The new owners were happy as they began their new lives. It had pleased him that it was so well kept, but just looking at the home of his youth brought both smiles and a bit of sadness to him. Everything he knew as a child was within those walls, from his first spacemen to his first books he had gathered in his room on second floor. Now he thought of his possessions inside the backpack and around his waist. When he decided to leave he realized that his most valuable possessions were his memories, experiences, and emotions that he carried in his mind. One day he might come back to see the haunts of his youth, as an old man visiting from Scotland, but now it was time to leave.

He closed the door of the Bolena house and walked quickly up the sidewalk into the darkness of the street. He picked up his pace and noticed a few lights breaking through the dark leafless branches of the trees that covered the hills of Squirrel Hill. Before he headed south on the first leg of his trip, he had to see Raoul and Dr. Alexander. His first stop would be Raoul's. He was an unlikely friend, but over the past three years they'd become very close, arguing vociferously over the social issues of the day while sharing their joint interest in history. The other part of his relationship with Raoul was Maria, his sister. That had been a bit more complicated, but certainly a highlight of the past two years. Kurt had fallen in love with her two summers ago.

Maria was a delight, and she spread instant joy with a captivating, seductive smile. When Raoul introduced them, she smiled slyly at him and lightly kissed his cheek. Thinking back on that moment, Kurt thought that he had fallen for her at the touch of her soft lips that day. Usually shy, Kurt asked if they could have lunch and she agreed. Within a month they were taking walks in Schenley Park, reading quietly together, and riding horses in the country. They became inseparable. It was after an afternoon ride in the country near a farm that was unoccupied, that they first made love. It was a time that Kurt still remembered. The relationship filled a major void in his otherwise quiet existence. He walked about a foot off the ground for months, but reality finally checked in to their relationship. Her teaching dream was paramount in her life. Ahead of her were the master's program and her doctorate, which she had qualified for in Paris. When they walked or sat in a café, sipping coffee or drinks, her future life in Europe was all she talked about.

When she actually left, he felt empty. She and Raoul, children of Puerto Rican immigrants, were the future of this new country, not an Anglo in his thirties. Kurt was too old for her future and too attached to the past of this land. Raoul and Maria were firm believers in the Atlantica Republic, and although they differed over the past, present, and especially the future of the area, they'd become true friends of Kurt. When Maria left for France last year, it was Raoul that had been his support in getting him through that difficult time.

Raoul knew his sister was a driven and modern woman of the time. She had no limit as to where she could go with her life and above all, he wanted her to have that chance. He felt for Kurt, but he knew it was only a matter of time when she would go to Europe and that Maria would probably disappoint him.

It had been more than a year since she left and he was basically healed, although he thought of her often, especially in moments of loneliness. Throughout this ordeal he and Raoul deepened their friendship. Kurt knew he could trust Raoul with his plan to leave Pittsburgh, and Raoul had already said he understood why Kurt felt compelled to leave, if he decided to do so.

Kurt crossed the Greenfield Bridge. A vehicle was winding down a path through the trees of the park as he reached the Squirrel Hill side. "Security?" he said out loud as he hurried off to Pocusset Street. He scrambled behind a group of thick, tangled bushes that ran down the ravine near the access to the Eastern Expressway. Leaning over, he looked down on the flashing commuter trains going back and forth on the honing tracks next to the express lanes of the carrier tracks. The train rode on a cushion of air and was like a wind blowing up the valley. From Kurt's viewpoint, the passengers were black dots in the framed light as they whisked by in a golden blur.

As Kurt's thoughts returned to the Security vehicle, he realized as a dissident, he could never belong to any of the small groups of patriots still fostering hopes to a return of the old days of the U.S. These groups maintained secret contacts with the Anglo new countries that bordered Atlantica, Columbia, and America. He'd thought about getting involved, but had decided conspiracy wasn't his game. He looked at the slowly moving Security vehicle that could, with its laser loop, immediately freeze locks on both rivers and main bridges in case of flooding or sudden landfalls. Atlantica had developed monitoring and mobiles systems to protect its natural and man-made resources. Much of the mobile equipment was developed in Russia. These creeping control mechanisms such as the one crossing the bridge in front of Kurt were monitored from space by satellites developed in the U.S. Kurt listened and watched as the monster van rolled across the bridge. He had no electrical equipment on him, only the solar-com unit in his backpack and his watch, which had power defaults, meaning only when activated would signals be sent. The world had become totally connected on land by fiber-optic systems and wireless communications by the light-link grids. Today, people could send information almost anywhere on earth or even to the revolving stations in space. Everything could be archived and was, automatically, but he relied on his leather-bound journal, wrapped tightly in the backpack, to record the history of this age. The downside of this time was that virtually all communication could be easily monitored even with personal scrambling.

He watched the van head up Pocusset Street. As it disappeared in the darkness, Kurt got up, adjusted his backpack and went in the opposite direction up another hill and into Schenley Park. This would take him over one of the old trails past what used to be a golf course right into the backyard of Raoul's apartment complex. Kurt came down the little embankment behind Raoul's place. He felt energized by the journey ahead of him.

chapter six

he day after Martin's violent encounter with Sloan in his apartment, he decided he needed to do additional checking on him. Security had been right all along. They had approached Martin two months ago when a routine data check revealed that Kurt Sloan was working odd weekend hours at the library. Some of his data downloads apparently had intruded on to some old, but critical information that had alerted Security. They knew Martin lived in the same house and asked him to look into Sloan, even suggested socializing with him. So Martin had done just that. Over the ensuing months he didn't have much to report, but since he began his surveillance, something bothered him about the Anglo, and last night's encounter was the last straw.

Martin slept fitfully after his volatile meeting with Sloan. Finally some time in the middle of the night he drifted off, only to be awakened by bright sunlight beaming into his room. He had one class scheduled for the morning, but he could skip that. The last thing he remembered before falling asleep was that he was going to spend the next day doing a background check on Sloan, and he would begin first thing in the morning. Martin was quickly out the door headed for the Tram stop. Classes were winding down, and he would be preparing for his Paris departure over the next month, but first he needed to address his concerns about Sloan. His talks with him, his secretive life, and his sudden outburst last night had justified Security's request of Martin to monitor Sloan's activities.

Martin grabbed a café con leche at the station coffee kiosk and jumped on the Tram headed to the terminal in Center City, Pittsburgh. In a few minutes he was walking toward the main Administration building on Grant Street. Martin went over in his mind a plan to find out more about Sloan. His first stop would be to a friend from Jamaica who worked in the Personnel Data office. He realized that he needed help in his research. Martin knew his suspicions were driven by his dislike for Sloan, but more than that, for the future of his beloved Atlantica and its revolution. He verified that Sloan worked at the library in the Historical Commission and had for ten years. He was the only Anglo except for the old director, Dr. Alexander.

Martin had to finish a lecture at the university scheduled for next week. It was late by the time he arrived at the house. He couldn't wait to get out of that dismal old place on the hill, especially sharing it with Sloan. He climbed up the sagging steps of the wooden house which was completely dark. "Looks like my friend is asleep, already," he said.

Martin tried the light switch inside the house. For some reason the power must have been off or there had been an outage in the area. He went into the kitchen area and fumbled around in a closet. He pulled out a flashlight and pressed the switch. The area around him was cast in stark light. He walked into the hallway and opened the switch box. The power had either shorted out or there was a problem somewhere in the system. He pulled the reset switch and nothing happened. "System must be down," he said and turned the flashlight to the steps.

He climbed up the wide, creaking steps to the second floor. What he found was upsetting. As he was passing by Sloan's room, he saw that the door was opened slightly. Normally Sloan was in his room at night, usually at his computer. Martin had always been curious about what Sloan was doing late at night on his system. After last night, he was more than curious, he was suspicious. He pushed open the door and turned the light into the room which appeared empty. The bright flashlight exposed the interior of the spare room. He ran the light across the walls with their faded, flowered wallpaper speaking of an era long gone. He looked around the room and immediately knew that Sloan had left, for good. His quick spreading of the light around the room verified that the room was totally empty. *Why would he just leave?* Granted, he had told Sloan that the building was designated to be demolished, but that would take weeks to put into affect. Sloan worked for the Administration. He'd had a great job for ten years. *Why would he go now, but more important, where would he go?* Martin would check in the morning to see if Kurt scanned in for work. Martin believed that there was more to Sloan's empty room than their argument the night before.

He searched the room for clues as to where Sloan had gone. He even crawled around on the floor, looking for anything that Sloan might have dropped in his haste to leave. Martin remembered that Sloan really didn't have many personal belongings. He was getting frustrated as he tore the bedding apart, "Where did that son of a bitch take off for? I didn't trust him for a second. He had that superior attitude of his people," he barked out to himself as he opened up the one closet that was also bone dry. "Got to find him," he said, as he sat down on the mattress.

Martin sat there thinking about Sloan and why he would suddenly leave. A lot would depend on whether he showed up for work in the morning. He thought about Sloan's job as a historian at the Library Complex. Martin remembered Sloan had mentioned in a smart-ass way that his research included work on the historical accomplishments of the United States, including the history of the underground water system. Martin recalled the media coverage of the Pittsburgh Aquifer system that was to be opened in a few months and the pressure being applied on Atlantica by the UN. He sat there puzzled, then said out loud, "Could there be a connection?" For some time he remained sitting on the bed in Sloan's empty room, his feelings of suspicion slowly leading to anger. "I'm sure the Anglo son of a bitch took off." Now Martin was stewing, and he thought about something Sloan had said several times last night, that if he left, he would go to Scotland, where his people came from.

"Where would he go and how would he get there?" Martin said. He knew it was very difficult getting space to Europe these days, especially for one who worked for the Administration. Closest place for an Anglo without a visa to get a flight would be Columbia, unless he could get to Toronto, which was very difficult for anyone. Either way he'd need something of extraordinary value to get space. There was no free flow of people into Columbia, and he had heard that a passenger needed either UN funds, Columbian dollars, or gold credits. "That's it," he said as he rose and went to the door. "He worked in the Historical Records, and he probably took something from there. Why else would he just leave?" He quickly left the room, walked the stairwell, and hurried down the steps. He was mad at himself for letting the Anglo get away. He had been right, and he should have followed his suspicions, but Martin was now determined to make up for his error.

Martin knew his feelings for Sloan bordered on hatred, but Martin realized it was probably more what Sloan represented than Sloan himself. He was a secretive person and had a sense of superiority, which Martin despised. Hating a person because of his leftover Anglo superiority was one thing, but realizing that he may have just left his position without some type of security check really upset Martin. *What if his job was classified?* He thought more about the recent media coverage of the Aquifer System that was soon to be completed and the fact that border countries were trying to obtain access to the water. Martin thought of various scenarios, one being that Sloan's position allowed him entry to data concerning the workings of the Aquifer. As unlikely as that was, he knew that he would have to sort this all out. If Sloan or anyone took valuable information about that system, it could be disastrous for his new country. He knew that taking unauthorized materials from a government facility was a federal offense because it was drilled into all new employees upon their indoctrination. Theft of government property, especially critical information, was punishable by long-term imprisonment, even life, depending on the materials. From Martin's perspective, it was mandatory by law to report defectors or anyone a citizen thought might be taking critical information. All reports were seriously evaluated by the Commission of Human Resources. In fact, if a citizen alerted the Administration about someone taking government materials and he or she was found guilty, rewards were given to the informant. The more he thought of Sloan's sudden disappearance, the thought of rewards became an intriguing incentive to Martin.

"Hell. Where would Sloan go?" Martin muttered. He looked out into the pitch-blackness of the late autumn night, and then slowly sat down on the top step of the silent house. He realized that he was in the center of this new order, just like the hurricane that had left him an orphan twenty years ago. Martin had studied vociferously how this new world had been created from the chaos earlier in the century. He studied the ways of the old world, and he smiled thinking of how the absolutism of the white race was gone. They'd set the stage for hundreds, thousands of years, but now it was the turn of the great human and colored majority to run at least a part of the world, their world. Let those white people, who had ruled, seclude and segregate themselves. The irony of ironies, one of his professors would say.

Martin recalled how the world had changed and how it had affected the white powers of the past. How the powerful Asian Society had combined with the African Union, creating the most powerful economic combination on earth. The production skills of China, Japan, and United Korea, combined with the vast natural resources of Africa, joined these two races, the Oriental and the Africano, for the first time in the history of man. The white race had been forced to give up their stranglehold on the world economy for their very existence. Martin had concentrated in twenty-first-century economics in his last years at college to better understand future economic trends. His conclusion was that Alleghenia, the most western state of Atlantica, could be the epicenter of future power. He was young, bright, and ready to assume his place in this historical struggle. He took a deep breath and became quiet.

Martin sat on the front porch of the house for a few more minutes, playing with the flashlight, letting it swing from his hand and play darting tricks on the empty naked trees. He would pack his bedding, data equipment, books, and clothes in the morning and have them delivered to the apartment the Administration was providing him.

Martin's thoughts returned to Sloan and how he would actually leave Pittsburgh. Because of Security he couldn't fly, drive, or take the overland monorail. He suddenly straightened up, remembering Raoul Lopez-Hernandez, Kurt's Puerto Rican friend, who lived in Shadyside. Sloan had mentioned him several times, as a good friend. He may know where he had gone and how he planned to get there. He punched out Raoul's name into his datafile and located his address. "I can be there in twenty minutes if I catch a Tram," he said getting up and looking back at the dark house.

Martin ran up to the almost-silent Tram as it pulled away from the stop. He looked at the screen. The next one would be there in a half hour. He saw a coffee shop opened and went over to it. *I need some caffeine anyway,* he thought.

chapter seven

"Kurt! Jesus, come on in. What a great surprise! Looks like you're going mountain climbing!" Raoul said, looking outside and then closing his front door with a solid thump. He stared at the huge backpack strapped tightly to his friend's back. "How 'bout a beer, *mi amigo!*"

"*Si, compadre.* One for the road, you might say," Kurt said, slipping the straps off his shoulders and dropping the pack onto the floor. He flopped onto the curved cushioned sofa that filled most of Raoul's small living room.

"*Dos cervezas* coming up," Raoul said, heading for the kitchen.

Kurt lay back on the air-filled cushions of the familiar sofa on which he and Raoul had sat on numerous occasions, drinking beer and solving all the world's problems. He settled into its softness as his mind and body relaxed. The comfortable relic reminded him of the world in which he grew up when he was living within the cocoon of his family's stability. His mind slowed as the events of the past days played like a movie in slow motion.

"Kurt? You look whipped. You want to go upstairs and take a nap?"

"No, I'm good. I'm fine. Just thinking about my family," he said reaching for the smooth, gray mug with foam flopping over its top. "Looks good," he muttered into the head.

"A new brew, an old recipe, my good friend. It will fire you up. So, *amigo*, what the hell are you up to," Raoul said.

Kurt sat up and said, "I'm leaving town, Raoul. You know I've been thinking about it, and I finally decided that I've got to get out of here. There's no future here for my kind. I'm an alien in my own land. Totally out of place in this day and age," he replied firmly, resolute in tone.

"Come on. You can hack it. Things are picking up. It looks like they're going to lift the restrictions on movement," Raoul replied, sipping on the beer and peering deeply at his good friend.

"Within Atlantica," Kurt answered. "That's a good thing, but that's also the crux of the matter for me. It's a state decision because it primarily affects Anglos, as if we are a lower-class or special breed. There is nothing about freeing up movement for Anglos out of the country. It's tighter than a drum for us. I guess it's something like it used to be for blacks back in the slave days. Besides, there are things going on that might make our lives more difficult."

"Like what" Raoul asked.

"Well, I think the powers in Atlantica are going to take over absolute control of the Aquifer in the coming months. There is too much power and money involved in that system, plus there is increasing pressure to open up the water to other countries. There has been a lot of media coverage about the pressure on the locals here in Alleghenia to relinquish control when the Aquifer is completed."

"Yeah, I've been seeing it on the broadcasts. Makes sense that the government would be concerned. After all, we do own it," Raoul said.

"No question, but there is so much at stake, especially when water is involved. We've got it and others need it," Kurt answered and took a long sip from the crock. "What the hell is this stuff?" he said, changing the subject.

"Thought you might like that! A new brewery opened last week. It's a Puerto Rican beer. Would you believe? Actually some people started up the old Allegheny Brewery on the North Side. Been empty for years. Good stuff, huh?"

"Got a bite to it. I like it." He paused. "Have you talked to Maria?" he added, asking the question he wanted to ask ever since he came through the front door.

"Just last night. Said to say hello to you and wanted to know what you were up to. She's fine. I guess she's leading her class in grades, so far."

"That's Maria, all right," Kurt replied.

"So what are you up to? What are you going to do?" he said, this time he changed the subject.

Kurt took a sip of his beer and looked him right in the eye.

"Why do you want to know?" Kurt responded as the vision of Maria's ivory face, coal black hair, and crinkled smile vanished.

"Wait a minute. What, you don't trust me? Why the hell did you come here, anyway?" Raoul said briskly, putting down his beer.

"I trust you totally," Kurt quickly replied. "But when the authorities realize that I'm absent without notification at work, they will check with my associates and friends. They know you are my friend. They'll come around to check with you, and you don't need that burden," Kurt added. Then he looked around and said, "Are you alone?"

"The good wife is with her mother and Carla's sleeping in the bedroom," Raoul quickly replied.

"Carla. Christ, if she knows I'm here and heard that I was leaving, I might as well turn myself into Security right now.

Jesus Christ, I gotta get out of here," Kurt said beginning to push out of the cushion. Raoul's large hand gently pushed him back.

"She's sound asleep, and beside she wouldn't tell them."

"Her boyfriend is with Security, Carlos, something or other, right? Raoul, let me say what I came here to say, and then I have to go." Kurt paused and began to speak in a whisper. "I'm leaving here. Going to try and get to England, to Scotland, actually. You know my sister is there and my parents were buried there," he said, moving closer into Raoul's face.

"I think you're making a big mistake, my friend. You have a great job. You like the work you do. I think you are giving up at the wrong time," he replied firmly.

"Raoul, maybe you're right, but this is your country, not mine anymore. It was my country. The whole world is different than when I was growing up. I see great struggles ahead for you and your people, but by the same token, I see nothing but more isolation here for my people. That's right, Raoul, my people. It's always negative to refer to Anglo-Saxons, as if it's something to be ashamed of. Bullshit. I'm sick and tired of being so defensive about my heritage. I'm proud of what my people created in this land. Just as proud as you are about your people." Kurt paused took another sip and said quietly, "The bottom line is that this is no place for me in the year 2050, Raoul. That's why I'm leaving."

There was silence while they looked intently at each other, and then Raoul said hesitatingly, "So what are you going to do?"

"I'm taking a hike, literally. I'm hiking to Columbia by way of the old Allegheny Passage Trail. You know, well you probably don't know. It's an old trail that goes all the way to the Columbia border. Once I get there, I'm hoping I can get passage to England."

"You know how tough it is to get out of here, especially for an Anglo. You said earlier they may lift travel restrictions for Anglos, but that's just in the State. For an Anglo it's hard to get visas for anywhere," Kurt said.

"I think you're taking a great chance trying to get to Columbia. That's a hard line place, my friend. They'll kill your ass just trying to get in. I heard there's a no-man's-land miles from their border. The got fences like they did in the U.S. fifty years ago. Look what good that did."

"Raoul, listen to me. All I want is a place where I can work and maybe make a difference in this new world. If it's with people of my own background, so be it. That's the world we live in. Some quiet place where I can live in peace," he said softly. They sat as a faint hint of Latino music played in the audio system.

Raoul finally said, "Peace, peace is what *you* want. We all want peace. It took my people centuries to peacefully gain control of their lives. Now there may be threats to take what we have achieved away from us by people of our heritage. You just said so. Sometimes I think nothing really ever changes in the power needs of all people. People get a little power and they want more, no matter where they came from. You leaving, my good friend, that's your decision. Me, I don't want to go anywhere. I think Pittsburgh with or without the Atlantica Republic, is my best hope. You know what we need, desperately? People like you. People without an agenda, who'd work for the success of the area, forgetting the politics or the race of the majority. We need skilled people of all backgrounds, even Anglos like you. Everyone is protected, even you, the people who only protected their own for four hundred years. I had to get that in there, Kurt. Don't you see, *mi amigo*, most of your people left. Whoever is left must be classified according to skills. Our Matrix Management System matches skills with need. Take you, for example. We need your research skills. I know you and how energetic you are about everything you do. While everyone works on the future, no one is paying attention to the past. That's a mistake." Raoul paused and then said, "I'm looking at you and I can tell your mind is made up to leave."

"You're right about me, as usual. Never could hide anything from you. Raoul, I've got to move on. If a Sloan feels confined, it seems he has to move on to greener pastures, so to speak. Just like my family did three hundred years ago. It might seem strange to you to go back from where I came, but it may be simply my genetic conscious."

"My genetic conscious calls me to grab this chance, here, right smack in the middle of what was Anglo country. No offense, old friend, but if I didn't know you better, I'd say you're leaving because you lost control. Your people have to be the boss. I think you're different than the rest, maybe not?" He stopped, then, calmly said, "You said Scotland, but where exactly is back where you came from, huh?" he quizzed Kurt.

"Paisley, a little town south of Glasgow. My sister went there when a lot of the emigration began. That's where my parents moved to and where they are buried. According to the historical data I uncovered, my ancestors left that very area in the 1600s and went to Donegal, in Northern Ireland. From there, two hundred years later, they came here. As for where I will end up exactly, I'm not sure. First, I have the big problem of getting to Columbia and getting on a flight out of there."

"Should I let you go? I mean I'm supposed to report defectors, especially one so skilled." Raoul was very serious when he said this and slowly drained his beer, while closely looking at Kurt.

"Only you can answer that, my friend," Kurt quickly responded.

"What about Martin, the guy that shared your house

that you told me was driving you crazy. Does he know you're leaving?"

"I don't think so. I'd be worried if he suspected anything. He wasn't there when I left. It's really odd. I just don't know why I seem to bother him so much. I think I represent the 'oppressors of old,' as he once put it." Kurt paused and looked at Raoul without saying anything. Then he stood up and offered his hand to him. "Anyway, Raoul this is *adios*. I have to get going because there's one other person I have to see tonight, Dr. Alexander. He won't like my leaving, but I have to say goodbye to him."

"He's going to be one sad man, not only as a friend, but as your mentor. I'm sure he's also going to miss that valuable historical work that you were doing for him," Raoul said.

"Well, I've given this a lot of thought, constantly. I'm thirty-five. There is so much I want to do with my life. So much I want to experience, to write about, but Raoul, the sacrifice is leaving such friends as you and Dr. Alexander. But, I have no doubt I am doing the right thing," he said as he stood. "I must get on to see him," Kurt finished and reached out his hand. Raoul clasped it with both hands. They came to each other and hugged tightly.

"I guess you have your route?" Raoul asked quietly pushing him gently away as they looked at each other.

"I do," Kurt said as he moved to the door. He opened it and turned, "Fortunately it's dark out tonight. So it might be slow going, but I really don't want to run into any Security patrols. I just want to get on my way. Anyway, after I see him, I should still get a good jump in the dark before daylight. My phones are off, but when I get where I can safely call you, I'll let you know where I am," Kurt said.

Raoul stood looking at Kurt in the doorway. He had a sad, empty look in his face, but slowly a crinkled smile spread over the handsome, dark, rectangular face of this new man of Pittsburgh as he looked at Kurt. "Until we meet again, my friend Kurt," he said slowly.

"That will be a happy day, Raoul. Please tell Maria I wish her the best." No other words were spoken as he walked out through the opening onto the small porch and into the well-lit area in front of Raoul's apartment building.

Kurt didn't look back until he was in the shadows of the woods across the street. He looked at Raoul's living room window framed by yellow light of the screen. He could pick out one shadow joining up to another. "Damn, Carla," he swore to himself and as he ran quickly down the path and began jogging in the pitch-blackness of this fall night.

chapter eight

artin looked at his watch. It was past ten, and the Tram was due in a few minutes at the Greenfield Stop. Once it came, it was a short ride to Shadyside where Raoul lived. He ran up the hill and down to the station, just as the Cross City was pulling in. It was ten thirty when he reached the Station. Based on his map scan, Raoul's St. Charles Street address was only two blocks away. According to the information in the datafile, he lived there with his wife and sister, Carla, who interestingly was engaged to a man in Security. Martin had taken note of that added piece of information. He walked quickly and in a few minutes he was looking at a large, narrow three-story brick town house left over from the Victorian era of 19th-century Pittsburgh. He couldn't see lights, but he went up to the front door and slid his ID card into the security slot. He hoped someone was up. There was no response, so he began to back down the steps when a light came on and the door opened slowly. A large man stood there in shorts and no shirt.

"Raoul? Raoul Lopez-Hernandez, I'm Martin McDonald, Kurt Sloan's friend. Sorry for coming so late, but I live in the same house as Kurt. I'm looking for him. Have you seen him?" Martin said quickly.

Raoul didn't reply. He stared at Martin for a few seconds as he held a mug in his hand. Martin could smell the beer.

"I know who you are. You came up on the scanner, that's why I opened the door. To answer your question, he was here earlier, working late, I think. Just for a few minutes," Raoul replied gruffly, not opening the door any more than halfway. "Are you worried about an Anglo, man?" he asked sarcastically.

"Well, yes, actually. I haven't seen him today, and there's something I wanted to talk to him about. He's always in his room working on his computer, but not tonight. It's a bit unusual, for him," Martin replied.

Raoul looked at Martin and said, "Man, are you a bit loco. I told you he was working late. Maybe he met someone. It does happen, even for an Anglo. Besides that, what are you doing here at this fuckin' hour?" he said beginning to close the door.

"No, listen, give me a couple of minutes. It's very important really and I need your help," Martin replied putting his hand on the solid wooden door.

Raoul looked at him and said, "McDonald, what do you really want with Sloan?"

"He's your friend, right? I need to talk to him. He was doing historic work for the Administration at the Castro Library with a Dr. Alexander. I have some important questions about it, for my own work. I stopped by to see him tonight, and it looks like his room is cleaned out, as if he left. So frankly, I got curious and I need to speak to him. He mentioned you as his friend, so that's why I came by so late. So my question to you, is where would a person like him go?"

"What do you mean, a person like him? Jesus, he's just a guy trying to survive in what used to be his country. But it's not his country, anymore, it's ours," Raoul countered, as they talked in the doorway. "Christ, you might as well come in now, I'm wide awake."

Martin came in looking around the rooms as he followed Raoul into the narrow room. "Look, I'll only be a minute, but if I'm hearing you right, he came by here, earlier. Did he say he was going somewhere? If he did, where was he going and why?" Martin asked anxiously.

"Hold on there, McDonald. I never said anything like that. He stopped by, I said that. I don't know if he took off or where he is. I assume he's going back to his room, in your house in Greenfield. I don't know what you mean by taking off. If you mean like in leaving, I have no clue that's what he's doing, but if he did leave, you'd be the reason. He told me about your conversations," he said sarcastically.

"He's an Anglo. He's the enemy, as far as I'm concerned. Has been and still is!" Martin responded.

"Jesus Christ, man. He's a man working for this Administration, our Administration. He's a man who stayed while everyone else he knows left. I know him. He's a good man. I don't know you, and I don't want to know you. You better get out of here, McDonald," he said, his voice rising in anger.

"Listen, this man works in an important department for this Administration. I don't trust him. I have to know where he is and if he has left. I'll find out whether you help me or not, but I want to know if he left for good, where's he headed, and why."

"Let me make this clear to you one last time. I don't know what his plans are, but as I said, if he has left, you may be the reason. Maybe I'm the reason. You don't get it. There is nothing left for him here. He grew up here. His family lived here for hundreds of years. My God, man, what's it to you where he goes or what he does. What, are you looking for? Points? For turning in an Anglo? How many points can you get for turning him in? He's a bookworm, a historian. He's absolutely harmless."

"No one's absolutely harmless. Besides, I have some questions for him about the work he was doing. He had access to the historic plans of the canals, roadways, walkways, subways, and water systems of the old country. That's important information, Raoul. Important to our survival and important to our enemies. If in the wrong hands, who knows, it could be used against us. In case you don't know it, water is our lifeblood."

"Well what do you expect me to do, McDonald? He is a friend. If he would leave, I can understand it. He has no family here. Maybe he decided he wants to live with what's left of his family. You must understand that. He's not the kind of person who would want to cause harm to anyone; that's just not the Kurt Sloan I know, Anglo or no Anglo. Go see the Administration. Have them check into the data. Certainly they can go back and check the work that he had been doing," Raoul calmly replied.

"You're missing the point. If he gets to another border country with any information, say, Columbia, a systems expert could extract valuable information that might give them an advantage over our government. That's what I would be afraid of; that's what I'm trying to avoid. Can't you see that?"

"McDonald, I think you're way ahead of yourself," Raoul replied. "Listen, go to the Administration. I have to get some sleep."

"Okay, maybe I'm wrong, but I don't think so. He may be your friend, but our government has real enemies. The problem I have, if he has left Pittsburgh for good, I don't know what all he might've taken. Your friend or not means nothing to me, because I don't trust him. Not for a second. I just want to talk to him. For your information only, this wasn't just my suspicion. Two months ago, Security came to me. They wanted me to get some information on Sloan because he's an Anglo working in a potentially sensitive area. He apparently began to do a lot of work on his off time, so they wanted to find out what he was doing. They came to me with rewards attached. I talked with him, tried to find out what he was working on, but all we did was get into arguments."

"You were also snooping around his room, McDonald. That I know and Kurt knew. So you're not much of a detective."

"Well, he must have something to hide, because tonight his room is empty and all his belongings are gone. He has left. Friend or not, he represents the old way of thinking, no matter what he may have led you to believe. Don't you see we just can't let him leave and take information that will hurt our country," he finished with an almost desperate flourish.

Raoul looked at Martin and said, "Listen, McDonald, I don't want our new country to be hurt by anyone, but I don't think Kurt Sloan is any security risk. He talked at times about visiting his sister in Scotland.

"Listen, I'm trying to put this all together. That's why I came here because you were his best friend and I thought you may have some clues for me. This may be very important to the security of *our* country," Martin said. There was a brief silence as the two just looked at each other. Then Martin continued, "If I heard you right, Sloan told you he might leave some day."

"Yes, a couple of times. He was very unhappy here, and he said he would like to go to Scotland. My God, he told you the same thing, so it's no secret," Raoul said.

"No, that's not in doubt. What is in doubt, is how. How, for Christ's sake, is he going to get there without Security catching his ass?"

"I have no idea. He can't get a passport without all the bells in Security going off, so he can't go anywhere by train or flights. He might be able to get a ride to Nuevo York, but he would have to be a stowaway on some transport vehicle, which is monitored closely. I don't know, maybe he'll just walk there, McDonald," he laughed; then he added, "For God's sake, lay off. If he did go, let the man alone."

"Sorry, I gotta find him."

"Look, no matter what you think he did, he's still my friend," Raoul said, his deep voice rising in frustration. "Friendships are rare, especially this one. Even if I knew where he was, I wouldn't turn him in. If you find him, at least hear the man out. Get his story," Raoul said.

"When I find him, then I'll decide. You know something my Latino amigo, you're much too old-fashioned. Much too sentimental. I gotta get going," Martin said as he turned toward the door. He turned back to Raoul and said, "Just talking to you has given me an idea. I'm going over first thing in the morning to his work center at the library. Maybe I can find what he was doing his last days there. Then I'll interview Dr. Alexander. Maybe he knows something, but if your best friend Kurt Sloan contacts you, here's my code. I'll expect you to let me know," Martin said firmly.

Raoul moved toward Martin and pointed at him, "Listen you son of a bitch, don't threaten me in any way. You hear me? Don't expect anything from me. I wouldn't give you anything about anyone. Now get the hell out of here before I throw your ass out. Now!" Raoul shouted as he moved toward McDonald, who held his ground for a second, then grabbed the handle and opened the door.

"You may regret what you said," Martin replied as he walked out into the dark night without closing the door.

"Fuck you, you Caribbean creep!" Raoul shouted out to the disappearing figure as he slammed the door shut.

Martin McDonald crossed the street and looked back as the lights went out. He looked around the area. It was pitch-black. He hadn't eaten since early in the morning and was feeling a bit weak. He had been going nonstop all day. The only place open was the 21st Cafeteria two blocks away in Shadyside which was where he headed. He had to slow down and plan his next move. Martin knew one thing, tomorrow morning he would find Dr. Alexander. He had a hunch where Sloan was headed, but needed to learn how he could get out of the country. Martin knew one thing, Sloan had few options.

Martin felt raindrops as he walked quickly up the dark road in the direction of the restaurant. He zipped up his jacket as light rain and the cold breeze blew in his face. The weather was changing as forecasted. He had never become accustomed to the cold weather of this area. He had never seen snow before he came here. At first it was exciting and different, but he soon got over that feeling when the freezing temperatures lasted for weeks on end. Those were the times when his mind drifted to the constant warm air and water of his Jamaica. Someday, he would go back a leader and help instill in that small country the qualities of this revolutionary land. Someday his people would be free and totally in charge of their lives. Things were changing, but not fast enough. He missed the color, the warmth, the people, but his life was here, and he had a job to do.

chapter nine

urt quickly got into his walking pace as he wound his way up a desolate Shady Avenue. He'd missed the ten o'clock curfew, but he'd tracked out on his planner a way through the Homewood Cemetery to Beechwood Boulevard, then onto a walking path built through Frick Park. The trail would get him within several blocks of Dr. Alexander's house. Once he left Dr. Alexander's, he could get onto the trail, which would take him to the old Homestead High Level Bridge and across the river to the beginning of his journey on the Allegheny Passage to Columbia, 318 miles away.

His legs felt strong, relaxed. He was glad he didn't have any more beer at Raoul's. It tasted great, but he needed to be as alert tonight as he had ever been in his life. The beer had calmed him and lessened the tension of telling Raoul of his plans. The conversation with Raoul was what he had hoped for, truthful, honest, and supportive. It had given him closure on several things, including his leaving Pittsburgh. His thoughts broke off as he noticed the grillwork of the Homewood Cemetery looming out of the darkness and the now misty rain, which had begun to fall. Wild vines twisted up above pointed metal bars. Glancing at his watch, he saw it was 11:30. The blue weather screen in his watch showed a rainstorm with high winds. Kurt suddenly felt that maybe the gods were with him. The moon was hidden and the rain would be a big help. Once he left Dr. Alexander, he felt he would make great time. He looked back at his watch and realized he would be there close to midnight. He knew the old man hardly ever slept even at his age.

As he walked, his mind began to wander which was what he loved about hiking. All you did was get into a gait, let your arms swing in a rhythm and let your thoughts roam. As a student, he was curious about everything, and he recalled a day when his teacher talked about the mind. Afterward he spent days reading all he could about the mind. The mind was defined as "the part of an individual that feels, perceives, thinks, wills, and particularly reasons." He knew his own mind was definitely in charge of his actions, especially at this crossroads of his life. *It's all such a mishmash of soul, mind, and gut reaction that's leading me on,* he thought.

This night was a decisive one after months of indecision. For years he tried to adapt unsuccessfully to the new culture. He was locked in his work and his narrow, confined life, but tonight, with his mission clear, he bristled with life. A gentle rain continued, and he realized it would be cold along the river later. Kurt shrugged his shoulders and picked up his pace on the next section of the road. As he turned a corner, he almost tripped over a fallen limb. He was amazed that he had not seen anyone since he began the climb. Soon he would be at Dr. Alexander's house. He wondered if he should have contacted him to let him know he was going to stop in to see him. As he reached the broad, low-lit Beechwood Boulevard, he felt comfortable with his timing. He was sure Dr. Alexander would be up and calling him would have been a mistake because messages, voice or visual, are monitored, filtered, and placed in a location grid. No, he should just show up.

Without warning, Kurt heard a loud whooshing sound coming down the steep street ahead of him. He looked up and saw the trim lights of a Skimmer sailing right at him. He dove to his left down an embankment and rolled under a huge bush at the bottom. The Skimmer, which was designed to silently glide at any height, was used by Security for surveillance. This one came to a halt, not more than a block away and reversed itself with its piercing white search beams running along the sidewalk. The beams came around and were now scanning for body heat. He rolled farther looking for something to get under that would reject the heat. The beam was now headed his way. He could see lights in the basement of a house several yards away. Kurt scurried quickly, low to the ground, following the embankment until he reached the cement block of the house. He crawled under some low-lying bushes that went right up to the lighted window. The beam went to where he'd been, as the Skimmer hovered above that spot. The beam was then aimed at the house and followed his path right up to the window. The pilot, realizing he was focused on a house, turned off the beam and sped off. Kurt lay there and breathed deeply for a minute. Inside he heard the Security System Connector react. He had to get out of there right now because Security was probably informing the occupants of a possible intruder on the property.

Kurt turned back the way he'd come, crossed the street, and ran as fast as he could along the other side. If he could run for at least five minutes more, he would be at Dr. Alexander's. It was tough running with all his gear, but he kept a steady pace. It seemed like a long time—his breathing was beginning to be heavy, but finally he could see the twin chimneys of Dr. Alexander's home. No fear of security systems in this house. The doctor didn't have them. He reached the large dark door and knocked firmly, but quietly. There was no response. He knocked again, looking back up the driveway for a sign of anyone. A light came on, and a scanner buzzed, no doubt screening the porch.

The door opened slowly, and Dr. Alexander was standing back looking surprised from inside the darkened foyer. He stepped forward, unsnapped a lock, and opened the door.

"Kurt, my boy. What are you doing here at this hour? Looks like you've been running from a band of hooligans. Come on in."

"Thanks so much. Not hooligans, but Security. They may have picked up my moving heat imprint."

"Moving heat imprint? What a nice modern way of putting things. Whoever heard of moving heat? Moving heat! I remember going to a Marilyn Monroe revival in college. That was moving heat," he laughed. "Sorry, you probably have no idea what I'm talking about," he chuckled as Kurt came into the foyer.

"She was an old movie star, I think," Kurt said standing on the small hallway.

"You are a historian of many things, I see, but before I tell you about Marilyn Monroe and moving heat, come along to my den."

They moved through the paneled hallway on a thick, cushiony blue carpet that hadn't been used much in years. It always reminded Kurt of his parent's home, soft and comforting. The den was unchanged from his last visit. This time of year, a fire glowed red in remission. He walked over and warmed his hands as Dr. Alexander plopped down in his leather chair.

"Now where was I. Oh yes, Marilyn Monroe. It was my second year at Harvard. It was in the Yard somewhere. They had old movies shown once a week in one of the lounges. One winter, I remember because there was a foot of snow on the walkways that night, all of Marilyn Monroe's movies were shown back to back. Funny, but there was a scene in one of them with a male star named, Tom, something or other. Tom, Tom, Ewell, that's it. He was the costar, great performance by that guy. Anyway, there was one scene of her standing on a sidewalk, when all of a sudden a gust of air came from an air vent below, subway or something. Jesus, Kurt, what a pair of legs. In those days if you saw a woman's underwear on the screen it was censorship time, but it was allowed. Now, Kurt, that was moving heat," the tall, old man said laughing. He looked at Kurt and said, "Here take off that backpack. If you're cold, push that chair over by the fire. There's a bit of a chill tonight, first inkling of winter." As Kurt began to twist out of his backpack, Dr. Alexander got up and helped him slide it off. Kurt dropped down into the leather recliner, as the doctor sat back down.

"Well I'm glad you're still focused on the important things in this life, Doctor," Kurt replied, thinking back to the Marilyn Monroe story as he stared at the low-lying logs sitting atop old molten ones, crackling from the licking fire.

"Kurt, a woman always represented to me the perfect mechanism in this world. A combination of softness and hardness, vengeance and caring, acceptance and rejection, every emotion in one package. I'll tell you, they still represent the ultimate mystery of life. But now, tell me what has you out roaming and ducking the evening Security patrol? I'm curious."

Kurt hesitated, not sure exactly how to start, but then just blurted out confidently, "Doctor, I am going home. I am going back to Scotland. I've talked to you about Scotland many times over the years. As you know, that's where my mom and dad are buried. It's where my sister and her family are and where the Sloan clan came from originally. In fact, if I'm not mistaken, that's where your family came from." Dr. Alexander nodded, but didn't say anything, and Kurt continued.

"Family, maybe that's what this all about, but the only family I have is in the lowlands, alive or dead. I've told you about my two uncles who left for Glasgow almost ten years ago and of course my sister, Margaret. They're all I have left in this world, as far as family is concerned. I want to make a new home there, and I know for sure that Alleghenia in 2050 is not my home anymore," he said with a crack in his voice.

Dr. Alexander didn't reply. He looked at Kurt and then at the fire. His face was angular, with a large spreading nose, which dominated his wrinkled, pink face. He had a full head of white hair, which was always in a bit of a mess. His look was austere, lean, and wise, but his dark blue eyes sparkled even this late at night. He exuded confidence and was a picture of health.

He'd been born in 1970 in the little town of Damariscotta, Maine, which was down east on the spectacular Atlantic coast. Growing up there isolated him from the rest of America. He didn't find out what America was really like until he went to Harvard. Boston and its environs were a rude awakening for him coming from the small village, populated heavily in the summer by tourists. He always talked about his summer jobs because they were the vehicle to his becoming a firebrand about American history and restoration of relics of the country. In ten years he had his master's, his doctorate, and was head of the History Department at the University of Pittsburgh. While doing this he'd mastered computer technology, especially programming. He designed programs about American History that even to this day were used at the university level all over the world.

One day, about two weeks after first meeting him, Kurt was amazed at a demonstration set up by Dr. Alexander. He retraced and rebuilt the Hadrian Wall in England using all the available topographical data and matching this with detailed maps drawn by the Roman engineers 2000 years ago. The computer display across the middle of England was remarkable. This was the early Dr. Alexander. He was more of a researcher and writer now, but his mind was still working on history with a goal of preservation for the future. His latest concern had been the preservation of the history of earth's natural resources, with emphasis on the Northern Hemisphere. But for Kurt, his most important work was in convincing the government of Atlantica to also preserve the history of the land they now governed. This is where Kurt worked, and he was in awe of this man. Dr. Alexander was the classic mentor, and Kurt had become an ardent student.

As he turned back to Kurt from the fire, the blue eyes sparkled. "You're leaving history, my son. The history of the world is where you are, now. A country, a boundary is meaningless when a universal revolution is under way. This is a universal revolution. This is France and America in the late eighteenth century; Europe in the mid–nineteenth century; Europe between the two World Wars of the twentieth century; this is one of the most important times in all of mankind. I really feel, for the fine historian you are, you're leaving at the wrong time," his eyes now locked on Kurt.

The only sounds were the tiny explosions from the low-lying, red-hot fire as it crackled away inside the large stone fireplace. Kurt stared at the yellow-to-orange flames flashing upward in an uneven serpentine dance.

Kurt did not respond, but Dr. Alexander picked right up and said, "What has happened politically, we can talk about. I believe the people in charge are benign. They want to create their own Eden here in Pittsburgh with its own water supply and system. That analogy might eventually be right on target. Am I getting anywhere?" he quickly added. "Oh, I'm so sorry, how about some wine."

"No thanks, I have quite a way to go tonight," he said firmly.

At that moment Dr. Alexander realized the seriousness of

his young friend and associate. He stood up and walked over to a wooden cabinet and rustled around in a lower drawer. Kurt could hear bottles rattling against each other.

He pulled out a bottle of red wine and turned back to Kurt, "This is good stuff for a cool fall night. Warm up the innards a bit. It's an old Merlot, Kurt. Not brandy, but a good bite to it. Sure you don't want a short one?"

"No sir. I need to be clear tonight. You go right ahead."

"I plan on it," he quickly answered as he popped a stopper from the dark bottle. "It's a heavy grape combination. Has a nice taste. At my age, I need all the power I can get so I can really taste the grape. This will do it." He ambled back and plopped down into the deep-seated chair. As he sipped, he looked deeply at Kurt, not smiling as he had before.

"You disappoint your old boss, Kurt. I never liked running as a reaction to adversity, and I am disappointed that you would make that choice. You are a superb historian," he paused and then continued slowly, "I think it's a grave mistake." He finished his sipping, but never took his bright, moistened eyes off Kurt.

"What happened, Professor? What happened to the United States of America? Why did it dissolve?"

"Because the majority of the people who gained control were of a different cultural heritage. They gained political control through the ballot box. It became the purest of democracies. Thus the most votes controlled the local, state, and eventually the national legislatures. One could say, that the vote destroyed what had been the world's beacon for democracy. But did it? What it really did was democratically and peacefully, for the most part, transform the United States from a white European-based society to a Latino, Africano, and Asian society. But isn't that democracy, Kurt? In its perfect state! What happened was that 'We the People' actually became the people. Not the white people who began the idea, but the majority of the people who lived within its boundaries. They gained control through elections, fair and square. So what do the losers do? They leave. Back to enclave white Europe or down to the South or up to Canada. That's you, Kurt, I'm sorry to say. Listen, adapt, my fine young man. Adapt. Join the swell of history. Study it. Write about it. I believe that's your life's mission. Whether this country succeeds or fails, it will be the center of the historical world in the coming years. They have problems, and some big decisions to make in the coming months and years which will have world implications. It needs to be recorded, firsthand for the historians of the future. In my opinion, at your young age and with your abilities, you should be the one writing of this time, in this country. I really believe that."

chapter ten

hey talked for another hour, heatedly at times, back and forth. Kurt thanked Dr. Alexander for his kind words of encouragement about staying, but Dr. Alexander realized that Kurt's mind was definitely made up. He finished his wine, and Kurt could see that he was beginning to grow weary. Kurt got up and walked over to him.

Kurt looked at the saddened face of this man for whom he had the greatest respect and said, quietly, "I must go. It's going on one o'clock. I can't dispute your logic anymore, but deep inside I know I must get away. Maybe in a year or so I'll feel differently, but I crave total freedom and"—he paused before continuing—"I can't even believe I'm saying this, but I want to live in an environment that is familiar. The loss of my culture bothers me. I'm proud of what the United States achieved, and what really troubles me is that the world has forgotten this. It's as if the United States never existed, and as a historian, Doctor, I'm proud of what was accomplished. Sorry—I'm not a bigot, you know that—but this land is a foreign country now, for me. I couldn't leave without letting you know what an inspiration you've been to me in my profession, but also as a friend. Your work ethic and absolute pure search for history has taught me so much." Kurt took both hands of the old man and held them tightly. They didn't say anything. Their hands stayed clenched, then slowly parted. "There's something else I have to tell you before I leave. Something I have to share with you for several reasons."

"Go ahead, Kurt," he replied quietly.

"Two weekends ago, I was working at the library. As you know I have had a lot of free time, so I thought I would do some personal family history, plus work a bit on the project you gave me to process the records that should be saved or destroyed. I know how important this project is to you and how you had to fight to even have them analyzed. I think it was two Saturdays ago, late in the afternoon, when I went into a room frankly I never knew existed. Inside I saw some cabinets which I opened. I was astonished by what I found. It was devoted to my father's work. It had all the original plans for the Pittsburgh Aquifer System, plus an addendum done in 2035. In fact some of his original notes and his signature were on many of the documents. It was a treasure trove. So, I downloaded most of the material that pertained to his work. I copied it to a chip, which I have on me. Right here in fact," he said tapping the sleeve pocket on his coat.

Dr. Alexander looked at him and then smiled. "I know, Kurt, I know. I knew you asked me if it was okay to do some off time work on the project and also to look for some personal history, but, when I checked the time monitors I was curious about the amount of time you were spending down there. So, I snooped around a bit. I went down there last week. You may not realize this, but when I had everything, and I mean everything, inventoried ten years ago, it was all imaged. I have every document prior to 2040 listed with content and its imprinted location. I could tell that you had found that special room because the sensors were disturbed on the door, the file, and even the documents. At first, I was concerned, for you, because that information, while not sensitive because it's just historical records of a great project, in today's climate, could be volatile. It contains valuable data on the whole structure of the System. So that scared me, actually, still scares me, since you copied the data."

"I just came upon the room. There weren't any special codes at the entrance. In fact, mine worked. Since it involved my father, I was ecstatic, so I downloaded the data. It was right there. Later, as I looked at the data, I realized that it might help me another way," Kurt said hesitatingly.

"How's that?" Dr Alexander replied.

"I needed a way to get to England, sir. I have no worldly funds, no UN monies, so in order to get passage, I required something of value. This data or some of it might be of interest to the government of Columbia."

"Kurt. Do you realize what you are saying?" he responded.

"I do, I certainly do, but, Doctor, there's another reason I would give them the data. Water is either going to be the salvation or destruction of this country and in fact of this whole hemisphere. If these countries cannot agree on a fair usage of this resource, then my father's work and the fate of the people are in jeopardy. By another country having access to the information, it might provide leverage for Atlantica to negotiate. All the data about the System supposedly was turned over to the Atlantica government in 2040 by the U.S. One thing for sure, Doctor, I realize now, after hearing from so many, that Atlantica plans on using the Aquifer for economic leverage. What I am doing may scuttle those plans. That was not the intent of the Aquifer that my father worked on for so many years," he said.

"I understand your feelings. You have every right to believe that and I agree with you. What you are doing may just do that. I didn't know what you had done with any of the data that you were researching, and I was going to ask you before you left tonight. As your boss, I will be asked where you are when they discover you have not scanned in. I will also be asked what you were doing in the old Aquifer files, so I'm glad you told me the truth. But more importantly, which I can't believe, it leads me to something that is extremely important, and we need to talk about."

They were both standing and Dr. Alexander said, "Kurt, please sit back down, I have a proposition for you." Dr. Alexander went back, sat down, and Kurt followed.

"I have to confess something. Listen closely to what I am going to tell you. I know how important your father's work is to you, and I totally understand what you did. In some ways you are a godsend because I have been trying for weeks to think of a way to influence the negotiations between the UN and Atlantica over the water. But let me explain a couple of things. I have vowed to secure and record as much history of this land as I can, with a government that wants to eliminate all reference to the USA. You're right, Atlantica and most of the world act as if the U.S. never existed. My concern, as a historian, is preservation of the past, not its destruction. That is my primary life's work as I near the end of my life. I am also appalled, like you, of the apparent attitude coming out of Atlantica, but what I have heard over the past months is what I've heard for years from Paris. The UN has feared that when the Aquifer was completed, it would become an economic wedge instead of a hemispheric source of water. Now, within the last month, my sources tell me that Atlantica will take over operational control of the Aquifer System from Alleghenia, which violates the federal charter, and furthermore they will use the Aquifer as economic blackmail to gain concessions from the UN and the surrounding countries. This must be stopped," the old man said in anger.

"Well that settles it for me," Kurt said. "But you said that you also had a proposition for me, Doctor?"

"This will take a few minutes, so bear with me, Kurt." He sighed and began again, "I want the UN to come in and take over the system. I have been in contact with associates in Paris who are close to the UN leadership. We have been trying to figure out some way for the UN to have leverage in their upcoming negotiations over water distribution. There was so much turmoil in the world during the past decades, that there was little concern for extracting valuable information about the actual operation of the Aquifer. It was all, in good faith, just turned over to the new government by the UN Commission. They received no copies of the plans or schematics. Now only Atlantica has the models and system software. Worst of all, we fear an open war over access to the water, especially since it will be at full capacity at the beginning of the year. My sources have told me that the Chinese and Brazilian Consortium working on the Aquifer have told the Administration that it will be able to generate full capacity by January, 2051. I also have found out that they aren't as pure in their intent as publicized. The consortium is to get twenty percent of revenues collected for the next fifty years, whether it's internal or exported. Another wrinkle, I'd say. So it is imperative, for all the people on this continent, living on meager water rations, that this system be utilized as it was designed. From what I can determine that is not the intent of this Administration. That's where your plans may provide a solution."

Kurt grew angry and said, "I knew they were close to having it completed. I should have realized the profit motivation is alive and well, even in this new society." Then he added, "But what's your proposition, Doctor?"

"Kurt, your data may provide the bargaining chip to make this government understand that if they don't cooperate, the system might be compromised. I hate using the word threat, but they may need to think that. How they can ignore the UN is beyond me, but if we have a chance to help the UN, we must do it. What you have in your possession may bring sense to the Administration. The UN has authority over usage of water resources worldwide. They have no schematics that would aid them in upcoming negotiations with the president of Atlantica, Roberto de Garcia. De Garcia is a revolutionary, but he is also an extremely brilliant man. He wants UN recognition for Atlantica's accomplishments during its Tenth Anniversary at the end of this year, but he also needs revenues. An agreement on shared water usage might do it. It's rumored they will try to gain trade guarantees out of the UN, using their water resource like oil used to be leveraged. Your operational information in UN hands might be helpful to the negotiators. Would you be willing to work with me on one last project?" he concluded, sitting back.

"What do I have to do?" he said unequivocally.

"Listen. Am I correct in understanding that you need passage to England? How are you getting out of here? It is very difficult for Anglos. You know that."

"I do and I have a way. The day after I found the Aquifer information, I came across another file with information on the Great Allegheny Passage."

"My God, I used to walk that when I was a kid. It was a beautiful trail. I think it's overgrown now. No one has used it for years."

"You're right, and the fact that it hasn't been used is even better for what I am going to do," Kurt said.

"What do you mean?" the doctor replied.

"I mean that I am going to hike that trail. It can't be in that bad a shape and shouldn't be monitored. As you might remember, I have been doing a lot of power hiking over this area the past year. My legs are strong, and I know I can walk that trail," Kurt said confidently. "My plan was to hike to Columbia and attempt to get passage there to England, hoping this data might help me with the authorities."

"Very clever, but dangerous, to say the least. They are a bit of a rogue country, but who knows, I guess that was about your only choice. Ingenious, I must say. The trail idea is a good one. You're right, that's the last place Security would be checking. By the way, do I have your code?" he asked.

"Why?" Kurt replied.

"I have another idea for you and one that would kill two birds with one stone. Listen to me. I am going to try and arrange for your passage to England with the stipulation that you provide the data you have to a UN representative. The UN can fly anywhere, so I'm going to make my contacts in Paris and see if I can't arrange for the UN to somehow intercept you on your way. This would help you from being at the mercy of the authorities in Columbia, who might not buy your plan. They may accept your data, but not your request for passage. If I can make the connection, it will help you avoid having to go to Columbia. They might arrest you, take the material, and throw away the key. It is a volatile place. They aren't the happiest country on the continent. If this works, you get safe passage and the UN gets the data that may solve the water problem."

"Well, that trumps my plan. This is incredible. I'd rather have the UN involved. Atlantica would have to listen to them as opposed to Columbia. The question is, how do I know if you've made the connection and if they want to get involved?" he asked.

"Let me think. I usually call various people in Europe. It's a great cover because I'm always working on my papers. I'll contact Paris as soon as you leave because it will soon be morning there. It will take me a day or so, but I'm sure I can make the right connection, get their approval, and find out how they plan on picking you up. We must develop a contact plan."

"Better yet, I don't know what I'm going to be up against out there. Starting in two days, I'll call you at noon. I'm sure on one of those days, I'll be in a location where I can reach you. You can then tell me the retrieval plan. What you need to remember is that a call can be traced within thirty seconds, so when we do talk, give me my orders quickly as to where I am supposed to be and who I am supposed to meet. Of course, this assumes you can arrange it. If you can't, I will go back to my original plan." Kurt finished.

"Noon, beginning in two days, that's good. That will give me plenty of time to make contact and develop a plan for your pickup. I also need a place where you can be picked up. Just a moment," he said and got up. He walked over to his desk in the library. After rustling around in a large drawer, he came back to the living room with a map. He unfolded it and spread it out on the coffee table in front of him. Holding it at one end, he offered the other end to Kurt. "Three days, hmmm," he muttered to himself.

Kurt watched as he pored over the map and dropped a finger down. "Fallingwater. That's it!" he exclaimed excitedly. "It's been empty for years. I know you know it."

Kurt looked at him and slowly a smile came to his face as he said, "That's so ironic that you picked Fallingwater. In the back of my mind when I was working on the trail, I saw that the trail goes near Fallingwater and for a while thought maybe I could take a short detour to see it for the last time. I used to go there with my dad. I love that structure and the setting. It's one of my all-time favorite places."

"Well if I can pull this off, it will be your launching pad for

England and possibly it will be the beginning of a truly new age for this continent." He looked back at the map and then up to Kurt. "Kurt, this was meant to be. I feel it—I know it, my boy."

They went over the plan again and finally there was nothing more to talk about. They looked at each other and both got up at the same time.

"Time to go, sir. I can't believe this has worked out this way. It's absolutely incredible," he said as he walked over to Dr. Alexander. They hugged tightly at the door.

"I'm so proud of you. So very proud and your dad, I know, is also proud. Godspeed," he said as Kurt opened the door and went out into the dark night.

Kurt walked down the sidewalk into the darkness. As he headed into the night, he knew he probably would never be back or see this great man again. Just as he reached the brick of the road he heard his voice.

"Kurt, remember. What you are doing and living is history. Write it down in your journal. Write down what you see and feel as you go on this journey. I said that the history of this new country is important, it is, but you are creating your own historical journey, which I believe will be even more important," he finished as his voice blended into the noises of night.

Kurt turned and looked back at Dr. Alexander standing in the doorway. He waved, shifted his backpack securely and walked up the street. The blackness outside seemed to grasp at him. Kurt heard the heavy door snugly close. His gut was tight with sadness at leaving Dr. Alexander.

chapter eleven

After his talk with Raoul, Martin went back to the apartment, showered and packed his personal belongings in his backpack. Something told him that in the coming days he was going to be busy working on Sloan's disappearance. If he was allowed, he wanted to be ready to assist in tracking Sloan. Just as he was fading into sleep, he remembered he was to make a presentation to his economics class in two days. He made a mental note to call his advisor and tell him he would be out of touch the next few days and fell asleep.

Martin was awaked by a dog barking loudly from the street outside the apartment. He yawned, stretched, and rolled out of bed. Light pored in through the window. As he sat on the edge of the mattress, his mind cleared and be went over all that had happened the prior day. He thought of Sloan and wondered where he would be today and then thought of all he had to do to begin his search. There was so much to do, but he knew he had to have a plan, a logical sequence to find Sloan. First he had to determine if his theory of Sloan's defection was correct. Raoul had not helped, but Martin's intuition was that he was covering for his friend. So he had to assume that the reason Sloan had stopped by was to say goodbye.

As he walked outside, the morning was gray and moisture was in the air, a typical fall day in Pittsburgh. He walked briskly over the bridge with the Castro Library looming ahead. Fortunately, the Cuban coffee kiosk was open in the park, and Martin devoured two sweet cakes dripping with honey and a café con leche as he waited for the library to open at 8 AM. As soon as the guard opened the heavy iron doors, Martin walked up the steps and entered the cavernous structure. He went to the second-floor archives where Kurt Sloan was supposed to have worked.

The air was chilly in the dusty, marbled 160-year-old library. Recently, the Atlantica government had authorized the imaging of all records related to the U.S. Government back to the year 2000. Older records, some from the late 1700s, when the city of Pittsburgh was founded by the British, were to be destroyed. Sloan's primary job, as he'd explained one night to Martin, was to process and eliminate unnecessary historical records. Those that might be useful were to be transferred to the Administration's permanent digital file system. Martin wondered if this work may have provided him access to valuable security information.

The library was a fascinating structure, and he found a booklet that described its history and why it was built. There were carryover stories about the poor boy from Scotland, Andrew Carnegie, who became a billionaire and then gave much away to the people of the area. Martin believed this to be fiction. He knew that Carnegie, like all the founders of this city, were white, English, and Protestants, some even poor. Martin's take on Carnegie's story was that he was a white man, in the right place, at the right time.

Martin entered a room, lined with shelves to the ceiling. He saw an old woman seated behind the desk, wrapped in a deep red shawl, bent over a large, pale green cloth-covered manuscript. The woman was running her finger along the lines of the book. Martin walked right up and stood over her as she continued to follow the sentences in the book. She never paused or seemed to notice him. He stood silently as she came to the end of the page and began to start along the top line of the right-hand side. It was then she noticed someone standing over her. She methodically put down her reading glasses and looked slowly up at Martin.

"May I help you, young man?" she said hoarsely.

"Maybe you can. I want to know if you knew an Anglo who, up until a few days ago, did research here at the library. His name is Kurt Sloan."

"Kurt Sloan. No, can't say that I can remember anyone by that name. What was his specialty?" she requested.

"Good question. I believe he was doing research on the history of this area. At least I think so."

"History you say. Of this area, you say," she said as she paused and then added, "Well, no one comes to mind. And why is this so important?"

"He's a friend. I need to know where he is because I have to tell him something very important. You see he's from the old Pittsburgh, probably your Pittsburgh. His family was here for a couple hundred years, and he was working on a project for the Administration going through all the old city records. Do you understand?" he said softly.

"First, you are correct, my Pittsburgh. Second, as to your question, I do understand. Look at this!" she said turning the now-closed book around, sliding it in front of Martin.

The faded green book had large, but barely readable script on the cover.

"HISTORY OF THE CITY OF PITTSBURGH," Martin said out loud as he ran his hand over the old cover. "So you're a history person, too, I see. Then you must know my friend, Kurt Sloan. Tall, about thirty-five, with brown hair."

"Oh you mean Mister Meager. I'm sure that's Mister Meager.

Marshall Meager I call him. I have names for everyone," she sighed as she looked at Martin.

"What would you call me?" he said.

"I don't know, young man. I haven't really looked at you long enough. You see, I have to look at people a while before I can give them a name," she finished.

"Mr. Mulatto, maybe?" he stoically replied, giving her a deep stare from his oval tanned face.

"Oh, I don't think so. That's a derogatory name. I only give pleasant names to my people," she quietly responded, pulling the heavy book back in front of her.

"Okay, lady. Who is Mr. Meager? Describe him."

"Oh, he's an ordinary man, but of the old ways. I mean he doesn't look like he belongs here, in Pittsburgh, now! He reminded me of someone from the old days. A silent, scholarly type. Sort of out of his element, one might say."

"Why would you say that?" Martin said.

"He never talked. He was always reading or thumbing his way through the oldest of books," she answered.

"But why did you call him Mr. Meager?" he said.

"He was like a squirrel. He would bring a small bag of food with him. Occasionally during his sessions, he would open up his bag and pull out some crackers. He would break off a piece and put it in his mouth without looking. He would just keep reading. It was odd. I spend quite a bit of time in this library. It's my home, yet it seemed that Mr. Meager was also always here and he never seemed to eat anything but his little pieces of crackers. A couple times I would ask him if he wanted to share one of my sandwiches. He would look up and slowly smile, but say no, that he had plenty to eat. He was a quiet bird. Also, he read very slowly and always took notes in an old, brown leather journal. He just looked to me like a Mr. Meager."

"So, why do you think he's the man I asked you about?"

"Well, he seemed a learned man and an Anglo. Not many of us around anymore, young man. In fact, none that I've seen lately," she answered spryly, looking him right in the eyes.

"Well that's their—*your*—fault. We didn't tell all those white people to leave. They deserted, just like your Mr. Meager may have done. The problem is that if he left, he may have taken valuable data with him which is why I'm here this morning. I need to know what he was reading when he was here, say the last couple of weeks. Do you know?" Martin said in a much harsher tone.

"He looked mostly at maps of the city, old maps from the City Planning Commission Division. He also read all the old newspapers. He said none of this material was in his work area. I assume his was more technical. This here is all the public information, newspapers, videos, and the like. That's what he said."

"So this is what anyone off the street can look at?"

"That's right. I guess his workplace had the more valuable materials. It's like when you go into an old bookstore, the old classics, first editions and the like, are in a locked case. As you can see, all of what I have here is wide open. We have no secrets here, which is why I don't know why you're checking up on such a nice, quiet man as Mr. Meager."

"That's none of your business, and his name is Sloan. One last thing, did he ever talk to anyone else in here about what he was looking for?" he asked.

"Only Miss Flipper."

"Who, lady, is Miss Flipper?" Martin sarcastically replied.

"Can't miss her. She's up there at the front desk," she said, pointing down the hall. "She's the head librarian. She's been here for years. Knows every book on this floor. Looks like, well, you should go look at her and decide for yourself if she isn't Miss Flipper."

"I think I will. I may be back, so you try and think of anything else about Sloan, ah, Mr. Meager, that you can," he said as he walked toward the main room on the second floor.

As he walked down the marbled hall, he couldn't help notice all the ornate decorations of long ago. Whether to refurbish this epic of the past was a decision the Administration had been putting off for years. Since all collections and books were available online, the remnants of the vast library buildings would no longer be needed and could be closed. The cost to repair it would be astronomical. As he walked along the dark corridor, he returned to the immediate problem of Kurt Sloan. *This is where Sloan was spending all his time; this is where he could have come up with some critical data,* he thought as he walked toward the main entrance.

He immediately saw Miss Flipper sitting behind a huge wooden desk that was raised on a platform, like a judge in court. She looked like a seal with glasses.

"Have a minute?" Martin said to the solidly built woman with her gray hair pulled back in a bun behind her head. She didn't acknowledge him as she leafed through a weathered notebook with faded alphabetical lettering on red tabs.

She didn't answer, but kept writing and turning pages. Miss Flipper was not ready to respond to him. He looked at her and thought of the other woman he'd just left. These are lost people, remnants from the prior Anglo rule. It must be bewildering to them. He remembered reading statistics for his dissertation of the Millennium Year 2000. At that time only 20 percent of the Pittsburgh population was black. Currently Alleghenia was almost split between Africanos and Latinos with a small minority of Anglos.

He stared at the woman who still didn't look up at him. She just turned the page of her book again. He finally cleared his throat and said more forcefully, "Miss, I need a minute of your time."

She still didn't look up, but slowly closed the book and shuffled a stack of cards before neatly putting them into a case.

iss Flipper, or Marge Dougherty, had been an employee of the Carnegie Library System for fifty years. Marge wanted to quit when the name was changed to honor Fidel Castro, but her pension earned in the U.S. was frozen, so she needed the work. She started as a clerk in 2000, shelving returned books. Her Irish-Catholic family had been in the Oakland area of Pittsburgh since the 1880s, coming over to work in the mines and mills. Her father had been a local fighting hero to the "Micks" of Oakland, fighting for the middleweight championship in 1965. He lost, but it made him a local celebrity. Marge went on to graduate in Library Sciences at Pitt, received her master's and spent her whole life behind the walls of this world famous library. It was her whole life. She never married. It was through books that she created her perspective on life. She never questioned the outside world, never paid attention to it. Everything came from the written word. She saw the decline and fall of the United States as inevitable because it, a decline and fall of a nation state, had been written about since history was recorded. What bothered her as she lived in this new world was the decline and elimination of the ethnic traditions of her childhood. The strong Catholic and Irish environments were gone. Most of her relatives had returned to the western lands of Ireland, especially her young cousins. She had thought many times of going, but she couldn't imagine her life without the books of her Carnegie Library, which she refused to call Castro. It was something she could not leave. Marge Dougherty looked up and said, "There, I'm done. Now you asked me something about time, right? A minute, I believe you asked for a minute. I've got at least a year, here, young man," she said in a deep and empty voice as she turned toward Martin.

"What does that mean?"

"It means that I'm seventy-four years old, and according to the edict that I received last week, all personnel will be allowed to work until the age of seventy-five. Of course there was a special notation to remaining personnel of the Carnegie Library, all six of us, that termination would be within the year. So, I've got a minute. Do you want to take out some books on William Shakespeare?" she sarcastically asked.

"It's the Castro Library, lady, if I'm not mistaken," he abruptly said to her.

"You are mistaken. That is for sure. Now, what do you want?" Miss Daugherty answered quickly and sternly.

"I want to know about someone who recently spent time in this department of the library," Martin asked.

"Who might that be?" she warily replied as she rolled her chair farther back from the counter.

"His name is Sloan. Kurt Sloan. He's about…"

"I know him well," Ms. Daugherty said. "He's a fine person, brilliant scholar. Probably the best history buff in the city. I still say city. To me this is still Pittsburgh. Yes, I know the gentleman. So what?" she coarsely said.

"I want to know, if you know what he did here at the library. What area, subject was he recently working on?" Martin asked.

"The man works here. He works for Dr. Alexander. He

had his own office and had access to all the files in the system. So what if he came into this part of the library? That's his job, for heaven's sake."

"I want to know what he was concentrating on, say the last few weeks," Martin said quickly.

"Well, everyone's entries are recorded. Now, he was also assigned to the old files, and in some cases they aren't recorded. Your Administration wants to shred some of the oldest materials on the history of this area. Priceless material going back to the 1700s. I can't believe it. Anyway, that was part of his assignment. A lot of that material is deep in the bowels of the basement. Mr. Sloan recently began to come here on his off days, mostly Saturdays and Sundays. On those days, he went down to the basement file."

"What's down there?" Martin asked.

"The oldest and most valuable ones," she answered stiffly.

"Like what?"

"Well, he was here two weeks ago and discovered some files that concerned the water system his father had worked on. You knew his father designed the Pittsburgh Aquifer System, didn't you?"

Martin's face froze. He was astounded. "No, I didn't know that. What did he tell you?"

"Nothing, he just stopped by, I think it was two weekends ago. In fact, he stopped by to see me on Saturday and Sunday. He seemed in the best mood when he left Sunday. The man is usually so serious and when he left, he actually seemed happy. More than I had ever seen him. I'm usually here in the afternoons on the off days. My life is here, you see. I love this place. I—" Martin interrupted her.

"Lady, I don't want your life story. I just want to know what he said when he came up from the basement."

"He just said that he had put most of the pieces together on his family history which he had been working on for months. As I said, he was so happy and so was I."

"What day was that?"

"Saturday. He also stopped by late Sunday and said everything was great. He said that he never realized how much valuable information had been preserved. Then he made a comment about reading something on the Great Allegheny Passage."

"What the hell is that?" Martin snapped at her with an incredulous look on his face.

"That was a hiking trail that Pennsylvania, our state, finished around 2006. It went all the way to the capital in Washington, DC. I was going to school, right here, when it opened. It was a big deal in these parts. It was supposed to be the most beautiful walking trail in the East. Mr. Sloan seemed so happy. I'd never seen him like that."

"Forget all the nice talk. I want all the entry codes for Kurt Sloan during the off time periods. That's what I want, not his day work."

"I can't do that," she said briskly.

"Listen lady, it might take me a few hours, but I can get the codes. I can get printed summaries of his requests. I can call right now. I know the Chief Magistrate of the Security Court. He'll get my probable cause and transmit a warrant for an officer of the court to search the library's databank. Take five minutes to trace his entries. But if I have to do that, I'll tell him of your uncooperative attitude. You won't even finish out the year here. You'll serve it down the Panther Hollow in the new Detention Center along the river. I don't care how old you are or how long you've been working here. This is important to me, and I know it will be to the Administration. So what is it? You going to help me, or is it goodbye to this place?" he stated directly in her face.

She glared at Martin. She sighed and said, "You're right," she acknowledged looking him right back in his face. "You'll get your access that way. Nothing has changed. Retribution still reigns in this world, black or white," she added with sadness in her voice and face. "What am I going to do, fight you, City Hall!" She walked around to the window that looked out over Panther Hollow next to the library. She turned back to Martin and said, "As I said, Mr. Sloan was only working on his personal family stuff in his off time."

"Lady, I don't want your explanation of what he was doing, just get me the entry data. Security needs to see proof of entry. So bring up that data, now," Martin demanded.

"Well, actually, the information is not in the system, just his entry points and the subject matter. I think what he may have seen was old hard copy, not data copy. I just know what he said to me," she replied.

"There must be something relating to these files."

"There is. Outlines, subject matter, etc. the hard copies."

"Bring that up, now!" he said, his voice rising.

"Don't get agitated, young man."

"I just want what he was working on and may have turned up."

She punched away at the thin keyboard, then looked up at Martin and said, "Here's an outline."

She looked at her monitor. Martin came around behind the counter and looked at the screen. He stared at the title MAP OF THE GREAT ALLEGHENY PASSAGE TO THE NATION'S CAPITAL and with topics listed below. It was dated 2012. He noticed a button to the side of the monitor which read VISUAL. He hit enter and a video obviously based on GPS positioning outlined a broad red line that began where the Allegheny and Monongahela rivers met, known locally as the Point and also the beginning of the Ohio River. The moving picture scanned the trail as if in a low-flying aircraft sailing over the facsimile of the trail as it had been in those days. It listed the mile posts through the mountains all the way to the Potomac River until it reached the capitol of the old United States, Washington, DC.

Martin knew where Sloan was going, how he was going to get there, and possibly where he was that morning. He was probably already hiking that old trail. He thought grudgingly that it was pretty ingenious. No one would have looked on that trail for someone trying to leave illegally. Emigration rules were strict for anyone, especially an Anglo employee. Security had been on highest alert to protect against any threats to the Aquifer. In this security climate, it would make it very difficult for Sloan to get through Security checks. To avoid the normal routes, this trail would be perfect. Martin was impressed, but how would he gain asylum at the border. Columbia was almost a police state and very difficult to enter. He would need something of value to convince the authorities to grant asylum and get him passage. His wages were strictly Atlantica credits, so he would need something else to offer the air service or their government. Martin suddenly was aware of the whole scheme Sloan was attempting as he looked at the screening visual which stopped at the entranceway to Georgetown. He understood it all. *Sloan is a traitor. He's trying to sell out my country,* he thought.

Martin looked away from the monitor at the old lady, who stood with her hands on her desk with a look of fear in her eyes as he said, "I thought you told me that all you could get was an outline? That was a GPS video concept. Don't play games with me lady. This whole thing is getting worse and worse for Sloan and for you. Is that all that is there?"

"I didn't know it was set up that way for that particular file structure. Most of the old files are just that, files. I think you will find the rest of them, in that section, just what I said, hard copy," she said.

"Whatever. Just generate a copy of that, now," Martin said to her as they stood beside each other.

She pushed a copy button and instantly a slender paper thin disc came out of the printer next to the terminal. Martin walked over and picked up the disc.

"Save that, permanently," he said to her. She hit another button. He looked at her for another moment and said, "Remember what I said. I'm convinced now that this man is a traitor, and you don't want to be an accomplice in the investigation that is pending. Do you understand, old lady?"

She didn't answer him, but looked at the screen, now fading back to gray. Martin looked at the thin disc he had, back to her, and then walked away. Marge watched him with tears in her eyes and slowly snapped the switch that turned off the data unit.

"God forgive me," she murmured to herself.

chapter thirteen

t had been two o'clock AM when Kurt walked down the dark path from Dr. Alexander's house to Browns Hill Road. He hadn't been able to see a thing. The rain had stopped, and periodically he had some help from a moon that peeked in and out of the mostly cloudy sky. He knew the river and the Homestead High Level Bridge were at the bottom of the hill. He needed to cross at the break of day when there would be little activity. He made a quick decision to find a spot to nap. More rain was expected early in the morning which would give him good cover when he reached the river. He'd moved inside a wooded area, found a large rock with a concave bottom that he could crawl into which would be perfect to protect him from any Security heat sensors. Large boulders abounded in the Pittsburgh area, left over from millions of years ago. He lay down, curled into a sleeping position using his backpack as a headrest, and within seconds, had visions of Maria, Dr. Alexander, his father, and mother, with her smile and quick vivacious laugh. These were his last thoughts as he drifted into a deep sleep.

He wasn't sure what it was, maybe the early bird calls or possibly the blustery wind and light rain, but he awakened and slowly opened his eyes. It was still dark on the rock. Kurt rolled off his perch and stood up. He looked at his watch which showed 6:25 and realized he had to get on the trail now and to the Homestead Bridge before the sun came up. He checked his backpack and when he reentered the path, he knew he was about halfway down Brown's Hill Road. Across the valley, he could see the dark sky giving way to the red of the sun that was breaking above the hills. The town of Homestead lay beyond the bridge, hidden in the darkness with lights that dotted the roadways. He could barely make out the structure of the high steel pillars of the bridge that crossed the Monongahela River.

He'd been down to the bridge last summer on a hydrofoil that he rented. He remembered clearly how the bridge was barely standing with its rusted-through metal and cracked cement supports. It was a local landmark, a remnant of a once glorious industrial past. It had been renamed after a local Africano baseball team of the early twentieth century, the Homestead Grays. Kurt had read in his historical research how the area had made a dramatic comeback after the steel mills were dismantled. He could see a walkway heading east along the riverbank. When the walkways were constructed, the riverbanks were left open as they were high above the water level. He stretched, ready to begin his first major test. Looking down the river, the walkway looked relatively clear. He remembered an article written years ago which said that accessibility to the walkway was being threatened by debris. Another design of the construction of the trail was that it was secluded, away from the noise and vision of the small businesses and communal districts that lined the valley from Pittsburgh.

Traffic on the river didn't seem heavy. He could make out two large coal vessels wending their way swiftly and silently down the dark river. "Nothing changed in that scene," he muttered, as he watched the cone-shaped piles of coal, a scene that had been part of this land for two hundred years. The barges moved around the bend in the river as the sun broke through the darkness and the early morning clouds. "I have to get going," he muttered, adjusted his backpack, and headed down the path next to the road.

As he half walked and jogged down Browns Hill, he could see ahead the roadway leading up to the entrance of the bridge. When he reached the bridge there were fallen trees and crumbled cement blocking the entrance. Kurt worked his way through the debris to the floor of the bridge where a solid bunker about ten feet tall lay in front of the bridge. As he stood figuring out how he was going to get around the bunker, he heard a loud whooshing noise. In a flash, he saw a commuter Meglev train roaring under the bridge on its way to Pittsburgh. In a few seconds, silence returned to the bridge.

Kurt looked at the cracked, but still-solid bunker in front of the entrance. It looked impossible to climb, so he walked around toward the side and found a slight opening outside the railing. He climbed over and squeezed through until he came onto the partially deteriorated sidewalk. He could see wide-open gaps in what was left of the roadway and walkways. Kurt walked gingerly across the remaining segments of the sidewalk, sometimes walking only on exposed beams, and then onto areas of the roadway that were still in place. At least two times, pieces of cement dropped heavily into the water below. As he approached the other side of the bridge, he went to the east side and looked over the railing. Down below he could make out a high ridge next to the riverbank, and beside it, a lower matted area that followed alongside all the way down to a bend in the river. That had to be the walkway. The ridge was actually higher than he'd remembered. It would give him better cover.

At the end of the bridge, Kurt came across another cement bunker which he handled the same way he had on the other side.

At this end there was an old steel ladder that went down to the trail below. It was in good condition, and Kurt dropped down onto the walkway. As he stood there he noticed graffiti on the walls of the bridge support. Obviously, others had been under the old Homestead Bridge. The slogans did not discriminate as they covered many groups. Some wrote of contempt for the Publicans, Blacks, Mulattos, and Latinos. Down a bit were anti-Anglo, even the worst white slur, anti-WASP. All were in different colors. Everyone was included. Another form of democratic expression was at least alive and well in Alleghenia. It seemed all factions felt the brunt of someone else's hostility. The section under the bridge had been incorporated into the walkway. The walking surface was rough, mostly a mix of dirt and gravel. He could see debris lying about ahead of him, but it was passable. In fact, it was perfect, because he could tell that no one was using it, at least at this location. He looked out at the river bending its way as always, undeterred by humanity. The sun lit the lingering darkness into a golden, shimmering mosaic. He tightened his pack and headed down the trail. The ridge to his right was approximately ten feet high. He noticed wild growth mixed with all sorts of discarded items, probably going back many years. This mixture was intertwined in heavy, dark green natural vines. As he walked along the brilliant river with the morning sun shining off the flowing water, Kurt couldn't forget what he was leaving behind. His whole life had revolved along this river. He was walking away from his heritage, his very heart and soul. For hundreds of years his family had lived, worked, loved, and died beside this great old river.

The walkway was dead silent, and he found a comfortable gait, beginning to feel some distance from his birthplace. He stopped and turned back to look at the Homestead Bridge, still visible with the sun blazing off the girders. His eyes then drifted to the river, the Monongahela. He always considered it a manly river because of its strong, tough history through the ages of the coal and steel industries. It flowed north, which in itself was unusual for rivers. Eventually it reached Pittsburgh, where it blended with the gentler Allegheny to form the broad and forceful Ohio. He thought of the natural constancy of rivers, which had sustained people along their banks for centuries. He thought it ironic that he was on a mission to try and provide people access to water, while these rivers flowed with a resource so abundant in this area. As he looked at the river this morning, it made him realize how critical it was to get his data to the UN so that this land could remain peaceful even though he would not be part of its future.

He hadn't walked more than a half-mile when he noticed a fabricated steel bench with a brass plaque affixed to its back. The plaque read DEDICATED, JANUARY 1, 2000, TO THE WORKERS WHO MADE THIS RIVER VALLEY, THE FORGE OF DEMOCRACY FOR 150 YEARS. Kurt looked at the plaque, shook his head, "They should see the 'Forge of Democracy' now," he muttered.

He covered the distance from Homestead to McKeesport in a little over an hour. The walkway was absolutely empty. He stood looking across the Monongahela and far down to the mouth of the Youghiogheny River. He looked at his maps and realized this would be the most exposed portion of his trip. He saw the two bridges he would need to cross. The first, a transit bridge, would get him over the Monongahela and the second, an old railroad bridge, over the Youghiogheny. Once he got over the Youghiogheny, he would walk along the riverside until he reached the entrance to the Great Allegheny Passage. Kurt looked up and down the broad expanse of the Monongahela this early morning. The river was quiet but activity on the streets across the way in McKeesport had picked up considerably. He sat down against the banked ridge. He needed to plan his next move carefully.

At that moment he saw a patrol boat splitting the waters of the broad Monongahela. The patrol boat was headed toward Pittsburgh. It was his first sighting of any Security on the river since he had left the night before. Kurt reached back into his backpack and pulled out his leather-bound notebook. He retrieved a map he had copied at the library. He looked up and scanned the riverbank across the way.

Kurt looked at the transit bridge that he would need to cross. The maps listed Security posts at both bridge entrances. Then he saw the patrol boat, which must have circled back, come toward where he was sitting. It continued past him until it reached the entrance of the Youghiogheny. It turned sharply and went down the river in the direction he was soon to be going. This mission might be more dangerous than he anticipated.

Kurt lay back against the ridge. He looked up at the sky and rested, but almost immediately, heard a loud whooshing noise that sounded like an old vacuum cleaner. He looked up and spotted a Skimmer swooping down river from Pittsburgh. It came zooming overhead and turned suddenly down the Youghiogheny River. What had they observed or picked up that would cause them both to go down the very direction he was headed? He realized he couldn't let that bother him. He had to get across the river and on to the Great Allegheny Passage and soon.

As it happened, the transit bridge was perfect because it had a lower maintenance track that hung under the main deck and the Security posts were unguarded. Kurt walked over across the Monongahela, looking below to the swiftly moving river. He climbed around a barricade and slid down the side of an embankment to the path below. He could see the rooftops of the City of McKeesport and hear traffic noises. It was morning and McKeesport was coming alive. Without hesitation, Kurt headed to his next crossing at the Youghiogheny. Once he got over that bridge, he would be on his way to the entrance of the Great Allegheny Passage or what was left of it.

chapter fourteen

artin was confident he knew where Sloan was headed and how he planned to get there. He also felt that Raoul knew more than he had told him, so he decided to contact him again. However, before leaving the library complex, he went to see Sloan's boss, Dr. Alexander. The older man was hidden behind a pile of layered folders. He had been very cooperative, for an Anglo, Martin thought. He realized that Kurt wasn't in his office area, but many times "Kurt would be in another part of the system for a day or so without reporting in to me," was how he put it. Martin explained to him that he was fairly certain the doctor's employee had left the area and that Martin did know where he had gone. Dr. Alexander was visibly upset at what Martin said and vehemently discounted it. Martin asked if the doctor could contact Sloan while Martin was there, so the doctor did. Apparently he got a message that Sloan would be in the field for a few days and would contact Dr. Alexander later. This seemed to genuinely surprise the old man. He had rubbed his face and looked out of his office window and then said to Martin that he was sure Kurt would be back as he said he would. Martin asked if the doctor had any idea where Sloan would go, if he would have left Pittsburgh. The doctor had no clue, but said that if he got more information, he would be glad to pass that on to Martin. When Martin left, he felt certain that

Sloan had even fooled his boss. Several times the old man had said he couldn't believe Sloan would have left him without an explanation. Martin could tell the doctor was devastated and said if Martin found Sloan, that he, Dr. Alexander, wanted to be the first to know because he wanted to bring charges against Sloan. "Sloan's work was important and no employee could just pick up and leave," the doctor had said as Martin was leaving. The doctor thanked Martin for alerting him. Martin was impressed with the old man and had picked up another clue about Sloan's destination when the old man had said what Martin already knew, that Sloan had talked about Scotland many times.

The information at the library and from Dr. Alexander was extremely helpful. It verified Martin's suspicions, but something was troubling him about the meeting he had with Raoul. It was early afternoon when he left the library, and he knew that Raoul was probably at work, so he decided to see if his sister was there. When Martin was asked to look into Sloan by Security he had been given a listing of his friends and associates. One piece of information Martin found important was that Raoul had a sister, Carla, who was engaged to a man in Security. Martin thought maybe she might be willing to tell him something that her brother would not. He had to try anyway.

It was early afternoon at the house he had been to the night before. When the door opened, he saw a small, dark-haired woman looking at him. She asked if she could help him, and Martin explained he was looking for Raoul.

"He's at work. I'm Carla, his sister, may I help you?" she offered in a soft voice.

"Well, maybe you can. You see, I'm a friend of Kurt Sloan, and I am trying to locate him. Do you know him and where he might be?" Martin asked still standing in the doorway as the woman kept the door halfway open.

She paused and said, "I do know Kurt Sloan. Come in, *por favor*," she said.

They sat down in the same front room that Martin had been with her brother. She offered him coffee which he accepted. The coffee was the dark, syrupy coffee favored by the Puerto Ricans. It was just what he needed as the morning session at the library, although productive, was time consuming, and he hadn't had time for any lunch. He sipped slowly on the hot, creamy coffee, as Carla sat down across from him. She was a sullen, but attractive woman. She had a lighter complexion than her brother. She sipped quietly and smiled at Martin with a hint of shyness. He decided to get right to the point.

He asked her bluntly, "Have you seen Kurt Sloan recently?"

She sipped again, but without hesitation said, "He was here last night, talking to Raoul. It was late. I think he left after ten."

"I must have just missed him. Did you know I was here last night, Carla?"

"Yes, Raoul told me."

"When Sloan was here, did you hear what they talked about, Carla."

"Not really, I was upstairs." Then she added quickly, "Kurt is a nice man, a very private person, but for some reason I have never trusted his loyalty to our country."

Martin asked her quickly, "What do you mean, not really?"

"When he was leaving, I heard him say something about going to Scotland. When he visited here before he talked many times to Raoul about visiting Scotland someday, but this time it sounded like he was leaving for there."

"That's important information," Martin answered.

"Well I thought so, too, so first thing this morning I called my fiancée, Angel Torres, who is a Security Analyst. He said he was going to immediately make a report. Angel told me that there were many pressing security problems and the possible defection of an Anglo historian might not be classified as high priority, but he would send in the report and Kurt's description to Security Headquarters. He told me that the data would then be automatically entered into the surveillance network which meant his profile would be displayed at transportation and public meeting places all over the country. It would also be in the news and monitoring networks. I didn't even tell Raoul, but I felt I did the right thing. Raoul will be very angry at me."

Martin said, "You are a patriot. You did *absolutamente* the right thing."

Carla then went on to tell Martin that Kurt had been a great help to Raoul when he had first come to Alleghenia. Kurt had encouraged Raoul when he was going to school at the university. She mentioned the relationship between Kurt and her younger sister Maria, who was now in France. Carla said that Maria saw something special in Kurt Sloan, but that relationship was over. Martin was interested in this information about Maria. As he left, Martin thanked her and said she would get a commendation when he filed his report to Security. She asked that if he talked with Raoul, he not tell Raoul what she had done. Martin promised he would not tell anyone, except that her help would be in his report. He then thanked her and left confident that he was really on to something.

As he walked back to the Tram station, Martin thought about what he was getting involved in. Curiously he felt energized and he felt a sense of pride that he was doing something to help his country. He knew he didn't like Sloan from the first time he met him, but was uncertain why. Now he had a better understanding of him, and it seemed like his intuition was correct. Well, now Sloan's name and ID would be over all the Security scans.

Martin realized that he needed more information to convince Security that his suspicions were valid. Since Security had been alerted to his disappearance, Martin decided to go to their Headquarters before it closed and see if he could get updated data and maps on the Great Allegheny Passage. He needed evidence to back up his story.

He hurried along Shady Avenue under the Tramline, listening for the next Tram. He climbed the metal stairs to the platform and sat down to wait. As he rested his back against the railing, he thought of the rumors floating around about infiltrators trying to gather information about the water resources of Alleghenia. The president of Atlantica was in Pittsburgh last week, and he spoke about the Aquifer System, which he announced would be at full capacity in January, 2051. He also reported there was significant pressure from the outside world for Atlantica to allocate the water resources to surrounding countries without, what the president said, was "adequate security or compensation." Martin was impressed with the president, who was adamant that this was *our* resource and no one else would decide how and who would benefit from it. Martin and everyone knew he was referring to the UN. The president added that Security had picked up increased chatter and knowledge about "outsiders" as he put it, attempting to obtain data about the Aquifer's capabilities, which, he added, "were state secrets." It was the last thing he said that Martin remembered the most. The president announced rewards for citizens who uncovered traitors in Atlantica who would "undermine the security of our nation." If information was proven correct, rewards would be given to the citizens, including paid scholarships for students to their next level. This announcement coupled with Security's request increased Martin's interest ever since his suspicions about Sloan had been aroused. He would be graduating soon and he already had his Paris scholarship. If he could obtain these additional educational credits, he could continue in Paris to achieve his ultimate goal, his doctorate. By age twenty-eight, he would have achieved the highest educational level possible. This would enable him to be accepted as a World Scholar and would open up many doors for him, especially getting a position with the Atlantica government in Nuevo York. Sloan may end up giving Martin his life's dream. It was both a very serious security event and a phenomenal opportunity for him personally. Martin could feel the raw excitement of exposing Sloan and also the rewards that awaited Martin for his work.

It was turning cold, and Martin looked up at the afternoon sky with dark clouds rolling in from the west. Sloan had a head start on him. He would like to begin a search in the morning, but he needed more backup information to convince Security of the need to find Sloan. He looked at the overhead clock. It was 4:30 PM. Martin pulled out his palm phone and punched information for Security. He was connected, and a woman told him they closed at six, but for data retrieval he needed an appointment. Martin asked if he could still get an appointment because he needed some maps. She asked for his name and said that the last time slot was open at 5:45 PM, which he accepted. As he closed his phone, he heard the rumbling of the Tram cars coming to the stop. Going to Security would give him a chance to check on Carla's story and see, if in fact, her fiancé had alerted Security to Sloan's disappearance, plus he hoped to get maps of the walking trail. The Tram pulled in to the stop and Martin boarded.

After a quick ride through what the locals called the Hill District, formerly a ghetto section of Anglo Pittsburgh, they reached the station at the base of The Bluff. As he got off, he looked up the steep hill above him where the Security Offices were located. Martin was famished, and he had time to get to Security for his appointment. He walked down to the Plaza Cafeteria next to the courthouse. He looked at the rounded sandstone of the strange, old building with the little bridge over the street that many of his fellow university students talked about as being such an architectural masterpiece. All he saw was a dark building, now filled with offices of the Administration. He remembered one student saying that the guy who designed that courthouse was considered an American genius, but Martin laughed as he paused and looked at its heavy, ugly walls, before entering the Plaza Cafeteria.

The Plaza was alive with Latino music, and people were eating even at this afternoon hour. He walked up to the line and waited as people in front of him picked up items from the counter and slid their trays toward the register. He made his selection and walked over to an empty booth that looked out of the window. He began devouring his lunch. Martin was alone for only a minute, when a young white woman, about his age sat down, smiled, took out a newspaper, and began to read. They looked at each but neither spoke. Martin went back to his plate, looking occasionally out the large front window at the courthouse.

He was lost in his thoughts when another person sat down across from him. Martin looked over. It was a young man, white, with a pencil-thin black mustache, who slid a tray over to the woman. He looked over at Martin, smiled, and immediately dug into a sub sandwich with ham coming out from between the dark bread.

The booth was quiet. Martin did not look at them. The coffee was hot, but good, and he knew he would need it to help him get through the rest of the day. He began to think and plan about the next day. His goal would be to gain permission to get a search under way as soon as possible and permission for him to go along with Security. His eyes strayed outside as he drank his coffee, stopping at the courthouse down the street. It reminded him of what this country used to be about. *How things have changed,* he thought.

chapter fifteen

urt reached the railroad bridge where the Youghiogheny River meets the Monongahela River. It appeared that the rusty bridge hadn't been used in years. He crossed over the Youghiogheny without a hitch, although looking down into the green, swirling water made him aware of the danger. The bridge's condition made him cautious with the extra pounds he was carrying. When he reached the other side, he sat down on the cement foundation of a demolished building that lay against the hillside. Kurt looked back across the river to McKeesport and thought that he had just finished the most exposed part of his journey. Now he would be following the Yough on his way to Connellsville.

He saw a wooden shack farther down against the hill that was tilted to one side. Kurt walked over and kicked open the rusty hinged door. He wanted to take a quick break before beginning the next phase. He found a small stool and sat down. He sipped water and had a snack while he watched the rivers collide where they met as they had for thousands of years. He would now be heading into the country and the mountains, away from populations. His mind drifted in thoughts of the journey ahead. His sister, what was she doing in Scotland? He hadn't seen her in years. Would he make the connection with Dr. Alexander's people and what did that mean? If that didn't work, would he get space on a flight in Columbia? Would either group buy his information as credible? It was a kaleidoscope of thoughts with absolutely no rhyme or reason. He took a deep breath and checked his watch. It was close to noon. He had to get going if he hoped to achieve his first goal of reaching Connellsville by midday tomorrow. Kurt had programmed the trail, the time, and the weather for the trip on his GPS screen. He knew the weather was supposed to be cloudy early tomorrow morning with rain expected and later in the week there was the possibility of an early snow storm coming off Lake Erie. He hoped the forecast was wrong, but for now, the rainy weather might provide cover. "That's the plan. Can't wait any longer, gotta get rolling," he muttered to himself. He took his last bite, stretched, and got up. Checking his backpack and pockets he set off, quickly setting a brisk gait.

He walked along the riverbank on a narrow trail. The path was cluttered with all types of debris. This was not the main trail, but it was completely isolated which was perfect for Kurt. He could see ahead a high wall with an arched entranceway. As he got closer, the path opened up and he walked onto a large landing of crushed limestone. It was the entrance to the Great Allegheny Passage as he could see in faded letters above the entrance. The wall had collapsed in several places, and he stepped over one low section onto the gravel walkway beyond. He saw stone, metal, and wooden debris scattered about, but the pavement was clear. This was a relief to him. Kurt looked back down the Monongahela River and then turned and began to walk. Slowly at first, but soon he was able to get into a quicker pace. As he did so, his mind wandered. If it wasn't for the finality and the circumstances of this trip, he would have been more relaxed and strictly enjoying this walk through history. He quickly realized he had to stay focused on the present, not the past or the future.

As Kurt walked, he listened to the river run beside him and the noises of various birds in the overhanging limbs above the trail. As he continued along the trail, it narrowed but was still solid even though the tiny crushed stone was moist and gave with his footsteps. What amazed him was the uniformity of the walkway years after its design and construction. It was still guarded by a sloping hillside. As he went deeper into farming country, it became more secluded. He was surprised by his pace. Many times he had to move aside branches, but for the most part, he didn't need to stop to clear the path. Kurt glanced at his watch and realized that he was close to his preplanned schedule. He felt extremely strong and alert. "This is good. Got to keep it up," he said.

Kurt came to a straightaway in the trail, and he could see far up the river where he could make out church spires. As he pounded along, the only sounds were from the water running to his left and occasional muffled sounds of life from over the ridge. The most surprising thing so far was that since he began his journey from McKeesport, he hadn't seen or passed another person on the trail.

Suddenly, as he turned the next bend, several church spires of different heights and colors appeared before him. This must be West Newton. He decided it was a good time to take a break as light was starting to fade in the late afternoon. Kurt loosened his backpack and dropped it on the bank. He sat down and turned on his GPS screen which flashed the weather for the coordinates. He checked the message and turned it off, so the signal wouldn't be picked up. The latest forecast called for rain tonight, and the possibility of a storm off Lake Erie tomorrow had increased with a significant drop in temperature. Kurt sat there for a minute, realizing he had to keep going into the evening. He had to get as far as he could before the cold weather and snow came. "I guess things were going too smoothly," he thought.

After the stop outside West Newton, the sky changed from fading light to darkness as night took over. This section of the trail hugged the hillside, and with the tree limbs hanging, he had perfect cover.

Near the end of the first day on the trail his body felt good, but gradually as he continued, tightness in his calves developed. The extra weight and the pace apparently was catching up with him. Kurt could feel the steps becoming laborious, and he realized he needed to rest. He rounded a slight bend and spotted a small cove about four feet up the hillside. He clambered up the slope and crawled into an oval-shaped opening. He explored the cave and realized that there was an old conduit cover leaning against the rear wall, partially covered by dirt and rocks. Whatever its purpose, it hadn't been used in years. This was a perfect spot out of the weather and any possible sighting from the air. He would await daybreak and the pending rain. He curled into a tight ball, covered himself as best he could, and laid his head on his backpack.

For several minutes he lay there wide awake. Somehow he needed to rest, hopefully sleep, if only for a few hours. As much as he tried to relax, his mind traveled over the bounds of his memory bank. From his father's laugh to a PBS special when he was a kid that showed the sun finally blowing itself up, disintegrating all the planets. Of course that would be in millions of years, but it made an impression on the young boy. Nothing, he realized, was absolutely permanent. Each moment was important in your life, yet absolutely insignificant in the timeframe of man's existence on this earth and even more so the existence of earth itself. This philosophy of living in the moment always put him in perspective as to the importance, the incredible importance of living for the present moment. Tonight, as he lay curled in a hole beside the Youghiogheny

River on the mission of a lifetime, he thought of his belief in the moment and that the only thing real and within his control was each tiny frame of time like this moment. That was his last conscious thought.

Kurt awoke in the dark, but he could tell by the sound of birds off in the trees, that daybreak wasn't too far off. He must have been exhausted from the past days because he had slept most of the night. He stretched his body, pulled up his legs, and rolled out of the cave. He slowly stood up as a group of low-flying crows could be seen in the gray light of the morning as they zipped by into trees above the hillside.

Kurt stretched his body again, looked at his watch and then to the river. Up ahead and across the river through the rising fog, he could make out a small town which he believed was Smithton. A few lights were sprinkled amongst the low-storied buildings. Smoke peeled out of several chimneys. He had been here as a young man when his family would drive into the mountains. These were fond memories of the times that they had spent together. This route was not only his way out, but was bringing him closer to his memories of his youth and his family and was taking him through lands that he knew so well.

Light was coming over the hills to the east and the fog was burning off. Kurt could see above him the first bank of high dark clouds in a tight ridge coming into view. The weather had been so typical of this time of year. Wave after wave of clouds would come in off Lake Erie, some with rain, but then, when the temperature dropped, snow. At that very moment, the wind began to pick up, as if listening to Kurt's thoughts. He checked his weather again. The forecast was for winds increasing to 30 mph, before a rainstorm arrived in the Laurel Mountains. It was time to move. Without hesitation, he grabbed his pack, tightened the connectors, hoisted it on to his back, and returned to the trail. Hopefully, by this time tomorrow, he should be in the mountains and on his way to Columbia.

He had walked for only a few minutes, when a light drizzle began, which soon turned into a steady downpour. He put up his hood and zipped up his lined jacket. The clearness had totally disappeared and a heavy black cloud bank took over the sky. The wind picked up and his weather meter clocked winds close to 30 mph. He walked blindly for close to an hour, and then the force of the rain quieted to a gentle mist. It was a relief from the large slashing pellets of the earlier downpour. He was able to see up ahead much better than he had before, so he picked up the pace. The bad weather made it unlikely that he would come across anyone on the trail, unless they were Security. As a precaution, when he came to incoming pathways, he would slow down to make sure there was no one entering the passageway.

Kurt knew from his work that the population in this rural community had plummeted over the past ten years. Most residents had either moved to the city, left the area or country altogether. The only growth industry was large organic agribusinesses set up by the Administration and worked by Latinos brought in from Mexico. He also remembered the Administration was attempting to revitalize a dormant wind-farm sector up in the higher ridges. Funds for these projects were coming from South American investment companies of the Southern Hemisphere Union. It was a good plan as the power generated was used by the local agribusinesses. Kurt also knew that the major farms and generating systems were monitored by Security, but so far he had not heard or seen any patrols in the air or on the water.

He was falling a bit behind schedule due to the rain, and the trail wasn't as secure now that it was covered in places with water. Much of the hard-packed paving had cracked, filling with water and dirt. Twice he took a few minutes to eat his rations. Finally, the misty rain stopped completely. His waterproof shoes had held up well during the day, but hours before he had lost feeling in his feet. It seemed like a month since he had his socks and shoes off. He would have to do some healing tonight because he couldn't afford for his feet to swell.

Ahead of him a curve in the path brightened suddenly as a short burst of sunlight peeked through the dense clouds. The trail still had some stone mileage markers, although most must have been taken as souvenirs He looked back at the river, noticing that the current had picked up dramatically from the new rain. He continued on the trail until he reached a large outcropping that came right up to a bend in the path, and he stopped. Slowly he looked around and could see both sides of the river at Connellsville. He could see no activity. The town looked deserted. He had been going at a strenuous pace, and the combination of the damp weather and impending night caused him to seek a place to rest for the night. He needed to ration his energy.

Grabbing hold of a tree that had grown up alongside the slope, Kurt climbed up the embankment. He could see what appeared to be the town center but saw little activity. Should he take the chance of going into town? He was tired and hungry. He craved something substantial like a sandwich and soup. Kurt realized the snacks and energy bars would do just fine. He had a goal, and he couldn't make a mistake now.

Kurt spotted a grove of trees behind the back of a ridge that protected the trail. He walked off the trail, up the mound and kneeled down between the trunks of the large oaks. He took out his small shovel from his pack and dug away at the hard dirt until he formed a place where he could rest his body and still see the river. He unhitched his backpack and slowly sat down. He pulled out his sleeping bag and got into it. It was cozy in the mound, and he could feel the tiredness leave his legs as he leaned against the wall. His eyes drooped as he heard the rapid current flowing past, then a dog's howling from afar. His eyes closed, and his head turned slowly to his shoulder. Shortly, he was asleep.

He awoke suddenly because he could feel raindrops hitting his face. Kurt opened his eyes, it was pitch-black, and there was a steady rain. Except for his face, he wasn't wet. He reached around and pulled the hood over his head. He looked at his watch and was shocked. He had slept for over five hours. It was the middle of the night. "Must have been whipped," he muttered.

He lay back, pulling the hood down over his face. He was wide awake. His mind was settled for a short time, his thoughts soon returned to his father. Under the circumstances of the new world of Atlantica, Kurt thought of his father's philosophy that "A person can only do the best they can." Kurt lay thinking of his situation and the day ahead. He said out loud, "That's all I can do, the best I can." Even though it was the middle of the night, he had a sense that he couldn't waste any time. He needed to put distance between himself and Pittsburgh.

chapter sixteen

"Y ou like that building?" Martin heard the voice of the man sitting at the table with the woman.

"Oh, no, actually I hate it!" Martin said.

"Why do you hate it?" the man asked.

"It reminds me of all the slave times of the Anglos, that's why."

"Well, yeah, they were depressing times no doubt, but that guy was a genius, for his time."

"What guy?" Martin asked sharply.

"H.H. Richardson," the man answered.

"Who the hell was he? Sounds like a perfect Anglo name, to me," Martin briskly answered, scooping up the last of his food.

For the first time the woman spoke, "He was the greatest architect of that time. The building and bridge you see there are world famous. It's called the Bridge of Sighs," she said, looking at Martin while sipping a light, lemon-colored drink.

"So what?" Martin answered her. "It still represents an ugly time in the world. Don't you agree?"

She looked at him and replied, "I do agree, but you know, some good things were done by those people," she answered shyly.

"Where are you from, girl?" Martin asked.

"That's none of your business," the man interjected. "June, let's just finish our lunch and get out of here," he said.

"We're both from Canada," she answered.

"That's a switch," Martin countered. "Many of the Anglos from here went there. So why did you come here?"

"We're both committed to this country and its goals. We're socialists and we want all people to have the same opportunity to succeed. My country buckled under pressures and allowed Americans and all sort of bigoted people into the country. So we came here to study," she ended.

"Study what?" Martin asked calmly.

"Comparative Societies is the name of the master's program. It's designed to compare world social structures and the governments that run them," the man answered.

"So why do you defend some guy named H.H. Richardson? An Anglo, who made a fortune off the capitalist system of that day?"

"Well we believe, June and I, that to understand societies and civilizations you need to appreciate their valid or positive points, not just discard all that they did. That's why we were so interested in Alleghenia, primarily Pittsburgh, to finish our master's degrees and develop our doctoral treatises. This is a perfect place to study the great achievements of the past inhabitants and their abysmal failures. That building over there is a perfect example. You know it was a jail for a long time?" he said excitedly.

"I didn't know that," Martin answered.

"You are right though. Although it is a masterpiece of American architecture, it also epitomizes what was wrong at the same time. It housed poor people, black, Irish, Slavs—those who could not pay for valid defenses. So you see, you've picked out the centerpiece of our thesis."

"That building is your centerpiece?"

"It is. It represents exactly what we are studying. We hope to go to Paris next year to continue in our Comparative Societies path," the woman piped in between her friend and Martin. "That's why we eat here all the time. We can see our doctorates painted on the sides of those dark, sandstone walls," she laughed.

Martin smiled and said, "That's funny. I'll be in Paris, myself. Maybe we'll bump into each other again. It seems funny to me to see such enthusiasm about a building that represents such bad times, but I understand why you're doing it. Well good luck, and thanks for talking with me. See you in Paris." He got up, took his empty tray over to the cleaning area, and walked out the front door. He looked over at the courthouse with a different opinion of its value. *Maybe there is something in what they said,* he thought as he looked back to the cafeteria window. They were waving at him as he headed down the sidewalk toward the incline that ran up the side of the bluff to the Security Office.

Martin got off at the top after a slow ride up the steep hillside. He walked along a narrow, cement street to a red brick building marked, SECURITY HQ. He looked past it to the city below. It was an incredible sight. He could look all the way to where the three rivers met. He turned the handle of the door, stepped into a reception area where a wide-shouldered black woman sat behind a counter. As he approached, she looked first at a clock on the wall and then at Martin with a broad smile.

"What can I do for you?"

He explained to her that he was searching for a missing Anglo who had already been put into the Security Watch list that morning. He explained to her that he believed the Anglo may be using a long-abandoned walkway to make his escape. He began to tell her of the urgency of his request, when she interrupted him and said she would be glad to help him and the

Administration. She understood the need to help and walked around to the front door which she locked. She said, "The office is closing," where upon she laughed and added, "Don't worry, Security never closes; this is just the Administrative Office." She asked Martin what exactly he needed. Martin went into an explanation of the data that Sloan may have taken and its potential damage to the country. He said he thought Sloan may be using the trail called the Great Allegheny Passage to make his escape and Martin needed maps of the trail, if Security had them.

When he was done, she cleared her voice and stated that she was Hillary Newsome and understood his concern. She would do all she could to help him. She had a broad, flat face with a wide smile. Hillary asked Martin for the exact spelling of Kurt's name. She entered the datafile and noted an entry in Kurt Sloan's profile at 8:30 AM that morning from Angel Torres, a Security Analyst. She added that Mr. Torres was one of their leading analysts and that he would not have entered the data unless he felt it had come from a valid source. She said based on Mr. Torres's request, all communication networks and transit facility systems in the state and country, had begun screening Sloan's photo and data profile as a Security Alert.

At that point Martin again stated that he thought that Sloan was going to try and get to Columbia by way of the Allegheny Passage and asked if Security would have a complete video scan of the trail. He repeated to her the original name of the walkway, the Great Allegheny Passage, and that it was built between Pittsburgh and Washington, DC around 2008. He added that it basically went southeast through the Laurel Mountains.

Hillary entered the data, looked into the screen, and said, "These are the coordinates and should cover that whole area. Do you want a disc or the hard copy," she asked.

Martin said both and she punched in her request. She said she was going to check the other offices while they waited for the report.

While waiting, Martin checked out the walls of the office which were filled with topographical maps and satellite pictures of the area. He had come full circle along the walls, when he spotted a topographical picture over a place called Ohiopyle, where he could make out a faded outline of a defined trail. He wondered if that was part of the walking trail that Sloan would be using. He noted how wild the area looked. The next few days would be quite an adventure if he had to go into that terrain looking for Sloan.

Suddenly a gray terminal against the wall started humming and a stream of paper began to come out of a slot located in the front of the unit. Hillary must have heard the unit and came back. She let it run, and when it stopped, she took the paper, folded the sheets into a book shape, and came over to Martin.

She handed Martin the folded hard copy and said, "At bit old-fashioned, but here you go, Mr. McDonald. I think this is what you are looking for. Here's the chip copy also," she said. "You can run that off your datafile."

Martin unfolded the first sheet which was in color showing a red stripe running through a map on the page outlining the trail. It was titled in all caps, THE GREAT ALLEGHENY PASSAGE. He folded it back into a neat book.

"This is it. When this report is finished, I will certainly make the Administration aware of your valuable assistance. Thanks so much."

"By the way, Mr. McDonald," she said checking her watch. "I would recommend you going over to Observatory Hill to the DataSec Office. They can provide you with a GPS scan of the trail just by having the coordinate perimeters which I would be glad to send them. It will produce an actual visual scan of the trail as if you are flying over it yourself. It's an amazing visual concept over the very trail this guy might be on. Would you want me to that?"

"That would be perfect, especially when the trail is being scanned. This will not be forgotten, I assure you," he said to a beaming Hillary.

"Take the incline back down and the Tramway to the Point. Their office doesn't close until ten. I'll send the request ahead and good luck getting this Anglo," she said.

Martin thanked her again and left. Darkness was moving in from the west in the form of dark, black clouds which to Martin meant rain. He was going to follow her advice and get this all done tonight. He walked toward the incline and waited for a few minutes until it came back up. The city below was still in the early evening light and from the sheer cliff that overlooked the city it looked like a sparkling pie wedge between the rivers. Across the rivers he could see his destination, Observatory Hill, the highest point in Pittsburgh where the Data Center for Security was located.

After two quick rides, Martin reached the center. He was guided into a small cubicle. A Security officer at the entrance checked his name and acknowledged his ID and clearance from Security. He punched a request into the keyboard and in a few minutes, a screen was filled with a satellite picture of the landmass between Pittsburgh to the left and a river in the far-right corner. It stretched to a wall that surrounded the western portion of Columbia. Then he watched an overview from a laser-guided satellite station that scanned the whole area that began at the Point all the way to the Potomac River. Martin could tell it was an older screening, maybe even from the archives of the U.S. because tape showed the walkway corridor before the wall had been put up around Columbia. It was dated

10/1/2038. He could see that the walkway was almost buried in growth at some locations, but still clearly defined, especially when it followed along the rivers. What had happened in the intervening years would make it more difficult for anyone trying to use it. "Sloan would never get far," he said to himself. The screen went blank, and the officer handed Martin a copy of the transmission he had just seen.

As he left, he knew he needed more proof of Sloan's intentions in order to persuade the Administration to authorize a search. They would have to be convinced that he may have taken Aquifer information and that he was probably using the Allegheny Passage to escape. At that moment, he thought again of Maria, Raoul's sister, whom he had seen with Sloan at the house. Carla mentioned her in passing, which may have been an oversight because she was now in France. Martin remembered the first time he saw her in the hallway coming out of Sloan's room. About a week later, they crossed paths on the front porch as Martin was leaving for school. They talked briefly, and Martin knew immediately from her accent that she was Puerto Rican. He also remembered her angular body and dark beauty from both meetings.

He thought about his reaction after the second meeting with the beautiful Puerto Rican woman. For some reason, his curiosity about Sloan grew when he saw him with the striking young woman. Because of Security asking him to check on Sloan, he decided to look into Maria. He found out that she had been accepted into the scholarship program in France. Martin realized that Maria obviously had a plan for her life, but he needed to get as much information as he could on Sloan and his intentions. Maybe Sloan would contact her if he got to Scotland. As he rode back over to the city from Observatory Hill, Martin realized he needed to communicate with Maria to find out if she might have some collateral information on

Sloan. Raoul wouldn't help him, but Carla had been very helpful. If Maria came through with any clue at all, he would have additional support for his request to Security to allow an official search for Sloan.

As he rode back down toward the city, the triangle formed by the rivers was outlined by lights along the riverfront. Martin was relaxed, knowing that he had accomplished more this day than he ever expected and he had much more to do.

chapter seventeen

artin spent a restless night in the apartment trying to think of way to get Maria's ID so he could contact her. He thought of going back to Security, but he needed to have an outside source. That was when he thought of his old professor from last term, Jorge Rivera, who now served as an assistant to Roberto de Garcia in Nuevo York. Jorge worked there in the Communications Network. His primary job was to do instant surveys on the populace by monitoring various broadcasts to get public reaction to the news. Jorge had known Roberto de Garcia for over twenty years. They both started in the Democratic Party in the Puerto Rican wards of Nuevo York when it was New York. It was with great reluctance that Jorge left his position with the University in Pittsburgh. He began as a professor with the university and became head of the Social Studies Department in the new University System until last year, when he was asked by his old friend, now President de Garcia, to join him in Nuevo York.

Martin had become close to Jorge his first year at the university because of his scholastic aptitude. Jorge asked him to help in a tutoring program for Caribbean students. They became close. Martin knew Jorge would help his star pupil locate Maria because he would realize the threat the defection of Kurt Sloan might mean to the Republic and to his friend, the president. Since Jorge was on the president's staff, he could surely locate a student on an Atlantica scholarship in France. Martin went into the Info Network for Jorge's number in Nuevo York.

It took a minute, but he was soon looking at Jorge. "Martin, *que pasa*? How the hell are you?" Jorge asked. "Do you know what time it is?" he bellowed.

"I do know. It's the middle of the night, my friend, but I would not have called you unless it was an emergency and this is an emergency, believe me, *senor*," Martin said.

"Okay, okay. What's on your mind?"

Martin didn't go right into his reason for calling as he wanted to calm Jorge because Martin could tell Jorge was upset at being called at this hour. For the next few minutes Martin talked old times with his professor. They had a common love for baseball. Jorge's middle name was Roberto, which came from Roberto Clemente, a national hero in Puerto Rico and ironically, in Pittsburgh. He had been a great black Latino baseball player of the late 20th century. They talked and finally, Jorge stopped Martin and bluntly said, "My friend, what do you want?"

Martin explained the situation and how potentially dangerous the defection of Sloan with data concerning the security of the Pittsburgh Aquifer System may be to Alleghenia and to Atlantica. Jorge was silent for a few seconds and then said, "I need her full name and last address." Martin gave it to him.

"Hold on. Turn to messages, Martin. Your ID address, also," he added. Martin did so and waited.

After a few minutes, Jorge came back on his unit. "Okay, go ahead, *amigo*." Martin pushed his unit, and a message and picture ID stared back at him of a beautiful woman with a Toulouse France address listed. It was Maria Hernandez. The record showed a Pittsburgh address, the one he had just visited, a Nuevo York address, and the current one in Toulouse. Also included was her call number. He thanked Jorge and promised to get back to him if he needed more help. Jorge had encouraged him and stated plainly that he would help Martin get to Paris himself. "You were my best and brightest," he said.

He immediately dialed the call number, knowing it was seven hours later in France.

"Your name again? I can't hear you very well and the picture is blurry."

"Martin McDonald. I lived in Kurt Sloan's house in Pittsburgh. Are you Maria Lopez-Hernandez?" he spoke as loud and as clear as possible into the handheld unit. There was interference and based on the ID picture and his memory of her, he couldn't tell for sure if it was her. The woman in the screen looked like the Maria he had seen, but the picture was out of focus. Suddenly, the picture cleared, and he knew it was her. "Yes, I remember Kurt mentioning you. What do you want?" she said anxiously.

"We met at the house in Greenfield," Martin said.

Maria lay propped on her elbow looking at the small screen of the man she remembered from Kurt's house. They had passed each other in the hallway, and Kurt had commented how he never saw this guy and really didn't like him. She clearly remembered their brief encounter. Afterward Kurt said that McDonald was a superpatriot and someone he really did not trust. Another time they met on the front porch and she remembered the piercing, hostile eyes that looked first at Kurt and then at her. The man had given her a chilled look that she could still see in her mind as she responded to him. "Is he all right? He's not hurt or anything?"

"Not that I know of, but I'm calling you to find out if you've talked to him lately. It's very important. He seems to have left

Pittsburgh for some reason, and very quickly. As you know I lived in his house and I'm concerned"

"I don't know why Kurt is of any concern of yours. You two weren't friends. Which makes me wonder, how did you get my ID?" she said angrily.

Martin had a quick comeback as he said, "The Administration needs very much to talk with Sloan. They gave me your number since I'm working on his situation."

"I assumed as much. So, I am surprised by what you've said. If true, it's a great surprise to me. I never thought Kurt would leave Pittsburgh. He really loved the city. It was almost an obsession, the history of it. He must've been really upset by something to decide to leave if he left. But he is a courageous person, McDonald. More of a survivor type than one might think. If he did leave, he will get where he is going, you can bet on that."

"Oh, he left. I'm sure of that. Do you know where he may have gone?"

"If he did leave, which I doubt, he would probably go to Scotland where his mother and father were buried years ago, and I think he has a sister there."

"I appreciate your information, but my real concern is why he left. Do you know why?" he asked bluntly.

"How would I know why if I have no idea where he is? Is that all? I have classes in an hour," she replied, anger returning to her voice.

"So you don't know if he's left and you don't know how he would be leaving. Is that correct?"

"That is correct and I'm cutting out of this call. But let me tell you, Mr. Patriot, I do know that history is his passion because he was chronicling the history of the demise of the U.S. and the creation of Atlantica. That's who he is. He's not a very complicated person. You're on the wrong track, McDonald," she said.

"Well, you don't seem too concerned about Sloan. His leaving is odd, especially as an employee of the government, but the troubling part of this whole episode is that I believe he has taken valuable information about our Aquifer. That's treason, lady. If you are aware of anything he is doing, you are complicit. Do you understand? France or no France, you would at a minimum lose your scholarship.

"Did you hear that?"

The picture faded slightly, and Martin could see a stunned looked on the beautiful face. She didn't respond immediately, but then said, "As I have told you, I know nothing about his leaving and certainly know absolutely nothing about any information you claim he took. I take that, McDonald, as a threat to me, and I will report this to the Embassy authorities. You have no right to accuse me the way you just did," she said. Quickly she added, "What is going on with you, McDonald? Why do you want to hurt him? This is a good man, Anglo or no Anglo. Is that it, McDonald? He's an Anglo? If he did leave, I'm sure he decided he wanted to leave because his country is gone, for God's sake. We've taken his country, his life away from him. If he did go, let him go, McDonald. Let Kurt Sloan have his life. I have a class. I have to go," she said and cut out the transmission from her end.

Martin looked at the white dot left from the vanished picture on the screen. He could tell she was telling the truth. As Martin sat on his bed with light beginning to show through the window, he knew, based on all he had learned over the past few days, that Sloan was using the trail to get to Columbia. Martin knew how tough Columbia's security was on transit visas, especially for a citizen and employee of Atlantica. He now knew that Sloan had critical information related to the Aquifer which would be valuable to Columbia. That has to be it," he shouted and grabbed his pocket phone, punching in Security Headquarters. "I'll get there as soon as it opens."

chapter eighteen

"Listen, McDonald. You can't come in here and demand a Skimmer just like that. We have been put on high alert with the tension between countries about the water resources and our immense borders are difficult to cover. Haven't you seen any news? Watched your scanner? Check your band now. You'll find a Community Alert," the stocky, broad-shouldered commander of Security said without looking at Martin. COMMANDER EMILE SLUDGE, SECURITY PATROL, his ID proclaimed. He wore a tiny communications headband which looped over his shaggy, red hair. Sludge was a light-skinned mulatto of Spanish extraction. He had a deep, husky voice.

"Sir, I am aware of the situation which is exactly why I am here this morning. By the way sir, who specifically is this tension with?" Martin asked.

"It's obvious, McDonald, primarily our neighbors to the east and south, Columbia, and America. We have water, lots of it. We will shortly have a delivery system, best in the world. They don't have either. It's obvious, McDonald," he replied briskly.

"If you will listen to me for a minute, I'll explain that the water system you just spoke of may be in danger of being compromised by an Anglo employee of Alleghenia, who has left without a Security passport," Martin said firmly.

Commander Sludge sat up in his large chair and said to Martin, "Let me hear more, McDonald."

"This Anglo, Kurt Sloan, works at the Historical Commission offices in the Castro Complex at University Center. He and I lived in the same house over in Bloomfield. He's disappeared from the house and work. If you check his work records in the System, you can see he hasn't been there the last two days. His supervisor didn't know he was missing or where he is. He just left."

"Okay, so what? I need more to go on than you just coming in here with this story. Maybe the man is drunk somewhere. Shacked up, whatever."

"He's not, I have checked with his friends. He's gone."

"What else?" Sludge asked more seriously this time.

"I have definite information that he may have taken critical data relating to the Aquifer System. I also have information that he is escaping in a most unusual way."

Sludge bent toward the front of his desk and asked, "The Aquifer System. That would be serious, very serious, and what's this escape method?" Sludge sternly asked.

"All the data I have collected convinces me that he is using the Great Allegheny Passage hiking trail that goes from here to Columbia through the Laurel Mountains. It's been unused for years, but he has secured maps of the route. I'm here, sir, to volunteer as a patriot, to look for him. I believe because he's hiking a trail in the mountains that the best method would be to use a Skimmer. It's the only way to fly over its length, find him, and bring him back to Pittsburgh for interrogation."

Sludge did not respond for a few seconds. He looked at Martin and then stood up. He walked over to the large office window, looked out and quickly turned back and said, "You may be on to something. First, we normally don't bring on volunteer security people and second, even if we decided to do so, I haven't an extra Skimmer. But if I had one, Headquarters wouldn't allow me to use it to find one man. Jesus, I've sent out Skimmers on seven red alerts in the last two weeks and so far; we've picked up five suspects. In fact right now, all of our available Skimmers are on duty," he said.

"All I'm asking for is a Skimmer to search the length of the Great Allegheny Passage for three days. I know we'll find him in that time. He may be a terrible security leak. What if the whole water system was compromised by one person? I know how he's getting out of the country. He's going by way of an old trail that goes right to the Columbia border. As you said, tensions between us are high, and they would love to have information on our Aquifer System. If they got such information, don't you think our leaders in Nuevo York would be devastated? It would create a national crisis."

Sludge looked at him and sat back down. He looked away and then back at Martin. "It's all speculation. You think this guy has information on the Aquifer? Do you know what he's got? We can't run this unit on guesswork, especially from a student, a nonprofessional. That's just the way it is," he said, and he stood up again looking at Martin as if he expected him to leave.

Martin didn't move. He looked up and replied, "With all due respect, Commander, I want to see whoever can make the final decision on this matter. As a citizen I have that right," he said firmly.

"Why should I tell you anything? You barge in here with some wild story about an Anglo taking down the whole fuckin' country. Anyone would need proof of your allegations. You know that guy may be an Anglo, but he's got rights too. If he's still here, he's got as much rights as you or me."

"Commander, I've worked hard to get where I am at this

point in my life. I believe in our country, and I know that this man is a threat. We all have too much to lose, so as a citizen, I ask again to be able to take my case to someone in the next level. That, by the way, is also my right. Read the Code of Civilian Rights, sir," Martin ended with a strong, firm voice as he stood to face Sludge.

Sludge looked at Martin and said, "Okay, your next stop would be to the Provost Marshal over at the Alleghenia Headquarters on Grant Street. Her office is on the third floor. If she believes this search is as important as you think, she can make it happen. Don't count on anything, but you might find her in a good mood."

"She? Her? A Provost Marshal? I thought they were like the police enforcer types," Martin said.

"They are and believe me, she is. They're the super police force of the various Republics in Atlantica. In Pittsburgh, our Provost is a lady. Don't let her hazel eyes and great legs throw you. She's a tough son of a...," he paused and then picked up, "I guess tough daughter of a bitch is more accurate," he said, laughing at his description with a feline like smile on his face. "Her name is Marshal Clay. First name is Dawn, I've never heard anyone use that name. To you she is Marshal Clay, period. Don't try any bullshit on this one. Tell her, if you would, that I took your request as a citizen very seriously and that I was abiding by the Code in recommending you talk with her. I will send a request to her office immediately that you would like a meeting as soon as possible. I could have thrown you out, McDonald. I get citizens in here all the time with all kinds of tales about neighbors, service delivery people, even other Administration personnel, but you, you're good," he said smiling that cat smile of his at Martin. "I have to admit, you are a convincing young man. You should be going into the law. But remember, if she for some reason approves your request, you are on your own. If she sends me the okay, I'll try and get one of our better pilots to take you. But you won't be going anywhere unless you get the okay from the Marshal. You understand, don't you?" he stated.

"I do. And Sludge, I remember people who help me. You're on my list.

"Fuck the list, make sure you know what you're doing or you'll be on my list. It's a short one, McDonald."

"Hate to push my luck, but when will I know?" Martin said as he was about to go through the door.

"You have and soon, maybe later today. Depends on the Provost," Commander Sludge replied without looking up.

Martin left Sludge's office and was quickly on Grant Street, the main thoroughfare in Pittsburgh. He had decided to go directly to Security Headquarters and wait for Provost Marshal's decision. If his request was granted, no time would be wasted, and he felt time was critical in finding Sloan.

The late-November air was brisk. Far across the Monongahela River, Martin could see the side of Mt. Washington, which loomed over Pittsburgh. This part of the city was still the center of this old town. He was walking beside the classic Headquarters of Alleghenia's Administration. The building had served for over a hundred years and fifty years in the same role for the City of Pittsburgh. It had been totally renovated years before by the State of Pennsylvania as a historic landmark, but while doing so, they had also completely brought it into the 21st century of wireless technology. It was now powered by solar energy which in Pittsburgh, one of the cloudiest locations in the Hemisphere, was a technical miracle. As Martin walked he noted business people, obviously from different nationalities. It made him think of the economic potential of Alleghenia, especially with its reservoir of natural resources. Thinking of this, it became clear why Atlantica would want to take control of these resources as had been rumored. Martin feared it could cause great friction between the leaders of Atlantica and Alleghenia, which made his discovery of Sloan's disappearance even more important. *If another country gains any important system information at this time, it might weaken our country's position especially with the UN getting involved,* he thought.

His discovery was becoming much more than a disgruntled Anglo leaving the country. It was becoming a potentially international bombshell or at least might create a conflict between Atlantica and the state of Alleghenia. This thought frightened Martin, as his loyalty was to Atlantica, but also he had a stake in the future success of his adopted Alleghenia. "Right now I have to protect them both by getting a Skimmer and finding Sloan," he said out loud confidently as he jogged up the steps of the Security Complex.

chapter nineteen

urt turned on his flashlight that lit a narrow path on the trail. In a few minutes he was in stride. The walkway was in very good shape with little debris other than branches and leaves. Kurt picked up his pace as his refreshed mind began to think of the miles ahead. He realized he had to contact Dr. Alexander when he got close to Fallingwater. From previous visits he knew Route 381 climbed out of Ohiopyle and reached Fallingwater. Kurt was hoping he could find a way over the river before Ohiopyle to save time and to avoid probable Security at the small river town.

To Kurt, Fallingwater was the most fascinating architecture he had ever experienced and in a setting that was dreamlike. That he was going near it on his way out was ironic. From those earlier times he'd fallen in love with Fallingwater. Its beauty and peace had overwhelmed him. The memory of the outreaching decks and layered stone in the dense woods of the mountains, with water running constantly underneath it, was remarkable. The memories began with a freezing day in the middle of winter when he was probably ten. It had been closed, but his father had received a special entrance card to visit. He would remember that day as if it was yesterday. It had been incredibly beautiful. Snow hung on the maples, oaks, pines, and drooped down the huge, black-green laurel.

He remembered hearing the stream roaring underneath as they stood inside the stone-floor living area in front of the massive fireplace. He had never seen such a place in his young life. Over the ensuing years, he'd been back at different times of year. Whether in spring, midsummer, fall, or the dead of winter, Fallingwater always affected him in such a gentle and calm way. As he walked in the darkness on his way there, he thought how the whole concept of Fallingwater represented the genius of the American experiment. Kurt studied the building of Fallingwater for a thesis in his graduate studies. This architectural accomplishment represented the greatness of America when a second generation Welshman, Frank Lloyd Wright from the Midwest, teamed with a Pittsburgh Jewish storeowner, to create what was considered one of the great architectural masterpieces in world history. The fact that Dr. Alexander chose Fallingwater as the contact point for Kurt to leave was almost too ironic for him to contemplate.

Kurt had been walking at a good pace when light began to appear in the sky ahead. Across the river he could make out what he thought was Chestnut Ridge and knew the trail would soon be turning south when he got to Indian Creek. There was no activity in or along the river. He was beginning to feel weak from his light food intake. It had been three days since he'd eaten a normal meal. His quick pace was burning his energy. He realized that at some point he would have to take a chance and see if he could locate some basic staples. If he came across a village he thought he might find a farmer's market or co-op, but for now his cravings would have to wait.

Kurt returned to the task at hand and picked up his pace as the narrow trail opened up a bit. He was lost in thought when suddenly he was jostled back into the reality of his surroundings. Laughter came ricocheting from the trail ahead, lots of it, and from many voices. He dropped down beside a retaining wall that came out of the hillside and listened.

There were several men, and they didn't seem to be moving. He tried to pick out what was being said. The loud laughter stopped. They sounded like they were around the next bend. Kurt looked up the embankment. In this part of the walkway, trees were hanging out across the top of the wall. There were no landmarks. He looked beyond the trees and could see the high ridges of the mountains. Kurt raised his watch directly at the sun and entered the directional guide. In the GPS window, his longitude and latitude showed, followed by the names Indian Creek N and Morgan Run S, apparently the closest north-south points of reference.

He tapped into the data again. Instantly it located him and the coordinates flashed. There was nothing around here. Just ahead, on the other side of the river, Indian Creek entered as it flowed south from Mill Run Reservoir. He crouched and listened. He could still hear the voices.

"What the hell are these people doing here?" he said, as he began to climb up the embankment. He noticed that one of the trees was large and thick, that it drooped over the top of the wall. He climbed the tree and hid among the twisted branches. Kurt parted them and looked down onto the trail. It was his worst nightmare, and it was early in the morning. They were Security, District Security, based on their pale green uniforms. They were dressed to the hilt in their crisp uniforms. Two were sitting in a dark green jetcraft, as it bobbed on the rippling water, while three more were sitting against the embankment. *Why there?* Looking up as far as he could along the trail, he spotted where Indian Creek entered the river. He sat scrunched in the branches as the group of Security men talked quietly now. He knew that creek well. Just three years ago, he had run its rapids. It was a beautiful, tight run, with great falls and dangerous rock formations that challenged anyone especially after days of spring rain in the Laurel Mountains.

The village of Indian Creek was located across the confluence of Indian Creek and the Youghiogheny. Kurt could see from his location that there were a few buildings and people on the street. Apparently, Security was patrolling the Yough and spotted an open entrance. Unfortunately for Kurt they decided to take a break. Three of them on the embankment were eating, and it looked like they were drinking something. *Probably beer,* he thought, as they passed around a metal container. Their laughter started up again. *I guess working for the Administration was not too bad a deal for them,* Kurt thought. He could tell from his vantage point that they were a mixed unit of Latinos and Africanos. Jovially taking a break, they looked content in their roles. *Well at least they're happy with the new country,* Kurt thought.

He sat back against the trunk, wedged between two forked limbs. His mind was working overtime as he tried to figure out what he should do. Wait them out? Go up to them and try to pass? Maybe he should just go over the top from here and get back on the trail. He remembered a small creek that fed into the Yough called Morgan's Run that was right past where these guys were parked. It wasn't on most maps, but it could be a secondary course for him to take. No matter how he got around the Security group, he had to cross over Morgan's Run. Its depth at this point worried him. *I just don't know if there is any kind of walkway over it,* he wondered.

Kurt didn't take long to think about it. Slowly he climbed onto the main trunk, then slid his way down. The trunk came down inside a walled cemetery with probably twenty tombstones and a large marble obelisk in the middle.

He stood and looked around, hidden from the Security group by the faded, white-washed wall of brick. It was for the Morgan family of that area. MORGAN was emblazoned on the gray base of the centerpiece. Kurt, always the historian, took mental note of the dates going back into the early 1800s. Morgan was a Welsh name, and there were a lot of Welsh in the area because of the abundant coal. The small gate door at the rear of the cemetery was locked, but the fence was not too high. He hoisted himself over the fence and dropped to the ground.

As soon as he hit the ground, he realized that one of the Security people had climbed the embankment along the trail and had a direct line to where he had landed. The uproar that followed was incredible. He heard shouting and could see the Security man on top waving his arms and scrambling down the side of the embankment. He could hear the voices of the others as they responded.

"Goddamn it, that was stupid," he said as he ran as fast as he could away from the cemetery and the Security men.

Kurt took off through a field of old apple trees behind the cemetery and headed toward Morgan's Run. He could see a small winding stream through the bare trees. He raced up to the fast-moving water and spotted a wooden walking bridge that looked like it was made a couple of hundred years ago. Kurt ran for the bridge.

As he reached it, he noticed that it was a suspension bridge, about thirty feet long. He grabbed the thin pipe that acted as a handrail for anyone who would use the bridge. Walking carefully he was quickly over as the narrow bridge swung and creaked. As he jumped onto the other side, the handrail broke away. Kurt turned as he heard the bridge creak loudly and saw it partially collapse into the water. He stood there holding part of the handrail as he saw three Security men, one behind the other, running toward the dangling bridge.

At the same time, he saw the jetcraft making passes over the river across the mouth of Morgan's Run, as if the skipper was trying to decide if he could skim in the low, narrow, and turbulent stream. He kept spinning around in circles at the entrance.

"Who are you?" came a shout from a tall Africano Security man as he reached the bridge across the creek. "What are you doing here? We need to talk to you. See if you got a pass to be out here," he shouted. The other two were right behind, and Kurt noticed one trying to put a scope of some sort onto what looked like a laser gun.

"Just a citizen of the world, taking a walk," he bravely shouted, as he swung the piece of handrail against the remaining wooden bridge support that angled into the water. He gave the support another whack and the bridge broke away from its base and crumbled into the water.

"That won't help you, goddamn it. We'll get your ass," the Security man shouted.

Kurt wasn't waiting for any more dialogue. He took off as fast as he could, running away from the walkway and through a deep-wooded area. In a few minutes he was on top of a ridge, which looked down onto the confluence of the river and the creek he had just left. He could see the three Security men back at the river climbing onto the jetcraft. He watched as they took off toward Ohiopyle, the direction that he had to go if he couldn't find another way to get across the river. He knew there were shortcuts over the ridges, but he had no idea where they were. This wasn't what he wanted. The adrenaline was turned on and he knew with this episode, he had become a hunted man. "I hope Dr. Alexander worked something out, because I have to get out of here. If they catch me on the trail to Columbia with this chip, I'll never leave this country. Never," he said to himself.

He adjusted his backpack, and scrambled down the high ridge. Through the trees he could see the river. He had to stay away from the trail for a while and according to his map, he could save some time by using the back fields ahead. From his vantage point, there weren't any signs of population, except a few empty barns near a two-track roadway that led into a deeply wooded area. That would be his route.

Within a few minutes he was on a farm trail, heading into the lower reaches of the mountains. Soon Kurt had regained a good pace as he distanced himself from the river. He was off the trail, but he should be able to find his way to Bruner Run which met the river above Ohiopyle. He had to find a way to cross the river upstream without drawing attention. Kurt had always been a good athlete and was in reasonably good shape from working out in the mornings before work. It was paying off as he began to pick up his pace on the up-sloping roadway. A half hour later, he came to another hilltop. He couldn't hear the river at all, but could see it off in the distance. He looked around, there were no signs of anyone, so he sat down against a tree to catch his breath.

From here he could see through the next batch of trees into what looked like an old orchard. Apples, he guessed. From the distance, it looked like the trees were still carrying much of the summer fruit. This year's crop hadn't been picked at this farm. Kurt figured that the farmer had probably left the area, and there wasn't anyone around who was hungry enough to harvest the apples. He felt isolated which was exactly what he needed. The chase by the Security patrol had jolted him, making him realize that he was now a fugitive or would be as soon as they reported their sighting and chase of him. He would need to be extremely alert the rest of the way.

Kurt looked back toward the river which was off to his left and the farthest he'd been from it. It was hard to tell anything from this distance, but he could see no activity on the water. He began to wind his way down the hill, through the thickening foliage and emerged at the edge of the orchard. The ground was covered with the mushy debris of rotten apples. At some time, this had been a productive apple orchard of some commercial venture. It was too large and well laid out to be just a corner orchard of a crop farmer. It stretched from the river all the way to a rise which must then dip and come back up against the base of a hill. He could see a farmhouse sitting off to the right of the rise about the length of a couple of football fields. There was smoke coming from the chimney. "Now who the hell could be out here in this desolation?" he muttered out loud to himself as he crouched beside a tree trunk. The sun had finally broken free of the dogged clouds and filtered down through the trees above him. He decided to take a chance and check out the house.

As Kurt walked amongst the trees, he reached up and grabbed several remaining apples hanging like leftover Christmas ornaments. He hungrily bit into the sweet fruit. Their taste made him shiver, but their bulk made his stomach feel a bit satisfied. The juice felt gratifying to his taste buds like nothing else in the past few days. He hungrily ate the first apple, threw it aside, and bit into the second one. He walked in the high grasses between the trees that were awaiting the first snows. Several pieces of farm equipment were strewn about as if abandoned in place. Through the trees up ahead the farmhouse was in sight. There was still no sign of life except for the smoke coming from the chimney. He stopped walking and looked back to the woods. No one was following. Then he looked down the field that sloped gently to the river. There was nothing in sight, and he felt relief that he wasn't being pursued, at least for the moment.

He turned his attention back to the farmhouse. "Maybe an old farmer who just couldn't leave, or is it a new immigrant who took over this place?" he said. The house looked empty, but it was not derelict. The yard around the fieldstone farmhouse was not filled with debris or junk. It was orderly. Kurt was cautious as he walked around to the front that faced the river. There was a wooden porch that fronted the house. He stood for a few seconds looking at the farmhouse, then said, "What the hell!" and he headed for the porch. As he reached the first step, he was jolted by a tall figure in a baseball cap who came from around the side of the house pointing the twin barrels of a shotgun at his gut. He jumped back in surprise and fear.

artin had spent most of the day waiting at different offices, but finally he entered the high foyer and walked up the granite steps to an upper level in the Security Center. In his idle time, he focused on his mission and its importance. He thought of Alleghenia's elder statesman and leader, Vincent Hawkins, whose portrait was on the wall. He had repeatedly stated, "We can't lose the momentum or we'll become slaves to new masters all over again." This seventy-five-year-old black leader of the Alleghenia Council was a true hero to the locals and since Martin had arrived had become one of his heroes. This was part of his dilemma, his allegiance to the federal government in Nuevo York and his growing attachment to Alleghenia. He had another more critical thought. If Sloan escaped to Columbia with the valuable Aquifer information, it might cause great harm to both Alleghenia and Atlantica. If Martin was wrong, the man still was a defector. But if Martin was right, it could help save this country and state that had given him his life's opportunity. By the time he spotted the entrance marked, OFFICE OF THE PROVOST MARSHAL, he was convinced he was right.

He walked through the Security gate up to a window counter. He was told by a black woman in a light blue uniform that he would need an appointment. Martin referred to

Commander Sludge and wanted to know if Sludge had wired the provost about an appointment for him. The woman looked down to her monitor, shook her head, got up from her chair, and walked back into the inner offices. Over her shoulder, she said she would check. Ten minutes later, she returned.

"Yes, Commander Sludge transmitted a request or at least a clearance that he had talked with you." She went on to say that it was up to PM to determine if she would see Martin. She sat down and began transcribing information into her system. After a minute with Martin still standing in front of her, she looked up, "Oh, sorry, take a seat, Mr. McDonald. It may be a while."

Martin looked down at her and went back to a low sofa and sat down. He waited for almost two hours and finally was summoned by a voice, not the woman at the counter. The voice told him to go through the door right in front of him. The door slid open into a long hallway. Martin walked down the curving hallway following arrows to the Provost Marshal's office. A door with a plaque on the wall stating PROVOST MARSHAL CLAY, opened. "This will be the test. I really need this one," he said to himself as he walked into a sparsely furnished office.

Martin and Provost Marshal Clay met for almost an hour. At first she said she had an only a few minutes, but the time extended as Martin explained the situation. PM Clay was a tall, willowy, and extremely beautiful black woman. Martin at times had difficulty concentrating on her face as she talked. She sat behind an open counter–type desk. Her long legs, extended and crossed, were a distraction. Fortunately, women, who were equal in all regards in this new society, were also allowed to advertise their sex, if they cared to. This one cared to. However, she was all business. Martin liked her no-nonsense approach. She could've been a model like the kind that he'd seen on Eurovision broadcasts coming from France. She had wide, sensuous lips that pouted when she listened intently. Her hair was dark and swept up to the back of her head. Martin was captivated by her deep, hazel eyes. PM Clay was a beautiful woman, however she gave the impression of being very tough. No wasted smiles. She seemed immediately interested in his story and his reasoning. She said little at first, but after his final explanation of why it was necessary to find Kurt Sloan, she turned in her swivel chair and talked out loud into a speaker.

"You heard all that, Watkins. Screen through to Sludge. I want him to find this young man a Skimmer somewhere, now. We have ourselves a patriot here. We can't ignore his request. It's important to all of us. When he leaves I want you to immediately arrange for pickup, preferably first thing in the morning." She turned and looked deep into Martin's eyes. "Our cause must always be concerned with the wisdom of its people. If not, then our whole reason for existence is destroyed. Thank you, McDonald. I could use your dedication and perseverance in this department. When you find the Anglo, come see me. I would like to meet this person," she said. Provost Marshal Clay then got up and walked over to the inner window, which looked down on the courtyard of the old courthouse. "I think I've lost touch over the past few years as to where we've come from. What those Anglos did to us. They controlled our lives for so long. When I was growing up it was better than my parents, and their lives were much better than their parents, but Anglo folks stilled controlled us. When a young man comes in here volunteering to find someone who might cause our country harm, I realize that we must protect what we have achieved." She turned from the window and looked at Martin. "I will never live under another's rule again. So get on with it McDonald. Catch the Anglo. I want to know when you bring him back," she said with a broad smile across her black face.

"I will, and thank you for your help," Martin said as he

turned clumsily, bumping into the oak table in her office. He recovered and walked out into the office area. Her associate, Watkins, a stocky, black Africano, told him that Commander Sludge had already been informed and would be coming back to her within the next two hours. The commander told her he had located a Skimmer, but needed a pilot. With that Martin asked if she could relay something to Commander Sludge. If it was possible, it would be best to find a pilot who knew the mountain terrain of the Laurels. Watkins took note of his request, saying she would contact him immediately.

He left the Security offices and decided he needed to do more research about the walking trail before he began the search. He needed to know the terrain before flying over it. The maps were old, and he needed anything that updated their condition or changes that might have been made over the years. The most important thing he realized was that he had to create a search plan and maybe a map for the pilot. Suddenly he was in a bit of a panic as he scurried down the stairwell to the street and into a Tramway station. Although it was late, he had to go back to the Castro Library.

As he waited in the station, Martin thought back to the times he talked with Sloan at the house. He realized that Sloan had brought to the surface the times in his youth when the white men were always right, always in charge, always looking at him in that superior way. Now he was looking for Sloan because he was trying to bring harm to Martin's world.

His mental drift ended with a loud roar and swoosh of a coming Tram. It was the "20" to Oakland, Martin walked aboard and found a seat by the window. His transmitter beeped. He listened to the message. The call was from the Provost's Office. He would be getting a call from Security later tonight concerning a Skimmer that would be made available for him no later than tomorrow morning. It was highly probable it may be available at daybreak, so he needed to be ready to go at first light. The delay was in locating a specific pilot who had experience in the mountains.

In a few minutes the Tramway stopped at the Cathedral station in University Center. Martin walked by the monolithic monument that stood empty except for a few lights at its base. He had changed his mind about this leftover university structure. He wanted the Administration to find a way to save it from demolition. What had changed his mind was his talk with several of his fellow Africano students, whose parents had been educated in the Cathedral of Learning. They told him how their parents held rallies and meetings during the days of the volatile thirties. These were the times when the minority realized they were the majority for the first time and that control was within their grasp. According to his fellow students, it was a glorious time, and it happened within the halls of this great cathedral. Martin saw an announcement this past summer that the Administration had decided to use it as a storage facility; however, there had been a groundswell of citizen opposition to this plan. Last week the Administration agreed, and it would reopen as a free university for students from around the world. He walked past its steps and across the park to the Castro Library.

Ten minutes later Martin was at a desk in the planning records at the library. He briefly thought about going back over the earlier material he reviewed which gave him his first clue as to Sloan's intent. He decided against that because he needed to familiarize himself with the trail maps and anything that updated their current condition. He became engrossed in the plethora of data that concerned both the terrain, primarily the area of the Laurel Mountains, and the Great Allegheny Passage. He read of its history and development from the late 20th century. It gave him new insight to the people who had occupied this land. On the one hand he realized the passion of people who cherished their personal independence and their dependence on nature. His take on the history was one he had read before. How the Anglo railroad barons raped the land of its natural resources for personal profits. Railroads were built right through the mountains over trails that the original natives had used for centuries. Of course, those peoples were overwhelmed, killed and scattered elsewhere by the whites, but the tracks and rail beds remained. As new transportation developed, the railroads lost their importance and went back to nature's domination. The tracks were taken up and sold as scrap, while the rail beds gradually were covered by development in the cities or by the overgrowth of nature. Then progressive Anglos realized that the trails in place could be used to explore, once again, the natural beauty and the terrain of this part of the country. Thus the old railroad beds that had been forgotten became the recreational trails of the early century. This gave him a better understanding of why this trail was there in the first place and why it was so important since it went from Pittsburgh to Washington, now the capital of Columbia.

Security beeped him, and the message was that a pilot had been located. Martin was told to be at the Skimmer pad at 6 AM. He sat for a minute, thinking of what he had to do tonight. He still had a few hours before the library closed, so he decided to finish the work in front of him and go back to the house and pack for his trip.

Martin worked another hour at the library and then headed back to his apartment. He packed his only set of outdoor clothes, a pair of walking shoes and a rain jacket given to him by Miss McDonald. By the time he got everything organized, it was close to 11:00 PM. He could feel the excitement building as he undressed and got into the shower stall. He lay down, dressed in the underwear he would be wearing in the morning and fell asleep almost immediately.

Morning came fast when the alarm in his watch buzzed. He had an hour to get to the Bluff. It took him several minutes to dress and hook up his backpack. It was five thirty when he left his apartment building in the dark and caught a Tram right away. In fifteen minutes he was downtown, looking up at the lights on top of the Bluff where he was to meet the pilot. Martin went into a coffee bar and ordered a café con leche and a scone. As he sat by the foggy window finishing his coffee, he picked up the weather scan for the next two days. Rain and a cold snap would be moving through which Martin thought might slow Sloan down. He took the last sip of the coffee, finished his scone, and headed for the incline that would take him to the Bluff to meet the pilot. His mission was about to begin.

chapter twenty-one

"Jesus Christ! You scared the shit out of me."

"Good, that's what I wanted to do. Get your hands up! Now!" said a firm, female voice.

He was looking into the deep brown eyes of a tall woman, waving the weapon right at his gut. "That's quite far enough, buster," she said to him.

Kurt didn't move. He looked closely at her and put his hands up slowly, as if in surrender, but more in a gesture of complete helplessness and a no-fear-from-me routine.

She didn't flinch. She just kept staring at him. Nothing was said. Finally she waggled the gun. "Sit down over there on that stump," she ordered.

He walked over with hands raised and sat down on a stump with tiny branches of new growth at its base. It was about ten feet from the porch. The stump was probably three feet across and a foot off the ground. He sat with his knees hunkered up in front of him. Kurt smiled slightly, hoping to ease the tension. She didn't respond. He realized he must be a sight to this woman out here in the far country. He'd dressed accordingly for a late-fall hike in his tan and pale green hunting outfit, which blended in perfectly with the leaf-strewn trail he had been walking. However, he thought he must have looked strange to her, and probably a bit dangerous since he hadn't shaven in three days. He looked at her again, and this time she lowered the gun a bit and spoke.

"What's your name?" she clearly, but firmly spoke down at him.

"Kurt Sloan," he quietly responded.

"Sloan? Anglo! Where are you from?"

"Pittsburgh."

"Sort of out of your bailiwick, aren't you?"

"Yes, I'm far from my bailiwick," Kurt more cheerfully replied. "That's a word I haven't heard for quite a while."

"What are you, some sort of English teacher? Course if you were, I can understand why you're wandering around these parts. No work for you in Pittsburgh from what I've heard. Just what are you doing here?" she said, "at Morgan's Run?"

"I'm doing research on the old Pittsburgh to Georgetown trail that was called The Great Allegheny Passage. It was built early in the century. I've been walking for almost three days. I just decided to get off for a while, and here I am."

"Just decided to take a walk and here you are. Just like that. Be serious, Mr. Sloan. These are strange times for an Anglo to be out exploring the countryside or have I heard wrong on the World Net?"

"No, you haven't heard wrong. Look, I'm an old Pittsburgher, born and raised there. When it was Pittsburgh, okay? I just had to get away," he said with great force, looking her right in the eyes.

Her suspicious look slightly subsided replaced by a softer, crinkled look. There was quiet for a few seconds as she looked at him. They stared at each other. Far away a crow was cawing. Finally she spoke.

"I used to walk that trail when I was a kid," she said in a distant, almost dreamy way. "My dad never let me go anywhere when I was young, but I used to explore the trail in both directions. It was my escape route to the world I used to say to myself." She kept the gun pointed right at him while she spoke. "Security was here about an hour ago. Said some Anglo had escaped along the trail at Indian Creek. If I saw anyone, I was to alert Security in Ohiopyle. I said to them that I never see anyone anymore. So now you come out of blue like some lost sheep. Where the hell do you think you're going, anyway?"

"I told you. I'm researching the old trail."

"Bull shit, Sloan. I'm a farm girl. I know shit when I see it," as anger built up in her tone. "They said you were a security risk to the government. Are you?" Before he could answer, she continued. "If you are, then this country is more screwed up than I thought if the likes of you are causing it grief. You don't look too dangerous to me."

"If realizing that you no longer feel good about your own home is dangerous, then I guess I'm dangerous to this country."

There was another silence. The crows were now trying to out caw each other high up in the empty branches of a giant oak, which straddled the walk in front of the porch.

"Come up on the porch, Sloan. You don't seem too dangerous to me. Don't make any quick moves. I grew up with this old double-barrel. You understand?"

"Yes, I do," he replied.

Kurt walked up the steps to a drooping wooden porch. He looked at the woman, who stood pointing the black-barreled shotgun at him. She was tall, large boned with golden brown hair tied in back with a band underneath an old black Pirate ball cap. He guessed she was in her early thirties with a clear complexion and penetrating brown eyes that mellowed in the light into the color of root beer. The eyes were what really hit him. He looked at them closely when he first reacted to her call to him. They were very liquid and bright.

As Kurt stared at her, he began to relax since running from Security even though she still held the long shotgun. She wore brown corduroy pants and a faded pale blue sweatshirt. The sweatshirt had Chatham College across its front in barely readable letters. He had her whole life in his first five minutes with her; farmer's daughter, college graduate, baseball fan, and a real looker.

"Except for those guys earlier and a few locals, you're the first person I've seen around here in a month. In one hour I've had a crowd on this porch all because of you. This place is isolated," she said somewhat defensively.

"You said Morgan's Run before. Just exactly where am I?"

"The whole area around here is called Morgan's Run. It's named after my family and has been for years since there's nobody for miles around here. You have a better name?" she said with a slight smile on her broad face.

"No, no, I was just curious. I've hurriedly studied the topos for the area when I left the river. I want to make sure this is the course that I need to be on, that's all. I thought I was closer to Bruner Run," he said looking down toward the river.

"Not too far from here. It's over that next ridge. So what do you want? What are you doing wandering around these parts," she said.

"I told you. I am just walking the trail."

"Mr. Sloan, why in the hell would those Security goons come from the river to tell me that some Anglo was seen heading in this direction?"

"I don't know why they are so concerned. All I know is that I am a history buff. My job is history. So I am exploring the old trail, the Great Allegheny Passage. The first part of your question was what do I really want. What I really do want, to tell you the truth, what I'd really like is some food. I'll pay you for it. As I said, I've been on the trail for almost three days, and if you have any food, I would be grateful. I have food cards, or if you don't use that, I have some gold coins. All I have had are dried meals, but I was looking for some real food." He fished into a side pocket of his packet and pulled out some coins. "I have a few gold coins that I could pay you."

"Gold coins? That's okay, you keep your coins. I have food. Around these parts we've reverted to bartering. Atlantica's currency is suspect out here. For example, about two weeks ago I went out to the main road and over toward Dunbar. An old friend of the family had died and I paid my respects. I was representing my family. I arrived at dusk. No one else was there. First time I'd seen a body laid out in years. Everybody gets cremated these days, but anyway, several people there were talking about how difficult things were. The only people around seemed to be in their eighties. The undertaker took apples, potatoes, and peanut butter from the family. Barter is back, at least in these parts. I don't need your coins; you may need them."

"Well, what could I barter for the food?" he asked.

"I don't need anything from you" she quickly responded.

Kurt looked around the porch and asked, "How do you exist here?" he asked.

"The old-fashioned way, by growing everything right here. Listen, Sloan. You seem okay, but I'm going to keep this gun near me. Seeming and being are two different things. I got this thing right here, but even with that sun beaming down, it's cold out here. Let's go into the kitchen, and I'll find something. You can tell me more about what's going on in Pittsburgh. It's been so long. I loved that city, went to college there a few years back. Even used to go into town on my powerboat, but I haven't been there in a few years. Things are so different," she said waving him toward the kitchen door using the shotgun as a pointer.

The kitchen was wood and ceramic. At some time, a lot of money had gone into the equipment. Now there were plants growing up against the windowsill in small containers with signs on them. He looked closer and saw they were various herbs. The kitchen was cavernous with an old wooden cutting block on a brick island in the middle of the room. A high, deep, and very wide brick fireplace had iron ladles, and cooking equipment hung from a rack besides the opening. The kitchen itself was spare now, obviously not used like it had been. There was a rectangular wooden table with two high-back chairs next to a framed window that overlooked the side yard.

"Do you want some coffee, tea?" she asked.

"Coffee would be great."

"I have some vibes working now on you, Sloan. You are what you're telling me and also what those bozos told me. Means nothing as to reality, yet I base most of my actions on my feelings. Dangerous way to judge, right?"

"A coin has two sides," he answered.

"That it does. Heads you're thief and murderer. Tails you're an old Pittsburgher looking for sanctuary from the authorities. I'll go with tails," she laughed and leaned the double-barrel against the kitchen island. "Tell me about yourself. How old are you? What's your background in Pittsburgh? Wait a second, go over to the cellar door and down the steps. Open up the springhouse and bring up the large silver can marked coffee. I'll grind us some real coffee."

For the next hour, they sat there and talked. They discovered that their backgrounds were very similar, in a way that made it easy for them to understand the other. She ground the coffee beans and told her story. It was after an hour that she said to him, "By the way, I'm Elizabeth Morgan."

chapter twenty-two

s they sat outside in two wood-slatted rockers drinking a very strong black coffee, Kurt Sloan and Elizabeth Morgan talked about what had happened in their country. She gave him the history of her family that Kurt found fascinating. The Morgans were one of the original pioneer families in the Laurel Mountains. Her name, Elizabeth Morgan, had been given to the oldest female since the 1700s when the original family resided in Virginia. Her direct family had lived on this land near the Youghiogheny River since the early 1800s as part of land granted to Josiah Morgan by King George of England. Morgan explored the area west of the Alleghenies with Col. George Washington. Josiah Morgan had been with Col. Washington on his excursions against the French and was with him when he attempted to negotiate the withdrawal of the French garrison in the name of King. Because of his work, he was granted thousands of acres including this parcel. It wasn't until the early 1800s that Elizabeth Morgan's descendants settled at the confluence of Morgan's Run and the Youghiogheny River. She was now, two hundred and fifty years later, the last Morgan living on the land. Her younger brother and two sisters had immigrated to Wales, the land of the original Morgans.

Elizabeth had refused to leave. She'd been here by herself

for three years. She'd planted each spring, gardened all summer, and harvested in the fall, just as her family had done. She would put up most of her vegetables for the winter and would shop periodically in the small town of Dunbar, not telling anyone that she was living alone. Occasionally she had visited the Jones family, her closest neighbors, to see how they were. They were elderly and close to her parents when they were alive. During this past winter they weren't well and within the last two months they both had died. Mr. Jones first, then Mattie Jones, his wife, died two months later. Elizabeth felt loneliness had finally done them in. Their dying left nobody within five miles.

Kurt glanced at his watch. It was past noon, and he realized he had missed the first call of Dr. Alexander. When he had a chance, he would check to see if a message was left for him. A few minutes later, Elizabeth told Kurt she had to go the freezer in the basement. He told her he was going to walk toward the river to get his bearings. Kurt walked a path to the banks of the Youghiogheny. Standing beside a pine next to the wall that protected the path, he looked slowly in both directions, just in case she was watching him. The river was empty, just a rapid current at this point. He went around the pine and punched in Dr. Alexander's code. In five seconds he was connected. He read the message. CONTACT MADE. WILL MEET YOU NOON, FALLINGWATER AT ONE OF THE NEXT 3 DAYS BEGINNING DAY AFTER DATE OF THIS TRANSMISSION—CONTACT WILL LEAVE AFTER 3RD DAY. CONTACT: CODE NAME COBRA. GOOD LUCK, DA. Kurt checked the screen. That meant the first day was tomorrow for the contact to be made, so he was in good shape. He felt a sense of relief for the first time in days. He had a chance, a good chance. The transmission took fifteen seconds, well under the surveillance time, so he headed back to the farmhouse. His mind raced, and he knew he might make tomorrow's contact if things broke perfectly, but he certainly would be there for the second day of the time frame. He climbed onto the porch and went into the kitchen where Elizabeth was dropping several containers on the island chopping block.

"You said you were hungry, Sloan. Do you have time for a farm meal?"

"Well, to tell you the truth, I'm starved. If you don't mind, I would love a farm meal."

"Well, it will be a change to have company even if they're a security risk," she laughed.

"What can I do to help?" Kurt asked.

"Take that container to the well outside and fill it with water for more coffee, please.

In a few minutes, the water kettle began to whistle, and she took it off of the stove. She poured the steaming water from the container into a glass vessel with a paper filter. The water dripped through the coffee beans and a large batch of dark coffee was ready.

"You know I haven't talked with a soul for so long, how about we go in the living room and you can tell me about Pittsburgh."

They went to the rustic living room with dark, cracked-leather chairs that surrounded a matching leather sofa. Elizabeth sat in one chair and Kurt in the other. For the next hour it was like old classmates at a reunion. Once he asked her about communications because she mentioned that her father had established a satellite cellular system about fifteen years ago. He asked her if it was still functioning, and she answered that it had given out during the winter. All she had was a wall system powered by her solar unit and occasionally she watched World Net. She received mail from her brother in Wales. Most of her current knowledge came through the World Net based in Paris. As for the house itself, she explained to Kurt that her father had it made completely self-powered when he installed a solar receptor in the late twenties. It still functioned perfectly.

Later, after another mug of the strong coffee, she took Kurt on a tour of the renovated brick farmhouse which he commented to her was a remarkable structure. After the tour, they talked more, stopping only for a snack of dark bread and apple butter. Kurt had trouble stopping himself from eating all of the fresh, hearty apple butter and black German-style bread. The fresh-made apple butter and bread reminded him of his home. He looked out into the sloping yard to the river far off in the distance. It was already late in the afternoon as they sat in the kitchen.

"I only eat twice a day, so the bread and apple butter will have to do you till later, if you're still here and still hungry," Elizabeth said with a smile.

"That was delicious, as you could tell. I think that's all I could have handled anyway. As far as leaving, I do have to go, but I have to ask you something."

"That's okay, fire away. By the way, there's a really nasty storm coming in over the river. The one yesterday was just rain, but there's to be a sharp drop in temperature along with thunder and lightening. Might not be to cozy out there on the trail." She pulled back a white curtain from the window. Look out there," she said to Kurt as if the storm had suddenly appeared. The whole sky was cut right in half as a dark black bank of clouds was meeting the clear, bright blue overhead. The trees along the river could be seen bending in an obvious pickup of a breeze.

"Security can't scan too well in that kind of weather, although their heat scans could probably pick me up. I may have to delay a bit. Could I stay until the storm passes?" he said turning back to her. "The barn would be fine," he added quickly.

"Well, you shared my precious apple butter. I guess you can

stay a while. If the winds get too bad, I might go to the barn, myself. It's older than the main house and built like a bomb shelter. Good choice. But I'd like to watch this one come in. Let's go into the side porch. We can watch the storm from there unless it gets too wild."

She walked to the sliding glass doors that led out into the side porch. He looked passed her into the glass-enclosed room that must have been an outside porch at one time. He could see all types of hanging plants, cacti, ferns, and assorted miniature trees. Over her shoulders as she walked through the porch doors, Kurt could see blackness rapidly filling the sky through the wall-to-wall windows. He also took notice of the woman as she stepped into the porch area.

Even though she was a large woman, he noticed when she walked, she flowed. She had taken off her ball cap and the luster of her light brown hair glowed. It was an electric moment. One he hadn't felt for a while. He locked onto her body as she pushed through the ferns onto the porch. He'd been running from Security one moment, and now he was following this fascinating woman. Life was one strange pursuit, no question, and another twist had just been added.

"Sloan. Are you coming? The storm is moving fast." He walked into the porch and as he did, he could see the rain slanting over the river. The remaining clouds of the beautiful day were racing to get away from the pending storm.

"This is going to go on for a while. I'll put on some water. Would you drink some tea or more coffee?"

"Some tea would be fine, if it's without caffeine, I'm wired."

"It is. Some kind of herbal mint, I believe."

"You have a good gas supply, I see," Kurt said.

"Our family has had a free supply of gas for over a hundred years. No matter what's going on with the Central Power in

Pittsburgh, I still get gas. I'll be back in a second. You can tell me of your plans. Where you are going. What's going on in Pittsburgh? I'll be back."

Kurt turned and watched her heading back into the house and going into the kitchen. His mind refocused on his task at hand as he admired the strong stride of his hostess. Based on the message from Dr. Alexander, he should make the connection at Fallingwater, possibly even tomorrow. If the storm got worse, he might have to stay over and leave at daybreak. Either way, he should be able to get to Fallingwater sometime tomorrow. Another thought he had was that maybe Elizabeth knew a short cut to Fallingwater. Maybe she knew a way over the hills or if there was another crossing over the river before Ohiopyle.

As the rain pelted off the glass windows, Elizabeth walked back into the porch holding a pot of steaming water on a tray with two cups.

"Here you go, Sloan."

"Please, Kurt, if you would."

"Kurt, this is perfect for this kind of weather. Wow, what a great rain. You'd be soaked already if you were walking that trail."

"No doubt about that. Now, what I wanted to ask you when this storm rudely interrupted was if you knew a short cut to Fallingwater. I saw a bridge back at Indian Creek, but that's where Security was hanging out. Just wonder if there is another bridge that's not on the maps. If so it would save me quite a bit of time getting to Fallingwater," Kurt finished.

She looked at him as the rain continued to beat against the glass windows. Elizabeth sipped her tea, steam climbing past her lovely, chiseled face as she looked at him. "Fallingwater! A man is leaving his land and Security is apparently looking for him, yet he has to take a detour to see a house in the mountains. Granted it's a classic house in the mountains, but you are a very interesting bird, Mr. Sloan."

"Miss Morgan, if I may be so bold. You, all by yourself in the middle of nowhere in a land that is going through traumatic upheaval, are, may I use your phrase, also an interesting bird. Birds of a feather, possibly," he said jokingly.

"Touché'," she quickly replied. "To answer your earlier question, there may be a way to Fallingwater without going all the way to Ohiopyle. The key will be if the Laurel Run bridge down the river that was added about twenty years ago is still up. I really don't know. I would have suggested the one back up at Indian Creek, but maybe the other one is still up. I'll give you directions and you'll know when you get there. From there on the other side, it's a climb, but passable. At least it was."

"So you've taken it?"

"Many times! As I said, Fallingwater always fascinated me as well. To be where it is and the classic grandeur of it in the middle of my loving mountains was and is a sense of pride. Mr. Wright, a fellow Welshman, was no doubt a genius. How he could blend a cement and glass structure in with the natural wood and vegetation along Bear Run is a testament to the creativity of the human race."

"That's sort of the way I've always felt. My dad used to take me there when I was a youngster. Since I was hiking the trail I wanted to see it once again. So here I am," he finished, looking and then listening to the outside weather. "It sounds like it is quieting down outside."

"It is slowing down a bit, but it's still windy and dark. You may not be going anywhere in this stuff if this keeps up. You want more tea?"

"Actually, I would. Our conversation has been great. I really haven't had anyone my own age or background to talk with in weeks—months, come to think of it. My best friend is a great guy my age but comes from a completely different background.

Not an Anglo from Western PA. My associates at work are from all over the place, the world actually, and my mentor, a great man is eighty. But for sharing thoughts with someone of my age and, what can I say, cultural heritage, this short time with you has been comforting if that is the right word."

She was still standing with her back to him. She turned and said, "Funny you said that. As I said earlier, since my parents died over three years ago, I really haven't had any socialization. My personality is basically a loner type. Even with my college degree and work I did in Brazil, I have really enjoyed the peace of this place. Surviving on the farm has been a full-time occupation, but I knew all along that I would have to get off my butt and do something with my life, and I knew it wouldn't be here."

"Do you have any idea what you would like to do? I mean you have a great education and some international work experience."

"I do have a great education and I loved my work in Brazil, but I can't seem to focus on one area. But I'm a Libra, which means, I weigh everything, usually too much. So the questions for me are what the hell am I going to do with the rest of my life and where am I going to do it? I know I can't stay here in these beautiful boondocks, it's too comforting here. My feeling now is that I would like to teach, somewhere. But where that is, I haven't a clue," she said sadly as she turned to look at Kurt. She recovered. "Let's say we have some dinner. I think, Sloan, you're going to have to wait until morning. It's dark and still raining. You'll lose your ass out there. I'll start something and we can have it a bit later. I think it's time for some wine from our cellar. Are you a wine drinker?"

"I am a drinker, period. Based on my heritage, a good dark beer; a good dry wine; or the mother lode, a single malt, is part of the package. So your wine sounds perfect, especially with the nastiness outside."

"I've got some of that mother lode, as you say, but for now let me show you the wine cellar," Elizabeth said as she walked past him into the hallway.

chapter twenty-three

ntonio Ramos-Craft was a white Latino. The man was formidable as he stood looking at Martin. He was called Warlock, was about 5'10", but weighed two hundred fifty pounds. Warlock was a major in the Atlantica National Air Service which was headquartered in Harrisburg. His uniform was dark green with white piping. The ANAS was the coordinator for all military air units in Atlantica. Major Craft piloted a Skimmer and was assigned as Martin's Security associate to search for Kurt Sloan.

The Skimmer that Warlock flew was ten years old. The jet-air propulsion craft had been built in Pan Mexico, a loyal Atlantica ally. Martin and Warlock stood on the tarmac of the small landing field on the Duquesne Bluff. The wind was blowing the directional flags west to east. They talked for a few minutes; then Warlock said to Martin that it was perfect weather, since they were headed east, and they should board and take off. Soon they were zooming down the Monongahela River headed southeast. During the next hour they sped over rivers, then on to the mountains. They were enclosed in a glass bubble at the front of the craft. Both wore mouth and ear pieces. They didn't talk for a few minutes. Martin was captivated by the scene below as he tried to get used to peering at objects as they came into view and then quickly passed. It took him a while to get used to searching with the naked eye and reading the scanner that was between their seats. It wasn't long before he could begin to make out the mountains. Down below, the river glowed with the morning sun.

Martin looked over to the pilot and said, "The name Warlock sounds familiar. Like from one of those old last-century movies that's shown late night."

"It's a name I picked up from my military days. It means deceiver, or even worse." He smiled in a crooked way. "The old meaning is one who is in touch with the evil spirits. A sorcerer," he replied this time with a smirk.

"A sorcerer? Well I hope we can get in touch with the guy we're looking for, who may be an evil spirit," Martin responded trying to develop a relationship.

Warlock nodded at Martin and said, "Just so you know, I take this revolution of ours very seriously. I know from what my grandfather taught me about the Anglos and how they controlled people so they could stay in power. What's funny, he was white of old Castilian stock. He was ahead of his time. So, I don't want us to lose our power, the country we have. We have control and we'll get more power if we stay together. I'm on a mission. I have my orders and from what I was told at the briefing, this is a big one. What I like about it is that it's a capture of an Anglo defector. I have been on many missions in my military career. I served in Brazil and the Turkish Campaign of the old U.S. Been a military pilot for twenty years, but now I finally have a war to fight that I really believe in. My mother was Latina, born in Venezuela. My daddy was as white as the driven snow, a colonel in the former U.S. Air Force, but he became part of the problem. He dumped my mother when I was a kid because of the military prejudices against Latinos. It was my grandfather who became like a dad to me. In fact he hated his own son. So you see, civilian, I have a stake in any job I'm told to perform for the government."

"You're a major? That's pretty far up there for a pilot, right?"

"It is. As I said, I was in the U.S. Air Force, just like my daddy. Fact, that's how I got there. Inside I hated his guts, outside I took advantage of his reputation. Now, I have a squadron in Harrisburg, but I take on urgent missions whenever asked. A couple of years ago, I left teaching military tactics for the civil war in Brazil as a mercenary. Then I was in Lithuania when liberation came here. I came back and signed up in Nuevo York. The government wanted me to go back to teaching again. Not me, I talked my way into solo work and set up my reserve unit for emergency uses. I still teach as a profession, but too much office work makes a man stale. I hate being stale. Life is meant to be lived, alert and sharp. That's enough about me. Tell me about this traitor who's trying to escape with secrets that might endanger our country."

"He's an Anglo deserter. Took something with him that may hurt our Aquifer System."

"Whoa, that's big time. So, our job is to find him very soon, I assume," Warlock said.

"Correct. We have to search an old hiking trail called the Great Allegheny Passage that goes between Pittsburgh and Columbia. The trail has been closed for years with no maintenance, but he's using it to escape. Our job is to find him, pick him up, and take him back to Pittsburgh before he reaches the wall at Columbia. That's it, in short form," Martin said.

"That's the way I like things, simple. Okay, so we sweep the trail. To do that, I've got various sensors, heat, voice activators, movement, video, of course. This baby can stop on a dime, land just about anywhere, hover, you name it. You have the perfect craft for this mission, McDonald."

"Great, Warlock. Looks like we have a team," Martin

replied.

"Looks that way, but I'll need your personal input about this guy. What's he thinking? What are his goals? That's where you come in because you know him. The more we know about how he thinks, the quicker we will find him."

"What's your main job. I mean in the ANAS?"

"My main expertise is usually to get someplace faster or find someone sooner than anyone," he replied. "By the way look down there at that fire."

He glided in over a large area along the river that was engulfed in flames. The inside of the rectangle was blackened and the fire had gone to the riverbank. The fringes of the flames could be seen spitting up into the morning air. It was spreading like a carpet being pulled up on three sides.

"What's going on, Warlock? Brush fire?" Martin said.

"Someone is probably clearing the land for next spring. Nuevo York wants all possible farmland tilled. I guess that's what they're doing down there."

"Where are we? You said we'd skim slowly toward the border, but I lost track," Martin said.

"Look at the monitor, McDonald, then over at three o'clock. That's the Yough Lake according to the monitor. I want to go to the end of our tracker video. At least as far as I can safely go, and then we'll come back, which takes us almost to Cumberland near the Columbia border. These videos of the trail you found are great, plus I was able to download from our library some original tracks of the trail about twenty years ago. Between the two, we have great visuals. Of course, we're looking for one man in this vast territory, but at least we know he'll be on this trail. We just went over Mt. Savage back there and Cumberland is coming up. We'll turn around and wind our way slowly with the Laser scanner. It'll pick up human heat from this altitude with no problem. I don't expect there to be many human heat centers along that old trail. Based on my calculations when you believe he left Pittsburgh, I can't imagine him getting any farther than Ohiopyle," he finished.

"You said human heat. You mean it can tell between, say a deer and a man?" Martin said.

"Yep, even between a big man, six two, two hundred pounds, or a small woman, five two, one hundred pounds."

Martin looked down at a curling stream that darted in and out of vision with the twisted and graded portions of hills that made this part of the country so uninhabitable. Only little river villages remained based on the latest map of the area that was done three years ago. Most of them were deserted. Looking down to the trail where it was exposed in some spots, he could see lots of debris, mostly tree limbs mixed with sloping piles of leaves. Up to that point Martin had little concern for his safety, but seeing the terrain, the mountains, and the absolute darkness that prevailed along the trail, he realized this would be more dangerous than he thought. Finding one smart man on this trail would not be easy.

"There's the Potomac coming up to your right, McDonald. It comes up and then turns southeast at Cumberland. I think we should land in Cumberland and talk to our command units in Pittsburgh. I had to get clearance from them just in case you wanted to land. It's cleared, but this is on the frontier, so be prepared for some tough questions. We should touch base with them and let them know who we're looking for and why. There was no sign of him on our first sweep, which was to be expected. In fact, I just wanted to scan the trail—let you see what we are up against. But my guess is he is somewhere near Ohiopyle. We'll go back over at one hundred feet. If he's anywhere on or near the trail, we should be able to spot him. I'll check in and we'll land. Okay?" he said.

"That's good. We've been going at this since daybreak. It's

time to stop for lunch. I'm hungry and this looks like a good place to land."

The Skimmer swooped in over the compact town crammed between the steep terrain. The river gleamed in the midday sun as the Skimmer landed on a pad near the center of town. It was the only craft on the heliport. They sat there for a few minutes awaiting the commander to approach them as instructed. Soon three individuals appeared dressed in drab olive-and-sand-colored uniforms. They walked up and rapped on the glass. Warlock propped open the window.

"Major Craft and Martin McDonald - under orders from Pittsburgh Security," he yelled down to the three standing stoically under the wing.

Martin observed the three. He noticed that one of them was a woman. They were all dressed alike, but she was the tallest of them. She had skin the color of coffee with cream. She was stern looking. Martin was very sensitive to black women in official capacities, because no matter what social or military rule, even in this Republic of equality, women still had a difficult time.

"Throw down your ID chip," said the black woman.

"Who are you? Identify yourself. That's protocol," answered Warlock.

"Fuck protocol! Drop your chip or this thing goes up!" the woman countered.

"This thing goes up or you go down. No one talks to me like that," said Warlock and he hit the starter. Immediately the engine opened up and they moved upward, the blast of their airburst knocking them over on the tarmac. They were up immediately and aiming their lasers, but the Skimmer was gone and over the steep hillside.

"Pittsburgh Center, this is Major Craft Do you read me?"

"We read you, Major. Why the liftoff from Cumberland?"

"I just peeled away because there's something odd going on down there. I think the fuckin' area is in enemy hands. They are definitely not friendly," he shouted into the speaker. The screen showed the monitor in Pittsburgh going to another frequency.

They circled the town several times and then swooped toward the west with the sun high above them.

"Major Craft Jesus Christ!" came the reply from Pittsburgh Center. "They've had intruders six times in the last week who had false ID. We've communicated with them and sent a new password that is also in your command module. Bring it up and use it. We'll ask for a new clearance for you and just use the new password," said the rapid-fire communicator.

Martin heard the interchange over the intercom and tapped Warlock on his arm. "Warlock, we have to get back there. This whole mission is too important not to verify that Sloan hasn't gone through here yet. Verify or whatever you have to do, but get back there. We'll leave as soon as I can find out something, one way or the other."

"Okay, will give it another go, McDonald. Control sent them the new password, and we have it, too, so we'll go back down as soon as Cumberland gives their okay. Nobody can be too careful, but I'll be damned if I'm going to lose one of these Skimmers to anyone. But I guess they have been breached here recently, so I understand. That was one tough lady."

"Good-looking, too," Martin added as they flew over the mountains. At about one thousand feet they were still well below the tops of the mountain ridges. Warlock winged in and about observing up the trail as it would occasionally appear.

"Until we get clearance, we might as well check around here." As they followed the trail, Warlock turned on his sensors and nothing came back indicating human presence. To prove its effectiveness he turned back toward Cumberland. For a while nothing happened. Then it went into a crackling sound with a red light flashing every second. Both sound and light became louder and brighter as they came closer to the Cumberland landing spot and the Security personnel awaiting them. Then he swooped away and both suddenly stopped. "That's how it works, McDonald. Pretty nifty, eh?" At that moment he got a message in his earphone.

"I hear you. Okay, we'll be coming in," Warlock talked into his mouthpiece. "You want the password from me? Whatever you say. Here it comes and we're heading in. Any problem with that?" he asked. He listened for a second and replied, "Roger and out."

The Skimmer picked up speed as Warlock turned in a ninety degree swoop and headed for a landing. In a few seconds they were coming down onto the heliport. The same three Security people were standing to one side. This time there was a group of militia, standing behind them with weapons drawn. They landed and the same ritual began again. They walked up and motioned for the window to come down. Their weapons were raised as before. The black woman was in the middle, with what looked like captain's bars on her shoulder and a deep scowl on her face.

Warlock looked down at the woman and cried out over the sound of the engine, "Octoberfest." He hadn't turned it off this time, and in fact the landing pods hadn't been lowered as they had been before.

"Munich," the captain shouted the reply. Then she added, "You can disembark now."

Warlock and Martin climbed down to the tarmac and were escorted over to a three-story glass-and-cement building without a word being spoken. Inside the captain asked for an explanation of their search. Warlock said he apologized for his takeoff now that he understood their security concerns.

He introduced Martin who went into an explanation of the purpose for their landing. The captain seemed to warm up a bit and said she would take them to Sector Intelligence whose mission it was to monitor all movement of people within a hundred miles. Martin felt better already. At least now he could search from this end and corner Sloan along the way. Martin was certain this was the way Sloan was coming.

Not long after landing it began to rain hard. Warlock asked if they could stay until the storm passed. As it turned out it was late afternoon before the rains stopped. The Security team gave them a tour of the facility. They explained the various methods of observation that were available. It would be very difficult for Sloan to pass this far without detection. As the storm slowed and finally passed, darkness was spreading in from the east. They were asked to spend the night and Warlock agreed. After a rousing dinner with the now friendly Security team, Warlock went out to check the Skimmer and get the latest weather scan. He came back in and told Martin to be ready to lift off at sunrise because it would be clear, but that the weather was going to turn negative again with rain tomorrow and snow possible the following day.

It took Martin quite a while to fall asleep in the dorm as his mind replayed the day. He tried to visualize Sloan walking that curving, almost invisible trail along the river. Martin felt that he had been right in insisting they land in Cumberland because Security was now alerted. Tomorrow they could concentrate closely on the trail back toward Ohiopyle. His adrenaline was flowing, he liked this cat and mouse game. His last thoughts were about possibly switching professions by joining Security when he got back from Paris.

chapter twenty-four

The storm was passing, but rain continually pounded the windows of the farmhouse. Kurt and Elizabeth talked into the evening like long-lost friends about mutual interests in history, families, and what they had been doing during the demise of the U.S. Elizabeth got up, stretched, and went over to the window that looked toward the river. Kurt got up and followed her.

"Looks like the barn tonight," he said.

"No question. It should be okay in the morning," she said. "You mentioned scotch before. How about a touch before we figure out something for dinner," she asked.

"That would be perfect," Kurt responded as Elizabeth went into the pantry off the kitchen. Kurt was standing by the window looking out into the dark night toward the river he had to cross tomorrow. Even though he couldn't see the river, he thought about how the water ran wild and free, abundant, while in most of the world it is scarce and people were dying from lack of it. It made him realize how valuable the collection of water in this part of the world was and why the Aquifer system was the most valuable piece of property in the hemisphere. It not only captured the water in the mountains, it captured water beneath, which Kurt wasn't aware of until doing his research. Late in development, the U.S. had added a state-of-the-art recycling system to purify used water. This ingenious purification system was another bonus in the Aquifer System. The concept would make water a recycled resource which was revolutionary. Kurt discovered this when he read the chip glossary which listed RECYCLING SYSTEM TECHNOLOGY as an addendum item. This new information would be critical data for the UN. It was no wonder that Atlantica wanted to maintain the secrecy of the Aquifer System just prior to it going on full capacity. It would give them unprecedented world leverage. It was unconscionable, which in Kurt's way of thinking, justified what he was doing, especially knowing how his father designed the Aquifer for universal usage. He realized his actions could be the most critical he would ever make and would define his future.

His thoughts were interrupted by Elizabeth saying, "Here you go, Kurt. This is now thirty-year-old scotch. It should settle you down a bit. You look like you're in outer space." She then proceeded to sit down and face Kurt.

"Oh, I was just thinking how brief our lives are and how constant nature is, like that river out there. Beyond that, since we have such a brief existence, it is critical to know you are doing what you are supposed to be doing. I was thinking maybe I'm at that point. You know what I mean?" he said

"Predestination!" she said. "You must have some Presbyterian in your genes. I do for sure. Jesus, my mother preached that message to me every day of her life. 'You're put on this earth for a purpose so find it, and do it,' she'd say to me. Here I am thirty-three years old and I have no idea yet what that purpose is. Suppose I never will at the rate I'm going," she finished.

"Well, you're right. My family did talk of predestination, but more in a literal sense of following your intuitions which I pretty much have done. I really don't go outside myself, very often."

"Me either. I don't know whether it was growing up on the farm, but I have always internalized my thoughts and beliefs. But I think when I went away to school a bit of a genie was set loose. It was the midthirties. As you may remember, things were in turmoil. I was out in the world for the first time. As a freshman at Chatham College, I exploded. I was an activist, if there ever was one. That was when Congress tried to enact voting rule changes that would have denied voting for new citizens. I even wrote protest songs. I was a real iconoclast for peaceful revolution amongst my own people. My family was horrified. My dad said that I was destroying the foundations of the American way, which I couldn't understand, since I thought the American way was to foster democracy for all. I remember saying to them that they didn't trust their own philosophy," she finished, slowly sipping on her drink. "Little did I really know."

"I was in college during those times," Kurt quietly responded. "I wasn't worried. Corny, but I was always proud of the way the people in this area handled problems of whatever nature. A significant influx of Latinos arrived in the twenties to work the coal mines and Aquifer. In the early thirties, blacks were running government offices. In the midthirties, these two groups, represented the majority of the Western Pennsylvania population. During this same time period, upper- and middle-class Anglos began to leave the area and settle in other parts of the country. Many immigrated to their homelands in Europe. Even blacks from the middle and higher economic classes began to migrate to Canada, France, and to stable African countries. The incentives from those countries were incredible. Looking back, even I supported the liberalization of social needs and taxing the wealthy. You know, yourself, how youth is always opposed to the status quo. I think it was just before the 2038 Constitutional Convention that I began to understand what was really happening. Before I knew it, everything changed. Three years later, I was required to learn Spanish and to speak it within a year in the workplace. The whole turnover happened so fast, for everybody. In the whole country," Kurt finished.

"You really know your history, Kurt. That was an amazing analysis of that time. For me, I was twenty-one, had just graduated from Chatham and went immediately to Brazil to work an archeological dig. I loved the work. It was fascinating and actually tied into my degree as a social historian. I'd get emails from my parents or I'd read that Pennsylvania, along with most of the Eastern states, became the new country of Atlantica. It was hard for me to believe. My hosts in Brazil were jubilant that the monster to the *norte* had disintegrated. New York was now Nuevo York. Looking back, twelve years later, I still can't believe it."

Kurt responded, "The United States lost its soul. It didn't know who it was anymore and tried to be what everyone wanted it to be, whether that was all of the citizens or all of the world. It lost its uniqueness, its character, its reason for being. Of course, for their part, the new Latino majority didn't want to adopt much of the quote 'American way.' They wanted a Latino-oriented country, period. So it was a combination of powerful factors colliding."

Elizabeth quickly responded, "You're right, but let me put on my social historian hat, too. There was so much more that undercut the country during those years. There was a complete loss of interest in our history, language, and the self-reliant, optimistic attitude of the citizenry. My main thesis was that the U.S. became segregated in a different way than the black/white issue. A new segregation developed between the elitist, educated classes versus the military classes, the very rich versus the lower classes, and the secular versus the religious community. By the time the social and then the economic underpinnings collapsed, everyone had chosen sides and there was no American unity. It was ripe for what happened. When the newly enfranchised illegals and the entrenched Latinos, along with the disenfranchised Africanos took over power, there was a shell of the old country remaining. There was no unity among the Anglos to counter the takeover, even democratically. They just retreated or left. They lost faith in their own history of accomplishment. Of course, the blinded media didn't help.

By that time, the U.S. was essentially part of Europe, philosophically, economically, and certainly, politically. The world and its media cheered on the demise of the giant superpower, as it became incorporated into Europe and the quote 'World Community.' In reading articles from the late-twentieth century and early in this century, the whole psychology of the country changed. It was a brash, innovative, self-critical country, but always looking ahead. Then it became ashamed of itself and became a subordinate of European and world philosophies. Absolutely extraordinary," she said.

Kurt added, "Absolutely correct, it was incredible. People from all classes and wealth transferred their savings and investments to British, Irish, Scottish, Polish, German, Italian, and Israel banks or investment houses, to wherever they were going. All funds were gladly accepted from Americans." He looked at Elizabeth, then added, "Anyway, the democratic revolution worked. We live in a country, Atlantica, made up primarily of Latinos and Africanos from throughout the Northern Hemisphere and around this world. Give it another ten years, and it will probably survive. Right now, the first major threat to Atlantica's current tranquility is how they handle the completion of the Pittsburgh Aquifer system. I don't know if you have kept up with its development, but how Atlantica reacts to the water needs of the people in this hemisphere will be its first real test as a country. I'm not sure the Administration knows how to handle the absolute power of water resources they have inherited."

They were quiet. Outside it was completely black. Finally, Elizabeth broke the silence, "As I look back at those times, we were right in the middle of one of the great social meltdowns in the history of mankind."

chapter twenty-five

he two of them sat quietly and finally Elizabeth looked at Kurt and said slowly, "It had been quite a time. I was teaching in Brazil. My brothers and my sister began to leave for Wales in 2038, but my father and mother refused to leave. I came back three years ago when they both got sick. Within six months of my return, they'd both died. At least I had time with them. I swear, my mom died more of anguish than illness. It was a real sad time, dismal, in fact." She paused and looked away from him.

"I'm sorry about that. In the thirties my parents moved to North Florida. After five years there, they went to Scotland with my sister. I think they went back to die. I saw them both just before they left the U.S. which was a blessing." He paused and looked at his drink, swishing it around. "So here we are in 2050 having thirty-year-old scotch in an alien country, our own alien country. Strange, isn't it! By the way, I'm curious about your personal life during all this, if you don't mind my asking."

"I don't mind, but what about it? And why would you be interested in my personal life?"

"Well, I was just thinking when you were fixing the drinks, how brief life is. I was thinking how wrapped up I can get in human historical change, as if that will have any lasting effect on this earth. No matter what we go through, it's all a blinking of an eye."

"What's that got to do with me?" she quietly said.

"I'm a bit in awe of your courage. Living here all by yourself when the rest of the world is in revolution and massive change. You've talked of school, family, this house, but why have you stayed out here by yourself?"

Elizabeth smiled and began, "Kurt, after my parents died, I didn't have a clue what to do. I was also scared. They had been my bedrock. So I decided to make this my cocoon. I know this place. No surprises. I feel safe in this house, plus I had no place to go. It is peaceful. Except for two visits from the Administration's real estate people last month, I've had no visitors in the past year," she said, paused, and went on, "This place is all I know, and as I've said, I haven't a clue what I'm going to do. But this day has been a bit of eye-opener. It has been great talking with you." She paused again and added, "I suggest that you should take advantage of this respite here before you shove off to wherever. Relax a bit. Take a little break from running away from those Security guys. You can't know how beneficial it is for me to just talk about what has happened over the past years. I still get the world news from the dish out back, but it's someone else's usually biased perspective or the worse things that are going on in the world. I never see anything positive."

"That is the way the media has always been, believe me," Kurt said.

"I know. Talking with you today has given me a chance to express some experiences and opinions. It's been a while since I have had that opportunity. Over the past year I've been thinking a lot about the battles, the struggles in the world. It looks to me like they boil down to ethnic, economic, or environmental disputes. The E-Factor, you might say."

"That's about right," Kurt responded.

Elizabeth continued, "Look at what we have today after all the reshuffling of populations; we have a world divided into religious, secular, ethnic, or cultural countries. Even what was the U.S. is now five countries based on segregated premises. As Anglos, what are our choices if we don't go overseas. We could move to America, Columbia, Libertaria, or even Canada. None of them appeal to me. America is very strict, religious, and white. Libertaria is libertarian to the nth degree. Columbia's close, but from what I hear, it's a quasi-military state. So what's left? Canada? Maybe, but for me, it's too cold and completely socialistic. So I guess overseas, say Europe, might be the best thing. But another aspect of all that has happened, which is a good thing with all the polarization of countries, is that there is no real war threat anymore, anywhere. There are noncombative disputes. Now that is an improvement in world affairs."

"That's a good point. However, as I mentioned before, Atlantica may be in the center of just such a potential problem that could become combative. That pertains to the distribution of water. Most countries have allowed the UN to monitor and enforce water disputes. That has worked so far, but lack of water in this hemisphere could create, here in Atlantica, the ultimate test for the UN," Kurt said.

"What exactly do you mean?" Elizabeth asked.

"East of here, Columbia has to import about everything, including water from America, which is by far the largest country on the continent. The problem is that America itself is having trouble supplying water to its own population, let alone exporting water to Columbia. They've said soon they will have to ration water for their own people and stop supplying Columbia. Out west, Libertaria and Pacifica are in fair shape, but Columbia and America are strapped for water. Even Canada, who annexed many U.S. border states is having difficulty with their water supply. Atlantica sits on the greatest water resource in the hemisphere and engineers from France and Brazil will have the Aquifer completed by the first of the year. Three-quarters of the hemisphere's population needs water and the Aquifer, which was designed by the U.S. for that purpose, is controlled by Atlantica. The story in Pittsburgh is that Atlantica plans to leverage the Aquifer in order to gain trade and economic credits from the UN. Back to your earlier point, this may be the first potential for war. People can't survive without water; it's that simple," Kurt said.

"I'm aware of the Aquifer, but haven't paid much attention lately to its development. That would be unfortunate, especially as it affects this area. Wouldn't it be awful if Atlantica, by not sharing the water supply, caused a war that could destroy all they have gained."

"That's my fear, but you make a good point." Kurt stretched and continued, "You're so right. This has been great dialogue and a much-needed break," he said eyeing his glass of scotch. "I was just looking at this scotch. It's warming me up, feels good, like I've taken a huge breath and settled into an easy chair. Nice feeling. It's so smooth."

Kurt sipped, then tipped his head back and finished the scotch. He got up and went over to the tall bottle. He took it in his hand, read the label, and poured another round into the glass. He then looked up and out over the river. He turned back to her.

"Sorry, you want a touch of this?"

"Sure. Do the honors."

Kurt looked at the bottle closely, smiled, and walked over and poured more of the brown-colored whiskey into her glass. He looked at her for a long moment.

"Better with age," he answered as he walked back and sat down. They were silent as they slowly sipped their whiskey.

Then he sat up, looked at her and said, "I haven't been totally honest with you, Elizabeth. I am walking the Great Allegheny Passage, and I plan on visiting Fallingwater, but the reason I am doing both is that I have decided to leave Alleghenia. It was becoming a prison living in Pittsburgh. So after years of internal debate, I decided to leave. That's probably why the Security patrol was looking for me."

Elizabeth looked at him and smiled, "You know, for some reason I knew you were trying to leave. Call it what you want, but I thought no one in their right mind would be hiking the trail in late November, especially one that has been basically unused for years."

"Well, your intuition is absolutely correct. I'm not finished. I've been listening to you talk and although this is definitely out of the blue, I want you to think about what I am about to suggest. Just think about it."

Elizabeth leaned forward awaiting his next sentence. Finally when Kurt hadn't continued, she said, "Well, what is it? What is your great suggestion?"

"Why don't you leave here? Go to England with me? It might be the perfect time for you. You wouldn't be by yourself and you could decide when you got there where you want to go," he said quietly and seriously.

Elizabeth slid slowly back into the sofa, looked at him, then outside, took a sip and put her glass down on the table between them. She closed her eyes and rubbed them with both hands. It was quiet again in the room, now only lit by the two twin brass lamps on the end tables. Elizabeth straightened up in her chair and looked over at him, saying, "To England, with you, now," she said quietly. "Why would you think I would go to England, with you?"

"I was just thinking, to a great extent, we're of similar backgrounds. You said several times you know you have to leave here. It isn't easy getting out of Atlantica, especially for Anglos these days. I have a plan to get out and it just might work for you, too. It's an idea, Elizabeth."

She took another sip of her scotch and answered, "Thank you, Kurt. It's a fine thought and I appreciate you thinking of me, but I don't think I can just get up and leave my farm. But as to your first point, it has been a good time for me, too, Kurt, believe me."

"Well, I'm glad to hear you say that because I've felt a rapport with you. The offer stands. Please don't take this the wrong way, but as I sit here, for some reason, I feel I know you a little. It's been a while since I've had such an interesting, intelligent, and how do I say this, reassuring conversation."

Elizabeth had relaxed back deep into her chair. She listened to him attentively, but didn't respond. She swirled her scotch around and around looking at her glass, the ice clinking off the sides. She put the glass down, arched her neck to look out of the now darkened window.

"Pitch-black out there and the rain has finally stopped. Forecast is for a clear, cold day over the mountains. Perfect for working outside or in your case, walking the trail," she said. There may be another storm coming day after tomorrow with snow. Can you believe that, this early." Another bit of silence, and she continued, "You used the word *lonely*. *Lonely*, what an interesting word! Being by yourself is one meaning and I think the other is craving company. I guess I was in the former category. For the most part, I was by myself for the past three years. Didn't really want anyone around, and then today, you came stumbling onto my land. It's the first time in quite a long time that I was with another person. I must say I agree with what you said earlier, it has been a wonderful day."

Kurt, sitting across from Elizabeth, looked at the lovely woman, who gave him a querulous look as she sipped her whiskey. He sensed a look of almost suspicion, but also a touch of acceptance like she was right being so hospitable to this stranger.

He replied, "Listen, I know I came out of the woodwork, literally, but from our talking, one thing has become clear to me. It's that we have a lot in common. We're Anglo, old Western Pennsylvania families, history professionals, and we seem to be able to communicate. Oh, and neither of us has a clue as to what we're going to do with the rest of our respective lives. I think all these coincidences mean something," he ended.

"Coincidences, maybe, but still we've known each other for half a day, so I think you're probably putting too much into what you call coincidences," she countered.

"I had a friend who was a forensic scientist who said that in crime there was no such thing as a coincidence. Usually coincidences were tied together by facts. But, I understand. Pardon me for speaking out of turn, but that's how I feel about our conversation, that's all. I'll head off to the barn and leave at daybreak if that is okay."

"Of course, I said that when you first came. If the weather didn't clear up right away, you could stay over. That still stands." There was another quiet spell and they both started to talk at the same time.

"Well, here's my—" Kurt said, but Elizabeth interrupted.

"How do you expect—"

She stopped, and they both chuckled at their cutting each other off. Elizabeth said, "Go ahead, Kurt."

"Sorry. I said I had a plan. Here it is. Since I am staying over, I am going to head for Fallingwater at daybreak. It looks like I'll have to go to Ohiopyle before I can cross the river unless an unmapped bridge turns up before there."

"Funny you said that because there may be such a rope bridge put in years ago for hikers to reach Fallingwater which would save you at least a half a day. That is, if it's still up," she said.

"Well that's great news if it pans out. I wanted to avoid going all the way to Ohiopyle because of Security and the time it would take."

"Ohiopyle and Route Three eighty-one are how folks go north from around here, so I'm sure there's a checkpoint," Elizabeth said, then added, "So if your plan works and you get to Fallingwater, what's next?"

"Well, I'll be off to the other side of Ohiopyle and hike my way to Columbia, unless something else happens. If I get to Columbia, I hope to seek asylum and get permission to fly to England. They have two flights a day out of old Dulles Airport to London."

"Then where are you going, Kurt?" she asked with more interest this time. "You haven't said exactly what you're going to do."

"Well, I'll first go to Paisley, south of Glasgow, where my sister is living. From there, it depends on where I can get a position. I would like to work at one of the National Universities, maybe in American history. That's my general plan, anyway," he said. Then Kurt looked at her with a quizzical look on his face and asked, "Have you had any insight as to what you are going to do, Elizabeth?"

"No, not yet. You've supplied me with much food for thought. More food for thought today than I have had for a long time. Something still bothers me. We have talked for hours about our personal lives and the breakup of the U.S. but the more we talk and I think about it, the more troubled and disillusioned I become."

arlock and McDonald were up before sunrise and spent an hour with the Security forces going over the trail data and potential locations from Cumberland to Ohiopyle which would be their area of concentration. Security magnified on the GPS screen potential sites along the trail that a hiker could use to avoid detection. They shared breakfast and by the time they got up to leave, all of the prior distrust related to their initial landing had been dissolved. In fact Warlock found out that he had served in Egypt with one of the Security men. They finished their breakfast talking of the campaign of 2030 when Gaza was finally settled between Israel and Lebanon.

It was right after the first rays of sun came over the mountains that Warlock fired up the vapor jets. Since they received the Security Flash from Pittsburgh, they talked about options available to Sloan in getting to and around Cumberland. Security in Cumberland relayed to them a report from a boat detail on the Youghiogheny that a solo Anglo man had been seen west of Ohiopyle. They had chased him, but he had eluded them. Warlock and Martin had done data inputs into their GPS network seeking alternate travel routes. In Martin's mind the most critical thing was the description of height, weight and heat that were close to what Sloan may look like in hiking clothes. The man who ran was white, which made the description valid because not many whites would be out walking the Laurel Mountain trails these days. Martin and Warlock looked closely at the printout of his trail options. As it turned out, Sloan had few choices. He could follow the Great Allegheny Passage directly to Cumberland or he could take branch trails that wound around the mountains which would take much longer. The most logical alternative path would be the Old 40 Trail which had been built over the remains of the first turnpike in the early 1800s. That would probably save him about one day. The only problem was that it went through inhabited and loyal areas built by refugees working in the logging industry the last decade. This was especially true around Frostburg. One possible choice was to take the Northern Trail which stayed above the old Mason Dixon Line before dropping straight down along Will's Creek Trail into Cumberland. They agreed that Sloan would probably stick with the main Passage trail, but they would do a pass over the Will's Creek Trail anyway before going back west toward Ohiopyle.

The sun was brilliant behind them as they headed west following Will's Creek which was flowing as a river that day due to unusually heavy rains the past week. They followed the trail without incident until Warlock turned the skimmer due west and crossed over a large mountain.

"Mt. Davis," he yelled into his speaker, "over thirty-seven hundred feet, McDonald. I can't believe that guy is going to walk this whole trail system. Let's get over to Confluence."

Looking down at the desolation of the mountains and thick forest covering, Martin began to think that Warlock was right. Sloan was not in shape to cover this much ground in such a short period. "You're right, Warlock. Let's get back to the Youghiogheny. From where he was spotted we know he was close to the trail. So he either doubled back or he is laying low trying to wait out Security. He certainly is not looking for us, that is for sure," barked Martin into his speaker.

"If that was him," Warlock countered. "Those Security guys on the trail are probably not the brightest in the world. He could have been a farmer, but that GPS feedback put him into the overall description, so we'll assume it was him."

"Good assumption, Warlock," McDonald countered jokingly.

"No smart-ass remarks to me. You want this guy, I'll get him. That's my profession."

He swooped up and over a power line, then settled again into his glide path. Warlock was now following a river west. "We're still over the Casselman River, McDonald. It goes all the way back to the Yough Lake," he said.

For most of the day, they circled some of the sites picked out by the Security people in Cumberland. Warlock said to Martin that he wanted to clear out everything east of Ohiopyle before concentrating there. Finally he turned west toward Ohiopyle, following the trail exactly and slowing the speed. It was early in the afternoon when Martin, who was looking at the line of the narrow river, spotted what looked like smoke. "Over there. What's that?"

"Smoke," Warlock shouted, as he banked over a cut in the hills.

"Something's burning. Can you get closer?" Martin shouted excitedly into his mouthpiece.

"I can hover right over it, except I gotta stay clear of all that smoke. I'll let you down if it looks clear," he shouted as he reversed his rotors and dropped down to the spot along the river where spirals of smoke were dissipating into the air.

Warlock maneuvered them just to the left of the smoke, which seemed to have stopped.

"Someone put it out," Warlock shouted over the vapor engine noise.

"I'll go down. Just move to the other side."

"Here take this," he said handing a slim laser gun to Martin.

Martin grabbed the shoulder harness, hooked his arms into it, and opened the side hatch. Warlock nodded to him. The auto winch dropped down toward the ground and in a few seconds Martin was gliding onto the soft, needle-covered turf. The sight of a fire was about twenty feet away and it was smoldering. Someone had just thrown water onto the pile of once-burning wood.

He drew the palm-sized gun and walked cautiously toward the blackened pile. Obviously by the footprints, someone had been here. "Don't move," said a deep voice from somewhere behind where Martin was standing. He could see no one and he froze.

"What do you want here?" came the voice again from deep curls of bushes wedged in between pines.

"Why don't you come out? I'm not here to harm you or anyone," Martin replied.

"Why that fuckin' government thing overhead?" came the deep guttural voice.

"We're looking for someone who used to work with me in Pittsburgh. Someone who would have come through Confluence on the trail."

"You're a long way from Pittsburgh. Confluence is down around the next bend. This trail is never used anymore. You got a weapon there. You can drop it, now. Is this person you're looking for dangerous?"

"Not dangerous to you, just to the government. As far as the beam in my hand, if I drop it, the guy up there looking down at us will blast you away. He's got a picture of us on his screen right now. I'd advise you to come out with your hands up so he can see you're weaponless."

"Nice talk. You're a cocky son of a bitch. While we were talking, my members have disappeared. Nothing you have could find them now. We flipped and I lost. I cover you until they're gone. I pay the consequences whatever they might be."

"Tell you what. I'll call off the Major up there," Martin looked up at the hovering Skimmer, "if you come out. We'll talk. I have no need to harm you, unless of course you're a fugitive yourself. The Major probably knows that already. He's probably sent your profile into headquarters. If there's no response, he'll back off."

At that moment a tall white man dressed in tan-colored leggings and jacket came out directly in front of Martin. He held a shotgun at his waist. He was well over six feet, narrow build, with a dark brown beard, mustache, and a shaggy head of hair that came down over his ears. His deep blue eyes flanked a broad nose. Martin looked at the man, who was probably in his thirties. The man looked up at the Skimmer, hovering over their heads, then lowered the shotgun to his side.

"No problem down here, Major," Martin spoke into his collar phone. "I don't see a place to land, so just hover for a few minutes while I talk to him," Martin spoke into his phone.

"You can put that down, Mister. I don't trust that thing you were pointing at me, and if I have to, I'll shoot it out of your hand."

"Not necessary," Martin said and he dropped the laser into a belt holster. "I got my security right above you."

The man looked up, then lowered the shotgun and moved toward Martin. He flipped his shotgun several times in his large hand, then threw it to the edge of the river.

"Who are you looking for?"

"A man called Kurt Sloan. He may be coming through on his way to Cumberland on the trail from Connellsville. May have passed through Ohiopyle or even Confluence and be heading through here. Have you seen anyone walking it?"

"No one uses this trail anymore. First, no one has time to walk for leisure and secondly, it's not safe. It's not like it used to be. In the old days, our people used it to get into Confluence. We sure as hell don't want to go anywhere. Families have lived in these parts for hundreds of years. We have some farms we're trying to keep going. Don't see too many people from Pittsburgh anymore, from any place for that matter. But we can grow enough for ourselves. Trouble is, we have no place to sell what we make. You understand?" the man said.

"I think so. Why don't you take your produce to the markets, to Bedford or even down to Cumberland?"

"We do. Problem is no one has any currency. Some people try and use old dollars. The credit chips from New York so far don't work out here. No one trusts that. The Pittsburgh credit line was okay for a while, but now no one will use it. Would you?"

"Well, I do, of course. So what do you end up using?"

"Anything of value. Over east, some even have voucher chips from Columbia. The new American currency is also traded, anything that others will trade for. It's like it was when my folks first came here. Last week I got paid in old gold coins from a collection somebody got from a house over in Meyersdale. Most of the people still here are old. It's not easy to just start a whole new way of life like they want us to do in Pittsburgh. Is that who you work for, that new government?" he said cautiously.

"I am on a special project for Security but I'm a full-time student. Just so you know, I totally believe in what they're trying to do. It's not easy changing a system that's been around four hundred years. They're trying to help all citizens like yourself and not just the rich, like it used to be. It takes a while to get a new system working right. You had any contact with the government representative? Have they come to meetings to explain what's going on?" he said.

"They were at meetings over in Meyersdale. All I know is that they talked about buying up properties to divide amongst other people. Mostly people from God knows where, who didn't do a goddamn thing to earn the land like the folks who have it. Most of this land has been in families for centuries. That didn't go over too well. But I did go, so I would know what they were up to. Not many showed up. People were afraid if they went to the meetings they'd be profiled. Once you're profiled, then what I heard, you're in their system, which means you eventually will lose what you got left, your independence, your freedom, and worst of all, your land. That's what we're all afraid of losing. Our freedom to live the way we want to. Do you know what I mean?"

"I know very well. I've never had freedom, sir, never. That's why this new country is trying to get freedom for all its citizens. You have to listen to them, give them a chance. You never had freedom in the old system. I mean only the rich were controlling things. Only the rich white people were getting anywhere! Now everybody can participate and get mutual benefits, equally: schools, housing, jobs, health care, and most importantly, opportunity is open to everyone."

"You sound like a politician. All we want is to be left alone to live. That's all. No offense to you, but not the way some black or Latino bureaucrat thinks we should live. What the fuck would they know about living out here? All those immigrants know is living in a big city. Look at you, this country is just right for your kind. It's yours now."

"No offense? My kind of what? Sir, I came here asking for your help!" Martin screamed. "I have a Skimmer and Security on top of your head. He could disintegrate you in a second, if I ask him to. I don't believe in violence, but your insults make it tough. This country is trying to help you. So I guess you're saying you don't want our help, but you are now a citizen of the country of Atlantica, and you will be profiled. Whether you believe it or not, it's for your benefit. It will make you eligible for the social benefits that you'll get for free."

"Nothing is free, young man, especially my freedom. You can keep your benefits," he countered.

"That's up to you, woodsman, but I can't let your insults go unanswered. Since you noticed, I'm both a black and a Latino on a Security mission. How many of you are here?" Martin said looking past the man to the surrounding woods.

"Not gonna tell you that, but we have families that live in adjoining farms and have banded together, like it was back in the seventeen hundreds. The older folks are still here, but most of our young folk went back to England," he offered.

"Why didn't you?" Martin said.

"We just couldn't leave our land. This has been our land. It's still our land. It's fed our families and it's still feeding our families. No matter what you say or want in Pittsburgh."

It was a bit strange as the two of them spoke about the new country with the Skimmer humming away overhead. Finally Martin, the advocate for the new way, realized he wasn't getting anywhere and was wasting his time.

"Believe me, what is being achieved is for everyone's good."

Now equally impatient, the tall man looked at Martin and said, "Sorry, I don't believe you. You need anything else from me? I got to find some lost sheep," he said raising his shotgun and putting it up on his shoulder.

"Wait a second," Martin spoke into his collar phone. "Warlock, can you hear me?"

"Yeah, what do you want? Are you ready to come up?"

"Not yet, but any profile on this guy?"

"Nothing's come back. Probably clean, McDonald. Let's

get out of here."

"Okay, but listen. Circle about a bit and see if you spot any heat groupings that could be sheep."

"Sheep? You did say sheep? Getting a little horny, McDonald!" he laughed as the Skimmer peeled away above.

For a few minutes the debate picked up again between the patriot of the new society and the remnant of the old one. Neither understood the other. In a few minutes, they stopped talking and looked up as the Skimmer moved in over their heads.

"About a mile south, there seems to be a small creek. They're at that creek. Hear me, McDonald?"

"Okay, Warlock." He turned to the large man. "See that, Mister, we're not all by the book. We found your sheep. They're about a mile south of here by a creek. Give us some time, things will work out," Martin said. As he was turning to leave he asked him one last time, "Are you sure you haven't seen anyone on the trail?"

"I ain't seen anyone. I don't spend too much time near the trail, except as I said to go into Confluence or back over to Rockwood. Maybe he hasn't got this far yet," the tall man said and began to walk away from Martin. He went four steps and turned, "Nothing against you, it's just difficult getting along these days," he said quietly. "Thanks for your help. I'll be off to get those sheep."

"By the way, how many of your countrymen are back there?" Martin said looking off to the thick wooded area behind them.

"Just me," he said as he moved off, laughing to himself.

Martin watched the tall woodsman disappear into the trees.

urt thought about Elizabeth's comments of how it all happened. He rubbed his face with his hands, then looked at her, replying, "That is the question of the ages. Thinking about the past ten years is sort of trying to recall a surrealistic dream. A snowball slowly gathering speed and before you know, it's an avalanche, taking everything in its way. The impossible, happened. I remember my first years at the university and my father saying, 'This country is different now, but it's going to be totally different in a few years, Kurt. Won't be ours anymore, Son.' I'll never forget that. 'Nothing you can do, Son. Votes dictate, not the other way around,' I remember him saying. He meant that majority rules and the majority had become people not from Europe, at least not directly. They never really attempted to assimilate. They wanted the benefits readily given, but didn't want to give up their own culture. Another issue was that for thirty years, eighty percent of the seventy million or so immigrants from Mexico and Central America were illegal. This country became so dependent on the illegal workforce that laws were changed and they were granted citizenship automatically after five years of residency. They also received all the benefits of citizenship even before they officially became citizens. At the same time, gigantic environmental projects, like the Pittsburgh Aquifer, were created by the government to spur on the economy. The competition from Asia created panic in this country. Who filled the jobs? Mostly immigrants without any allegiance to the U.S. or incentives to speak the language or learn the history of their benefactor. This was the beginning of the alienation between Latinos and the multigenerational U.S. citizens. That struggle began early in the century and never ended. The culture of the Latinos quickly became the culture of many sections of America, primarily in the southwest and the northeast. It was quite a time at the universities where I went. I can remember they taught equally in both English and Spanish, as did most public schools. Later, of course, it wasn't surprising that when I began to work, my bosses were Latinos and Spanish was the language of the workplace. Many Anglos had already begun to leave by moving to other 'culturally friendly' states as the slogan went or began the exodus to their homelands in Europe. So that's when I began to realize the real impact of the catastrophic illegal immigration trends of the early part of the century. I went back and studied that time period. It was as if most people just wanted their yards cut instead of caring about the loss of their language and culture. I don't blame the Latinos one bit. The great majority had one goal, a better life for themselves and family—the American dream. But their numbers, language, and culture overwhelmed our country. Okay, I'm done," he said.

"I didn't understand the full impact of what was happening. My God, I was working in Brazil. Actually I remember thinking that the U.S. was the epicenter for a world movement of equality. I was naïve because when I came back to the farm when my parents were sick, I realized that idealism and realism are usually in conflict."

"That's the crux of it," Kurt said. "The irony of all this is that, as historians, we are experiencing one of the most important historical time periods in human history. To think that a country which called itself the United States of America and based its existence on fundamental rights for all citizens would by its very nature of democracy destroy itself. The question for these ages is just that. Did it destroy itself or was it the natural evolution of democracy?

"Who would have thought fifty years ago that we would no longer be the most powerful nation. Who would have envisioned that its own belief system would be the catalyst for its destruction? It's an extraordinary story and one that we are witnessing firsthand. Here we are, two history professionals, living the times that will be written, spoken, and videoed for the new centuries to come," Kurt finished, almost tired from his mini-dissertation.

"Well that sets the table," Elizabeth added, smiling. "But this conversation started with a suggestion, I believe, of traveling with you to England. What did you mean by that?"

Kurt looked at her for a few seconds without speaking and then said, "I guess I spoke out of turn, but I was thinking what a great background you have. I am sure you could find work in England. It's going to get harder to get out of Atlantica the way things are going, and I think I have a good shot at getting passage. I'm sure it would work for you," he added. "Besides, as I said, this little powwow of ours was certainly unexpected, especially in the middle of what I'm trying to do, but it truly has been quite a few hours I've spent with you. Most enjoyable. However, I really do believe that you're going to become more vulnerable here. There is no security out here unless I come around once in a while."

Elizabeth laughed, "No, I can handle my own security. I have and I will."

Kurt took a sip and continued, "Besides, your professional talents would be wasted. Because of your background, you would be a valuable asset in England, for anyone doing research on the social development and destruction of the great American experiment. Before I made my decision, I had numerous transmissions with professionals in London, who were positive that my historical roots, my experiences here, and my working background would find a receptive ear with government personnel placement. England wants American historians and especially ones with a social understanding of what America was and is becoming. You fit the bill. So that's why I asked you to think about going to England," Kurt finished quietly.

She didn't answer. Finally Elizabeth replied as quietly as Kurt had ended, "You come here, out of nowhere and in a few hours you want me go to England with you. That scotch is older than I thought. Things have changed in this land of ours. However, I appreciate your concern, I really do. You know what you have to do, that's obvious. You are going off to Scotland. But I think I'll stay put for now." She paused, got up from her chair, and said, "It's late and I'm also hungry. How about you, ready for some of that good old-fashioned country cooking I talked of earlier?"

Kurt smiled and said, "I'm sorry if I railed on a bit, but I also hear my stomach calling. Let me help," he said.

"No, you fix a couple more drinks," she said as she walked into the kitchen area. She turned back to him and said, "I want you to know I appreciate what you just said, believe me. What you've done is reopen a debate I have had with myself that I thought I'd settled months ago."

"I'm glad I caused that," Kurt said.

The room was quiet as the two looked across the room at each other. Then Elizabeth got up from her chair and said, "Okay, let me get some grub ready. You can get your butt out of here at the crack of dawn." She looked out the window and said, "It's hard to believe, but it's actually clear out there, Sloan. You can see all the way to the river. You should have good early morning weather."

Kurt got up and looked out. "You're right, doesn't seem to be any clouds tonight. If I grab some shut-eye and catch the last of the moon at daybreak, I'll be out of here with lots of light and before anyone is stirring around," Kurt replied as he followed the flow of Elizabeth Morgan into her kitchen. As he looked at her, he had a sense of closeness, a sort of compatibility.

It was ten o'clock by the time they finished supper. They'd eaten and talked more until almost midnight. Elizabeth fixed up a sofa in the sunroom, and Kurt fell asleep immediately from the scotch and exhaustion of his mind and body.

Several hours later, Kurt awoke as light poured through the windows. His mind came alive, and he pushed up on his elbows. Outside, the morning was in full bloom. He looked around and realized where he was as the memory of the preceding day filtered back into his brain.

He was in the sunroom which was filled with plants seeking the morning rays. Kurt was up and stretching his body. He felt rested with a clear head and a body that didn't ache.

"Good morning, Sloan. Looks like you had a good rest. Must've needed that!"

"Where are you?" Kurt answered.

"In here. Coffee's brewing. Should be done in a minute."

Kurt walked around several large bending ferns and remembered the small corridor that went into the kitchen where Elizabeth was standing. She was stunning, wearing a white robe with a golden sash around her waist. The robe draped down to the top of her feet which were surrounded by fur.

"Did you make those slippers?"

"Actually they were made by my mother, oh, twenty years ago. She made them from a rabbit pelt my dad brought her.

Apparently a trapper from up in the mountains gave them to Dad. It brings my parents back just by wearing them. Anything do that for you?" She kept stirring a bowl and looking out of the large sunlit window, which was over the sink area.

"The watch I wear. My dad gave it to me many years ago and it still works. Weather, GPS, directions, but nothing as comfortable-looking as those slippers." Kurt looked over at Elizabeth and said, "Not to change the subject, but what are you making anyway?"

"Well, you're going to need a lot of energy, and frankly, I felt like a great big breakfast. Since I haven't got a lot to offer, except loads of wheat flour, I'm making pancakes. Also I have a lot of syrup. In fact there are jars of it down in the cellar. That should do the trick. How'd you sleep?"

"Unbelievable. I must have gone out in a second. Woke once, then went right out again. Missed my early departure, but I sure feel rested, and my mind is clear. I'll have to leave as soon as I help you clean up. Did you sleep okay?"

"Great. I must say it's nice having company. This will be ready in few minutes," she paused, then continued. "So you're still bent on your trek to Columbia?" she said as she kept focusing on the bowl and her stirring of the pancake flour.

"That's my plan," he responded

"Is it that dangerous that you have to sneak out by the old trail? I saw on the news that emigration has been restricted for Anglos, but can't one just travel within the borders?"

"Well that's what is funny," Kurt responded. "The party line is freedom for all citizens which is part of their Constitution, but the reality is that more recently it has become a closed, autocratic society, especially for Anglos. There has been a growing suspicion of us, maybe because of the pending opening of the Aquifer System. Maybe that explains the Security patrols and the increasing concern about Anglos and plots

against the security of Atlantica. I've never heard any of my
few Anglo associates' talk of any plots," Kurt said, pausing,
then continuing, "Of course, my leaving, I guess, is a plot, of
sorts."

"What does that mean?" Elizabeth quickly asked, as she
finished stirring the pancake batter.

"I meant, that I'm leaving. After all, I am an employee of
the Administration and I've just left without notice," he said.

"That is bold. So that's why they are sending out Security
to look for you?" she asked.

"Probably because I work in the Castro Library System. I
do historical research and have access to sensitive materials."
Elizabeth began to drop spoonfuls of batter onto the grill.
"They probably are a bit jittery and don't know how to handle
you. They probably can't figure out why you stayed in the first
place, and now you just disappear, so they're suspicious," she
said.

"You're probably right." Kurt ran his hand through his hair.
"Listen, I'm going to wash up, so I can get moving. I need to
check my stuff and take a shower. Is that inside or out?"

She laughed, "No, it's just down the hall. I've got a reservoir
on the roof. It's cold, but it will work. But, how about holding
off, this will be ready in a minute," she added. She returned to
the stove. "In thinking about what you said yesterday, it sounds
like you were really on the fence about leaving for a long time.
You apparently like your work, but living was becoming too
restrictive."

"I loved my work. I was preserving the history of Western
Pennsylvania. The Administration wanted to destroy hard copy
records going back to the 1700s. Dr. Alexander and I fought
to preserve them. I felt like I was an archeologist trying to
save artifacts. The added factor was that I had a great man and
mentor to work with."

There was silence, and Elizabeth said, "Okay, let's get on with breakfast, the day is young, and we both have much to do."

"You're absolutely right. I'm ready," Kurt replied.

Elizabeth scooped up some potatoes that had been frying separately, along with some strips of thin meat slices, and placed them on plates. "Venison, Kurt. One thing I have plenty of here is venison. Makes me sad every time I have to kill one, but there is really an overabundance in the woods. Hope you like it," she said.

"I'm starved and that looks incredible," Kurt said sitting down at the table.

Elizabeth came over to the table with a large white platter filled with steaming dark brown pancakes. "This should do the trick," she said as she sat down across from Kurt. "Oh, I'll get the coffee!"

"Sit still, you haven't stopped since you got up," Kurt said as he went over and picked up the large pot of coffee.

He poured dark, black coffee into a cup by her plate and then into his own cup. Returning to the table and sitting down, the two of them just sat for a few seconds without saying a word.

chapter twenty-eight

"I wonder if anyone says a prayer before eating anymore," Elizabeth said.

"It's been a while for me," he said, pausing and then he went on, "Would you care if I offered a prayer of thanks?" he said.

"Please, I was hoping you would," Elizabeth answered.

"Power of this universe, thank you for all the blessings of this life that we each lead. Watch over the spirits of our families, and bless the years ahead for the both of us. Also, a special thanks for bringing us together. Amen," he finished.

"That was perfect. Now dig in, Kurt."

Kurt took three of the pancakes from the platter and soaked them with the rich, dark syrup.

"These look unbelievable."

"Old family recipe," she answered.

They both ate quietly. Elizabeth, fork in hand said, "Well, it sounds like you're all set then. Is it hard to get boarding space?"

"Very hard," Kurt replied cutting a pancake.

"So what makes you think you'll get space?"

"Well, I said before that Security was looking for me because I'm an employee who left his position without an explanation. I haven't checked in for two days. They probably have put out an alert on me. I've wanted to tell you this earlier, but now is the time for me to give you the whole story of my journey," he said, putting down his fork and taking a sip of coffee. "When I was thinking of leaving Pittsburgh, I knew I would need something of value to offer the authorities in Columbia to both gain asylum and passage for a flight to Europe. I had no euro funds or gold credits. I told you I worked in the Historical Commission. Several weeks ago I came across some original data on the Pittsburgh Aquifer System, the system that is the source of Atlantica's survival over the next years. What I didn't share with you was that my father was the chief engineer on the Aquifer project. I had been looking for information on our family for a personal history I wanted to preserve. I could never find anything on the Aquifer except newspaper articles, which I copied. Then two weekends ago I came across valuable data about the working design and infrastructure of the Aquifer System. When I stopped at Dr. Alexander's to say goodbye, he informed me that he had been working with the UN in trying to coerce Atlantica into sharing the water. Apparently, Atlantica has threatened to hold the other countries of the hemisphere hostage for economic concessions. That violates the UN mandate signed by all countries, including Atlantica."

"So what does that have to do with you and your hike to Columbia?"

"Everything," Kurt quickly responded. "When Dr. Alexander learned of the data that I had and my plan, he said that he was going to contact the UN to provide an escort to take me to England in exchange for this information. If it works, it means I won't have to go to Columbia and more importantly, the UN would get the data and be better able to negotiate with Atlantica. Not only will I be able to get to England, but this transfer might avoid major confrontation between countries."

Elizabeth was silent; then she asked, "Where are you

supposed to meet the UN escort?"

"At Fallingwater. Dr. Alexander looked at a map and selected that site."

"That explains a lot, but help me understand something. What value would this information be the UN?"

"When the Aquifer was taken over by Atlantica, all of the plans, designs, programs, and original data were turned over to Atlantica. No one else had access to them, which was a real blunder by the UN who handled the transfer of power from the U.S. government to the new countries in 2039. Any information they can obtain about the system's operation might give them counter leverage with Atlantica," Kurt finished.

"Wow. That's quite a tale, all here in my farmhouse. Sounds like the destiny of this world has come to my doorstep," Elizabeth said and then added, "So what does this mean to you?" she asked questioningly.

"I found something else that same weekend. Maps of the Great Allegheny Passage which is why I'm using the hiking path along the river," Kurt said.

"My God, you really did all that? You actually took that data? You must've been desperate. Is Alleghenia so terrible that you would take such drastic means to escape to England. That troubles me. It is very self-serving. The old 'do whatever you have to, to get whatever you want.' That attitude turned me away from society years ago. That's why I went to Brazil. Why I've been happy in my seclusion here."

Kurt's face tightened, and he replied, "Maybe you should have stayed in Brazil. Maybe you should stay here on this farm because there is a world crisis looming and it's right here. This country is slowly denying us civil liberties and destroying any remnants of our whole culture. But more importantly, this country is going to deny water access to others for their own monetary benefit. It makes me livid and you, the great liberal of twenty years ago, don't understand that? If you don't like what I've done, that's fine, but it's obvious you and I are on two different wavelengths," he said, putting down his fork and standing up. "I really appreciate all that you have done for me."

Without turning around to look at him she said, "Over the past three years I have been removed from many of the challenges you have experienced, which is why it is so difficult for me to understand your actions. We clearly have different perspectives," she slowly answered and looked at him.

Kurt said quietly, "I'm sorry if I was abrupt, but you hit a nerve. I have been processing this whole debate for months, years, so you got both barrels."

"Maybe I overreacted to what you did, but I think you're judging this new country too soon," she said.

"I don't think so, but if life here is okay for you, fine. Do what you have to do, Elizabeth, but I have to pursue my life and my life's work," he said walking into the hallway near the back door. He leaned over and picked up his backpack.

There were a few seconds of silence between them and finally Elizabeth said, "So, it's off to Fallingwater?"

"It is. I asked you earlier about joining me in England. Well maybe you could at least hit the trail with me to Fallingwater. You know the trail. It might be good for you to get away from here for a day," Kurt said.

"You're serious, aren't you?"

"Absolutely, besides I've grown a bit accustomed to your company and your supply of scotch, which we could take with us for a bit of a celebration at Fallingwater," he said quickly with a smile.

Elizabeth took his hands and held them. She looked up at him and said, "It's like I've known you for a long time. Odd feeling, I must say."

"Is that a yes? You will go to Fallingwater?"

"All I said was that I feel like I have known you for a long time. The truth is that I do like you in such a short time which goes against all my usual instincts. You have literally blown my cover. I have been insulated from the world, and you have exposed all the realities going all around me. But the biggest reality, is that I am in a cocoon here. I will not be a butterfly if I remain here, so against all my usual past reticence, I'll go to Fallingwater with you. To be honest, my gut feeling is that I should go all the way to Europe. The reality is there is absolutely nothing here for me but memories," she said, tapping her head. "So, I guess, Mr. Sloan, we better get ready to leave."

chapter twenty-nine

"Okay, Warlock, coming up," Martin spoke into his mouthpiece. "No strangers left in the area. He was looking for his sheep and you found them. Bring me up," he said scooping up the tiny laser gun.

Martin hooked on to the dropped cable and was quickly lifted up to the Skimmer. He stared down at the woodsman who had stopped in a clearing and was looking up at them. The man kept staring at the Skimmer as it began to head west. Warlock had the Skimmer at its lowest cruising speed, and Martin could see the man disappear again in the next wooded area. Occasionally Martin thought he saw specks of movement as they picked up speed over the remote valleys of the mountains. Here was a lost generation of people, cut off from their old society, now living like nomads in the lands of their forefathers. It was a role reversal of great magnitude, Martin thought. *Probably thousands of white folk are wandering around these mountains outside of Pittsburgh proper, surviving on instinct, not wanting to live the new way.* He couldn't take the man out of his thoughts.

"McDonald, we'll have to make a decision soon. It's late in the day, and I'm bushed, but it's your call. We could do some night scanning back to Connellsville. Who knows, we may get lucky. He may think nighttime is his best time. We could do a complete sweep, maybe drop down at Ohiopyle for the night. I think we should do a couple of runs and then take a break before we finish up later tonight. "

"You're the pilot, Major," he answered. "I'd like to go, but you're doing the flying. What's that down there? I can barely make out a small town by the two rivers. Is that Confluence?"

"Yeah, that's it. We're losing light, but you can still see the rivers coming together," Warlock answered as he swung the skimmer over the town.

"Can we put down there?" Martin asked.

"Easy. If you want. But I think we should go on to Ohiopyle since this old baby's got the Red Sensor System. Pick up anything in the darkest of nights. We could see if your friend is trying to walk it at night."

"Great idea! Let's do that instead. That's probably when he's traveling." Martin said.

"The trail goes northeast following the Casselman River before looping around southeast to Cumberland. I don't think he could have gotten this far, so I think he's somewhere west of Ohiopyle. That trail has been out of commission for years. So we do the whole trail one more time and then head to Ohiopyle.

"Good. Well, let's get on with it."

The craft swooped over the small town by the two rivers and swung around toward the west. A solid dark bank of clouds began moving in from that direction.

"Just checked weather and there's a storm coming in from Lake Erie. We'll get back here before that son of a bitch hits tonight. I have weather scans showing heavy winds and rain later tonight and then snow possibly later tomorrow. The temp is going to drop below freezing. It won't be nice for your buddy on the trail, believe me."

"Assuming he's on the trail," Martin said. "It's just amazing that we haven't spotted anything of him."

"It's a lot of ground to cover, McDonald, but we will find him. The way it's been raining lately, that white water will be churning. He's going to have to be careful along that river. As far as I'm concerned, that's good luck for us. If he gets this far, he might try and go over to the old interstate, but that would be suicide with all the various Security forces.

"I'm circling again so I can give our flight plan to Headquarters and see if they have any reports from our outposts," Warlock shouted.

Warlock began to talk into his mouthpiece. "Pittsburgh says the flight plan is good. So that's it. Let's get on with it," Warlock said.

"Okay, Major. We might get lucky tonight or first thing in the morning with the sensors. We might surprise him," Martin added.

"Agreed. I'll notify Pittsburgh that we confirm their recommendations, that we're going to patrol tonight, and stay over in Ohiopyle."

Martin turned away and looked out through the darkened sky to the rolling mountains that spread north. There was a defined break in the oncoming blackened sky, nighttime darkness and an oncoming deep blackness of a storm. The Skimmer flew quietly and literally sailed over the treetops as Warlock apparently wanted to get as close as he could to the trail down below. Martin watched the screen of the heat-sensing equipment looking for any white outlines that might be a man. His eyes, weary from the last few days, briefly closed. Martin's thoughts were on what was going on around him, and he couldn't stop thinking about the woodsman. In a way, it was as if Martin had stepped back a couple of hundred years into the past when those kind of people dominated the landscape below. Suddenly, he was jostled awake by a sudden climb toward a mountain.

Warlock noticed Martin drifting as the Skimmer climbed. "Relax, McDonald, nothing yet. I'm going to do some maneuvering along the trail. I have the scanner on. You just listen for any beeps. If you hear continual beeping, begin to look for an outline."

Martin looked at the red screen, and his head rested back against the seat. Once this was over, he had to concentrate on finishing his degree in Pittsburgh next month. He thought of the new, exciting world in which he lived and in which he wanted to excel. It was an odd world, with segregated societies, but it was at least orderly and peaceful. Europe had become a partitioned conglomeration as far as immigration was concerned. France, the Benelux Countries, Italy, and Germany had imposed strict immigration quotas, except for educational visas. Martin smiled thinking of what had happened to the U.S. Martin again opened his eyes and looked at the absolute pit of blackness outside. Suddenly a row of lights and an outline of houses with docks appeared. Warlock slowed and did a circle over the grouping of houses. Each had walls surrounding them, but there were no people visible from the Skimmer. *Probably vacation homes at one time,* Martin thought.

"Just checking to see if there is heat down there that shouldn't be. Those places are empty according to my data, McDonald. Nothing showing on the screen, though," Warlock said into his earpiece.

Warlock circled the Skimmer several times over the houses and then took off into the black ahead. The one thing that stuck in Martin's mind as he thought of the small cluster of houses he had seen earlier were the walls that each had. They were in the boondocks and still they had walls. Strange, Martin thought, how countries and regions had adopted the same idea to keep people of different religions or culture from entering unless of course they were to do labor for the rich ones. *Atlantica has no walls,* he said to himself. *That's why I'm there, and that's why it's going to make it.*

Martin was jolted back into the moment by Warlock whose humming had become singing. Martin glanced over at Warlock who was wide awake with a smile on his face as he continued to hum a melody Martin had never heard. The man was in his element. As Martin sat there he realized that after what they had done the last two days they had made absolutely no headway in finding Sloan. He had to be out there or Martin had made a horrible mistake. There had been no signs of Sloan. The only clue was the sighting on the river the other day, and there was no definitive identification of the person chased by Security. Martin did know if they didn't find Sloan by the day after tomorrow, the search would be called off. If so, all of his future goals might be compromised. He sat looking out into the darkness, trying to think of some clue he had missed.

chapter thirty

"Well, I've got much work to do if we're going to get out here soon. I need to check the outbuildings, barn, and the outside of the house. I've always had it ready for a quick exit because I never knew what might happen or who might show up. I need to see if there is anything that needs to be brought inside. I don't think there is, but I'll lock the old place up tight as a drum.

"Fortunately, the upstairs is about the way it's been since my parents died. The neighbors got most of the furniture from the rooms except the things down here. I only lived on the first floor. No one is monitoring my calls. I'll call a cousin, Ann Murray, in Chalk Hill, whom I haven't seen since last Christmas. She knows the farm and used to stay here in the summers when we were very young. She could use the livestock and the poultry. I'll tell her where the key is in case there is anything else her family might need in the house.

"I'll name her as the agent of record for the property. I'd thought about Ann over the past year as the person I would turn the farm over to if I ever did decide to leave. This will work. I'll call her from the barn and then walk the perimeter.

"One favor. Just leave a written message somewhere that she would know. If Security is monitoring the area, they might pick up the call. I'd like to get out of here without raising any suspicion at all about your farm."

"Good point. I'll text a one-line message to her that she will understand and then leave instructions in the basement. She knows where the safe is behind the foundation stone."

"I'll give you a hand. If we can make some headway this afternoon and depending if the Laurel Run Bridge is still up, we could be there either late today or early tomorrow morning before the contact might be made. But the great thing is that you're going with me to Fallingwater. How sweet it is," he said smiling broadly.

"What's ironic is that I also haven't been to Fallingwater in years. Just like you and your father, the last time I was there was with my father when I was in college. Remember that hiking bridge near Fallingwater I mentioned earlier, if it is still up, it could save us so much time. The terrain is very rough going up the ridges. There is a back trail left over from the Mingo Indians, who had a village on the river. If I can find that trail we could go that way after we cross the bridge. The critical thing is whether the hiking bridge is up," she said.

"You're right, it will save a couple of hours and we would avoid Security at Ohiopyle. Whatever happens, we can camp somewhere on the way up to Fallingwater and go in sometime tomorrow morning," Kurt said.

Elizabeth answered, "The good thing is that the area has been practically uninhabited for the past ten years, so I don't think we're going to come across anyone."

"I'm ready, but I have another favor. Just think, while we're hiking, about coming to England with me. If you want to split in London and go to Wales to see your brothers and sister, that's fine. But I would love to see you leave here with me."

"I did listen to you, Sloan, closely. If there is one message you made loud and clear is that there is much going on in the world. I am young and...," she paused and then continued,

"I don't know. Let me think on it."

"There is one thing I just thought of when you were talking about your cousin and the farm. As you said, the Administration will probably confiscate it. But once you get located, you can submit a real estate claim through the UN. You have to take all your legal, real estate data, so you can file the claim. Five years ago, I submitted a claim for some land my family owned in Washington County of the U.S. It took three years, but my sister received a fair credit distribution which she used to purchase a home in Scotland. I also had a couple of friends do the same thing in France. You can get a settlement if they take the farm."

"Well, that is certainly good news. That was one of my greatest fears if I left," Elizabeth replied.

"I thought it might be. Another thing, in my selfish opinion, I have a great sense that we are developing a very special relationship. I would like to be able to build on that."

"You're right, I feel it. There's something working here, no doubt in my mind. While we were talking, I've been thinking at two levels. Been sizing you up and really working over my situation. I have been contented here. When you think there's nothing out there, down deep, you're scared. Then along comes this man, who seems like, I hate saying this, a real nice man, a good man. Oh, God, there, I've said it. Enough of this dancing around, I've already decided. It's time to move on. I'm going to pack it up and go at least as far as England with you. Then I'll make a decision. We'll just have to see how it works, okay?"

"Okay, that's great."

"The bottom line is that I like you and even trust you," Elizabeth said with a quick smile. She went on looking intently into Kurt's eyes. "I think I know you a bit. You've struck a couple of chords with me, but the primary one is that I really have to change, to move on with my life. So, yes, I'm going to Fallingwater and the way I feel now is that once I walk through that field toward the river, I am not turning back. From there, I'm not sure, but that is one hell of a start and my hope is that we get there with your Dr. Alexander's help. I prefer his motivation and plan. It just feels safer. Hopefully, you can make that connection at Fallingwater. But we have to get moving." Elizabeth took a deep breath and went on, "So, today, this moment, is all that matters. The past and the future are now ," she said.

"That's potent," Kurt said, "Sounds familiar."

"I was paraphrasing T.S. Eliot," she replied.

"T.S. Eliot?" Kurt asked.

"He's my favorite poet and some of my favorite lines are from his poem, 'Burnt Norton.'"

"I read Eliot. Burnt Norton? That's in *Four Quartets*, right?" Kurt asked.

"I'm impressed. It goes like this. 'Time present and time past are both perhaps present in time future. And time future contained in time past. If all time is eternally present, all time is unredeemable.' I've thought about that quite a bit recently and ironically I know it's appropriate for my decision. To me it has always been a clarion call that all we have is the reality of the present."

"I believe in that philosophy of the present being what you really know, even though I am committed to studying the many moments of the past," Kurt responded.

"That's a great analogy. So, Sloan, let's energize this present time and get ready to leave."

"What about the livestock? The chickens?" he asked.

"I'll do one more feeding, and Ann will pick it up tomorrow. She may eventually end up taking them to her place which I'll tell her is okay. We have lots to do before we leave."

"Great, while you're doing that, I'll double-check in here

and come out to help you. You'll have to get all your gear that you'll need and pack it. I'll carry the bulk of the heavy stuff. Oh, you should hide any valuables," he said looking at Elizabeth.

"That's in my message to Ann. She'll take all that with her when she opens the safe."

Kurt smiled at her and added, "Those shoes look like great walkers which reminds me, make sure you take extra socks and a slicker for the rain."

They spent the next hour preparing to leave. Elizabeth sent a text message to her cousin, and she got a reply that said Ann would be coming tomorrow to check out the farm. They went through the house and stowed family items deep into the recesses of the cellar with Elizabeth methodically marking each item and entering them into a small notebook. Some old artifacts were stored in the safe along with instructions for her cousin. They also buried four metal canisters in the barn under the privy floorboards. Her father had designed the house and the barn very well. They then carefully loaded up Elizabeth's backpack, and Kurt rearranged his to carry additional items. Elizabeth added an old solar sonar detector which was in the house. Kurt attached it on to his pack which they thought would pick up sound approaching from the air, ground, or water. That and his night-vision binoculars would be helpful to them. The bottle of scotch, that was about empty from the night before, stood up against the kitchen window. Kurt poured the remainder into his canteen cup. He took a sip and passed it over to Elizabeth. She sipped and looked around the kitchen.

"Great stuff. In fact, I stashed away two bottles for whenever we get wherever we end up."

"Who knows where that will be?" Kurt answered, paused, and said, "So, that's about it. Might as well be on our way," he said, as he looked around the kitchen of the old farmhouse.

"Well, I guess this is goodbye to my homestead, my youth,

my parents, and the security of these walls. I'm heading out into the brave new world of 2050. I may be back, and then again, I may not be," she said, her voice breaking a bit. She tipped her head back, swallowed the balance of the scotch, and put the cup in the sink. "That, I'll just leave right there."

As they looked back on the Morgan Estate, it looked ready for whatever might come in the form of weather or people.

"Okay, let's get moving. We have a tough row to hoe," Kurt said as they headed to the river. In a few minutes they were at the embankment above the trail. Elizabeth looked up the field to her home and then followed Kurt.

chapter thirty-one

he two walked briskly along the river, Kurt leading and looking for any debris or obstacles that might block their way. They had walked for a short time when Kurt said, "Let's stop for a minute. I want to take a reading."

Kurt pulled his GPS scan from his right jacket pocket. He looked at the converging linear plot. "Okay, we're on track. We should be coming to the rapids at Laurel Run."

"I'm sure the bridge was still up last year," Elizabeth offered, adjusting her backpack .

Kurt put the GPS scan back into his pocket and said, "From where we are, it looks like we have another mile to go before we reach the bridge. That will be great if it's still there. If so, that's where we cross. As I said, if worse comes to worse, we'll go all the way to Ohiopyle. That will be the most dangerous because Security will probably be there. Let's just hope it's still up," he concluded.

Kurt started off, picking up the pace. He began to have a gnawing feeling in his stomach that could only be described as fear. For some reason, he couldn't get those Security goons out of his mind. By this time he knew that he was being looked for by Security. Personnel would have cross-checked with Security when he hadn't registered for work for two days. Dr. Alexander could make excuses, but that wouldn't stop

Security. It would bring out an alert, but he didn't think they would know about the data he downloaded. Then he thought, of course they would. If they were suspicious of him because of his disappearance, they might check his work site and the data he had worked on. That patrol would certainly report a sighting at the entrance of Morgan Creek. He knew firsthand they had patrols all over the rivers in Alleghenia. It was common knowledge that roadways and airway ports were thoroughly screened. He was puzzled by how heavily armed the Security team was that he saw on the river. Now he wondered about the wisdom of bringing Elizabeth with him. Was he putting her in danger?

His steps lengthened, and he could hear her breathing behind him, steady and strong. They would know soon whether the Laurel Run Bridge was still up.

Kurt picked up their pace again as his body felt loose and strong. They strode in unison with the increased noise of the current. Besides the increasing level of the water, the only other noise was the crunching of their feet hitting the ground and the shuffling of loose pebbles.

"It can't be too far until we get to Laurel Run," Elizabeth called from behind him.

"You're right based on my GPS map," he answered over his shoulder. "I don't want to take a chance to check again because the transmission might be picked up in Pittsburgh," Kurt said, turning back to her without losing pace. "The river curves a bit, so it's hard to tell exactly. Maybe a half hour at the most," he added.

The two plodded along as evening closed in around them. Whatever the power or reasoning, instinct prevailed, and two lone individuals had joined in a partnership, heading for the unknown in a unique bond. They could see up ahead the rapids across from the entrance of Laurel Run. They neared where the bridge was supposed to be. Kurt stopped, and Elizabeth caught up, and they could see that the bridge was down. Kurt could make out the aluminum pyramid left from some type of bridge, but that was all.

"No luck so far," he shouted over the noise of the high-running river. "We can take a break here. I know there is an old railway bridge at Ohiopyle. It would have been made out of solid steel and cement, so I can't believe that it would have been taken down. We'll take a short break and then head on out. And hopefully that hiking bridge you mentioned will still be up."

"Hikers talked about that bridge which is before Ohiopyle. It was part of what they called the Great Gorge Trail. I've never seen it, but a neighbor mentioned to me that some hikers had come from the East using that bridge. Of course, it could have been scrapped as well," Elizabeth said.

"We'll just find out. Somehow we'll get over there. That water is really running," Kurt said. He slid his backpack off and dropped it on the trail. "Let's have a bite, rest for a while, and head on out. We need to get across at the latest before daybreak. We need to make that contact."

Elizabeth sat down next to a pine trunk that had invaded the side of the trail embankment. She opened her backpack and pulled out several boxes and a canteen. "Here, Kurt, have some of these."

"Thanks," Kurt said as he dropped down beside her and opened the crackers and cheese. He looked at her, smiled, and said, "How are you doing on this adventure?"

"Actually, I'm loving this. This is the first great walking I've done in a couple of years, but these boots are a bit tight. I'll have to watch for blisters, but let's get going, I'm fine."

"Everything depends on which bridge we end up taking," Kurt said. He stood up. "Well, let's find out about those bridges."

He got back on the trail. "You can lead for a while."

They regained their pace with Elizabeth in front. They had not taken more than a few strides when suddenly they stopped as a muffled whir of air was heard. It grew louder and closer. The sound wavered, came closer, and then seemed to pull back. It was nearer, that was obvious.

"Over here, get down beside the embankment," Kurt shouted. Elizabeth ran over and ducked down beside Kurt who was lying flat against the high dirt wall of the trail. "Don't move," he said.

"What is that?" Elizabeth said.

"It's called a Skimmer. Haven't heard one of those since I left Pittsburgh. Only the Security Forces have them. Sounds like it's coming right up the river. Seems to speed up and then slow down. They can travel at three hundred kilometers or slow down to fifty. Right now it's drifting with the wind. That's the way they're built. You can hardly hear them, only the wings moving through the air making a whooshing sound."

At that very moment, the Skimmer came alive, and it zoomed by their spot. A gray shape ringed by lights swooped by over the river. It flashed by fast, but Kurt picked out in blazing white lights the letters ANAS.

"ANAS," Kurt spoke back over shoulder. "They're out of Harrisburg. Maybe it's routine surveillance, maybe not. Just do not move. We have some cover above us with all those rocks, so maybe they didn't pick us up. He's looking for something, and the odds are it's me. It looks like he's deliberately following the river and the trail at this point," Kurt said.

As Kurt finished talking, the noise drifted away for a moment, and then it was back in a flash. It flew by them again and headed back the way it had come. Kurt looked up and could see another flash as it banked to follow the bend. Just as quickly as the sound came on them, it was gone. Again there was silence in the wooded spot.

They could be looking for me, and you'll be dragged into my defection. They want me, not you. He stood up and helped Elizabeth get up. "You could avoid all this. Head back now and get back to your cozy farmhouse. If you have doubts about making this trip, please go back," he pleaded.

"Enough, Kurt. I've made up my mind. This was the right choice for me. If you still want me to go with you, I'm going. This is where I want to be, okay? We'll find a bridge and get to Fallingwater in the morning," Elizabeth answered firmly.

The silence of their spot by the river was instantly countered by a thunderous roar of air being moved by the sweep of the Skimmer as it roared overhead. They both looked up startled, and then they dove for the embankment. The craft above seemed to stop in midair. Then it slowly peeled away in a circle.

"Jesus, before they come back over let's get up to those rocks," he yelled and almost dragged Elizabeth along as he ran to an outcropping of rock. It was part of a chimney-looking formation that ran alongside the hill. In a few seconds they were squeezed tightly inside a crevice in the rocks. Above them in the dark they could hear the whirring sound of the Skimmer holding its pattern.

chapter thirty-two

arlock was guiding the swooping craft along the river when suddenly he cried out loud, "Son of a bitch. What was that?" he shouted. "Something's down there. Just a second ago. Now there's nothing being picked up. I'm going to swing back over that spot. It's on the system. Run it back."

Martin, who was half asleep, quickly came alive and looked at the scanner. He hit a button that caused a one-minute replay. There was an obvious blurred reference by the walkway.

As Warlock banked over the same spot, there was nothing. "Not picking anything up now. Whatever was there must have headed for those rocks by that hill," he shouted.

"Can you land anywhere?" Martin shouted back.

"Nowhere around here. River's narrow at this bend and it's moving fast, plus the wind is picking up. No opening anywhere around that I can see. Nothing on the scanner either."

"Send me down. I'll look around!" Martin shouted directly into Warlock's face.

"McDonald, just use your mouthpiece. I can hear that way. Don't panic, for Christ's sake. Might've been a goddamn bear or something, two actually. Your friend didn't have company did he?"

"Not that I know of. Heat registered in the high percentile for humans, but only for a flash. Went off the scale so fast, I don't know what the hell it was. We went farther east than I thought we could today. Let's come back by here tomorrow. Glide more. This thing is quiet, but it does make exit noise," Martin spoke into the mouthpiece.

"Okay, I'll put this down next to the falls in Ohiopyle. We can spend the night and get going first thing in the morning. I was there last spring. Nice little airpark. I've already sent them my Code Graph, should get a response shortly, and then we can land. I could use a couple cold brews and a few hours solid sleep.

"I know we're close. I just feel it. Listen, we'll go back out at dawn. If he starts up at daybreak, we might surprise him. First, I want to come back here. Gliding, so we can see if we can spot whoever ducked up to those rocks. Based on this GPS scanner, if that was him, we can concentrate on the trail from Morgan's Creek, all the way to Ohiopyle and then to Confluence. That Red Sensor is great, McDonald. By the way, Central relayed me that they set up two guards at Cumberland and sent a team on the trail from there. By pinching from both sides, we should have him by tomorrow. That's assuming he took this crazy trail in the first place. Maybe he went some other way," Warlock shouted in a derisive tone.

"He spent much time studying this trail, especially the last few days. He's on this trail, somewhere," Martin said confidently.

"By the way, I've been thinking. What happens if your boy has nothing on him? What grounds have you got to hold him? We may be a bit strange as far as building a new society, but you know how due process is the backbone of our Constitution. No one fucks with due process, no matter if the guy tried to kill someone. You'd better find something on him, some proof," he said back over the screaming whoosh of the Skimmer.

"I have a signed warrant. The original's in the system. I

know the Code. I studied it. I know you can't search someone without it, so I got it before I left yesterday. Judge Julio Cintron authorized it. I got it, don't worry," Martin said forcefully. He looked past Warlock and down at a grouping of lights in the pitch darkness. "Is that Ohiopyle, Warlock?" he said to the commander and pointed below them.

"That's it," he shouted. "That's where we're headed. The Skimmer banked and flew in low over the water and then swooped in toward the small town by the river.

"By the way, McDonald, based on what my data screen is telling me, the average man walking nonstop, with a fifty, even a hundred pound backpack, would be somewhere between Confluence back there and where we just saw something."

Martin was quiet, studying the screened map and asked, "Anything else of importance between Indian Run and Confluence, other than Ohiopyle?"

"Nothing. Well, there is Fallingwater, if you look here." Warlock said pointing to his pocket screen with a topographical display of the quadrant they were flying over. "It's on your screen." He reached over and tapped a spot on Martin's unit.

"What exactly is Fallingwater?" Martin asked.

"An old relic of the last century. Nothing there of value, especially for a man fleeing the country. He won't be there. If he is a fugitive, he's on the trail, probably moving at night."

"Seems I read about Fallingwater in Sloan's stuff," Martin replied. "Makes me wonder," he said as he looked at the topo.

At that moment, the Skimmer swept over Ohiopyle and began a glide pattern. "River's running hard. Look at it there," Warlock pointed down to the river running between beams of powerful lights.

Martin peered down at the settlement as Warlock brought the Skimmer down over a solid-concrete pad next to a two-story stone building with a red and blue flag of the Atlantica Republic.

"This will do for this short night, McDonald. Let's get our asses out of here."

Martin and Warlock climbed out, both stretched their cramped bodies before walking into the encampment. Built into the surrounding hills were glass-enclosed homes with a sign announcing, RESIDENCY AREA—ATLANTICA MILITIA, OHIOPYLE.

"Over there, McDonald. There's an inn still open."

"Good, I'm starved all of a sudden."

There was only one person working the Old Stone Inn at that late hour. The woman had been sleeping, but she told them that it was always opened as it had been for over two hundred years. They sat by a window in the stone structure as the woman started up a fire. It was chilly in the dining area. Warlock quickly downed his first draft of the dark beer and a second was put in front of him.

"Feel better already, McDonald. It's amazing what a good beer will do for one's spirit," he said as he sipped from the foaming second mug placed in front of him. Martin could see the transformation in the older man's lined face as he relaxed. Warlock put down the mug and looked at him.

"McDonald, how in the hell are little holes in the wall like this place going to survive the next fifty years. We're halfway through the twenty-first century and everything is in the cities, everything. I'm a country boy. Don't like the cement and metal of the city, but that's all there is today."

"This little town is at the headwaters of a river which flows all the way to Pittsburgh. It's got to be protected. The rivers of the Alleghenia dike system flow from many sources, both aboveground and under. Much of the water is diverted into the Pittsburgh Aquifer, so we need these outposts here to protect the rivers."

Warlock took a long sip from his glass. He wiped the droplets off the side of the pint, put his glass down, looked at this young black man with the strange accent and said, "You know, McDonald, I didn't like you one bit when I first met you. Thought you were a smart-ass. Still think that, but I was just realizing that this new country of ours needs to have firebrands like you. I've got my job, and I'm the best at what I do. But you, you could work in the top floors of that government. You got a good brain. I'm just afraid those that run the Administration will get fat and lazy."

"Can't happen, Warlock. That cannot happen. We have the chance of lifetime to make this country work, for everyone. I will do what I can to see that happens," Martin said.

"Here's to equality," Warlock said, raising his glass.

Then he added with a yawn, "What do you think, maybe that's enough for tonight. Let's get a few hours sleep."

"Fine with me," said Martin. "You did all the work. I drifted off during the flight, but you must be whipped, so let's go," Martin responded.

"That was good beer, and by God that chili will stay with me for a while."

They walked along in the quiet outpost, back to their Skimmer. They took sleeping bags into the empty waiting room near the landing pad. In a few minutes both were asleep.

"Excuse me, sir. You need to wake up."

Martin had been totally exhausted when he finally fell into a deep sleep. He had set his watch alarm for midnight. He was startled when he felt a tug on his shoulder. He was completely disoriented. The tugging became a shake. He rolled over, slowly opening up his eyes into the brightness of the room's light. He could see the dark brown eyes of a boy, shouting at him to wake up. Martin was up in a second.

"Who are you? What do you want?"

"Sorry to wake you up, sir, but someone is snooping around the Skimmer." The small, nervous voice came from the young man whom he now recognized as the boy who had shown them to this room earlier. Martin looked into deep-set eyes with water dripping off his hair. He wore a hooded rain jacket, which was soaking wet. A booming roll of thunder sounded at that moment.

"What do you mean?" Martin shouted, and the boy pulled back.

"There's someone in your Skimmer, sir. Seems to be two of them. My room's right off the landing pad. After I dropped you off last night I went back to room and was just about asleep when I heard noises coming from the Skimmer."

"Warlock. Warlock," Martin shouted over to the curled-up and snoring figure in the far corner of the cubicle. Warlock still had on a tiny earpiece with music that had put him to sleep.

"Warlock," he shouted again as he stood over him. He shook him violently.

"My God, McDonald, what the fuck is wrong with you?" he shouted as he rolled over and onto his feet, snapping his pants buckle.

"Someone's fooling around with the Skimmer. Let's go," he shouted to the startled, but calm commander.

They raced out of the room. The boy watched them storm by and followed. As they approached the Skimmer, they could see dark shapes inside the glass bubble.

Warlock was at the Skimmer bay first. He tried to pry open the side door. He pounded on the door. Martin went to the other side and did the same. "McDonald, come here," Warlock shouted. Martin ducked down and over to Warlock.

"I'm going through the escape hatch underneath." As he said this, the side door opened and flipped upward. A figure filled the narrow doorway, turned, and came down the dropped step ladder.

Martin could not believe what he was looking at. First, a tall, obviously black woman in a tan jumpsuit stepped onto the tarmac, followed closely by a shorter black woman similarly dressed. They didn't say anything as they stood side by side almost at attention. Martin couldn't believe his eyes. They stared at him with a calmness on their faces that was disturbing to the normally aggressive patriot. Warlock looked at them with a quick sense of fear in his face. They both wore sidearms.

Martin was astounded by the two black women. The older woman was about two inches taller with a thicker, muscular body. She had dark piercing eyes with a dramatic crew cut of black hair. The smaller of the two had her dark brown hair pulled back tightly and had a softer, gentler look with liquid gray eyes.

"Who the hell are you?" he said. "And what are you doing here, and why are you carrying weapons?"

The taller woman took a step forward toward McDonald and at that point, Warlock came up to McDonald and pulled his weapon from a side holster. It was a slim paralyzer gun. He straightened up and said, "Lady, stop right there, and both of you take those weapons out of their holsters. Now!" he shouted.

The taller woman stopped and turned to the other lady saying something that Martin or Warlock could not hear. She then turned back to them and in the same motion unsnapped her holster and pulled out a large, black gun. The other woman who hadn't spoken, did the same. They both held out the guns toward Warlock.

"Just drop them," he said.

Martin walked over and picked up the guns, looked them over, and went to the women and said, "One more time, who are you, and why are you carrying these things?"

"We're runaways from the National Guard in South Carolina," the taller woman replied. "We left Charleston, hoping to get to either Pittsburgh to be specific, or maybe hitch a ride to New York or I guess you call it Nuevo York, now."

"What's with these weapons?"

"What do you think? I told you we're with the South Carolina National Guard and in a foreign country."

"Your names and IDs!"

The tall one looked at her partner and back to Martin without replying.

"Did you hear me, lady? Your names and IDs, now!" he snapped.

"My name is Isabelle Dupree," said the older of the two. "Besides my National Guard duty, my profession is, was, a professor at Emerson College in Spartanburg, South Carolina. This is Elena Carver, fellow Guards person and also an associate at Emerson. We are trying to get away from the Carolinas. Maybe you don't know what it's like in the new Anglo country of America down south of here, it's a lot like Post-Reconstruction days of the Civil War. That is if you know what Post-Reconstruction was all about."

"I understand Post-Reconstruction, believe me. So why Pittsburgh?" Martin asked, as he looked past Isabelle.

Isabelle hesitated and said, "We want a free life. We want to be free to do whatever we can achieve with our abilities. We have seen media reports on the new country of Atlantica, which is seeking Africanos with degrees to work in the government. We looked at a map and decided this area was a back way to get into Atlantica from the Carolinas. From here we could go east to Nuevo York or west to Pittsburgh."

Warlock lowered his pistol and said, "Let's see your ID."

"All we have is our ID from school." said Isabelle, as she

pulled out a card from a small, black case that was in a sleeve pocket. She handed a picture ID to Warlock. "Look like me?" she asked, with a slight uplift in her eyes.

"Jesus, that's a bad picture. Sure this is you?" said Warlock, very seriously. "I mean you're a good-looking woman, but this is bad."

"Man, I know you're kidding. We may be Gypsies, but don't give me any of your male bullshit. That's me, all right. That's an ID, not a Miss World shot. Beautiful me, so what of it?" she answered right into his face.

"Lady, I was rapping on you. It's a good picture. How about you?" he demanded of the smaller, younger woman. She reached into her back pocket and brought out a small leather pouch. From a packet of data cards she took a picture ID and gave it to Martin.

"Elena Carver, twenty-two," Martin said looking closely at the ID. "Twenty-two-years-old and running away from home." Martin looked back at the card and then at the two of them. "How did you two get this far?" he asked.

"Well, we both served in the National Guard. One of our close Anglo friends totally understood why we were upset at staying in America. Things were okay and fairly liberal, but our potentials were limited. We wanted a chance in the outside world. Our friend, a pilot, was sympathetic. Since we were in the Guard, we would have had to get special visas to travel out of the country, which would have been a year's wait. We decided to leave. Our friend monitors the perimeter of the northern American border, so he waited for bad weather to make an incursion as far north as possible, which is how we got here. We left this evening, flew low in rain just above treetops until he dropped us here no more than an hour ago," she finished.

"That's quite a tale, lady, quite a tale," Warlock replied.

"So you came here, but why?"

"Our pilot thought it was such an isolated post and yet close to the Atlantica Turnpike. Actually, we didn't care where he dropped us, just as long as it was within Atlantica. A lot depended on our reception by the first Security people we met, which I guess is you two."

"That's probably the first correct thing you've said yet. We are Security," Warlock answered angrily. "What were you doing inside my Skimmer" Warlock asked, his anger building.

"To be honest, sir, we were tired and had no clue what we were going to do next. We knew we were in Ohiopyle and were happy about that. After our friend took off, we saw your craft. We came over and were trying to find out where it was stationed when you two showed up," she said calmly and convincingly.

"That's really interesting," Martin finally spoke up. "We're changing your plans again, ladies. You'll be going to Pittsburgh all right, but under guard. You'll be going with us. After Security interrogates you, they can decide what to do. I don't buy your story, especially with you packing weapons."

Turning to Warlock, who had put away his pistol and was checking the landing gear of the Skimmer, Martin yelled, "Major, keep your weapon out. We have to get ourselves moving as soon as possible. These ladies will in our custody until we can get them back to Pittsburgh. "

"That's good, McDonald," Warlock said. "Nothing tampered with as far as I can tell."

"I'm going to take them back to the HQ here, and they can question them. We need to get some sleep, so we can get going in a few hours." McDonald brought up his laser gun and pointed it at the two women. "Okay, you two, let's get moving. Maybe local Security can get more out of you."

"Sir, all we want is our freedom. Taking us to Pittsburgh is fine. You can check us out or whatever else you need to do," said Isabelle.

"We'll find out who you are," Martin replied. "If you check out, fine. Makes it easier, but nevertheless you're going to Pittsburgh with us, as our prisoners. *Comprende?*"

At the Ohiopyle HQ, nothing came up in the initial security check on either woman. Their numbers or visuals were empty. Even the old U.S. system, which was integrated into the Atlantica database, came up empty. This bothered Martin, especially with the older woman, but he didn't say a word. They were going to Pittsburgh anyway. Two more trophies for him with the Administration, that was all he knew. If they were innocent, as refugees they would be treated accordingly. But if they were infiltrators, they would be jailed. He had to find Sloan and get them all back to Pittsburgh for Security to sort it out. Local Security took the two women into a cell. Martin went back to his room. Just as he was falling asleep, Warlock entered.

"I checked the Skimmer and it's okay. Let's change our plans. Because of these intruders, we lost a few hours sleep. We'll leave at daybreak and get in a full day."

chapter thirty-three

urt and Elizabeth huddled in the darkness waiting for the Skimmer to leave. Almost as quickly as it came over them, it was gone. Silence finally surrounded them, and they decided to begin the final trek to Fallingwater. They continued along the river, only their narrow-beam lights clearing the darkness ahead.

Suddenly Elizabeth, who was leading, shouted back to Kurt, "Kurt, it may be a mirage, but it looks like the rope bridge is up ahead." Kurt played his light over the bridge. He also noticed in the beam of light that snow had begun falling quietly over the river scene.

"The bridge was built for hikers going to Fallingwater. Here is a plaque naming it the Wright-Kaufmann Bridge."

"It looks sturdy enough," Kurt said as he passed her and took a step on to the crosswalk. "I'm going first since I have more weight. You wait until I get across."

The bridge creaked and swayed. Kurt and Elizabeth crossed without a problem and saw a shelter at the entrance of a trail. "Let's stay in the shelter. It's a good time to break and wait for the snow to lighten. I don't want to lose the trail or you in this mess," he said.

"I am certain this trail goes to Route Three-eighty-one. Once we reach it, Fallingwater is about four miles away. You are right, I'm not sure about this trail, especially in the dark and the snow. A break is a good idea."

In the shelter, Kurt and Elizabeth talked about their objectives for tomorrow and decided to get some sleep before they began their final ascent to Fallingwater. They awoke after a few hours' rest. The snow had stopped, and it was still dark outside. It was the first time they had to hike uphill, but they had good traction and in less than an hour reached Route 381. From that juncture, they began to hike the two-lane road, taking them up over six hundred feet. From the time they left the bridge near the river until they approached the entrance to Fallingwater, they encountered no traffic on the road nor tracks in the snow.

Kurt and Elizabeth climbed between barricades that had fallen in disarray at the Fallingwater security booth. They reached the parking area and walked up to what was the Visitor Center, now dark and overgrown with branches from the unattended shrubbery and bushes that surrounded it. Kurt found a way around the Center and led Elizabeth to a path until they reached a field at the bottom of the trail. Kurt remembered this area from his previous visits and knew Fallingwater was ahead. They walked carefully up the walkway and began to hear the sound of Bear Run churning under the famous structure. They reached the final elevation and looked down at the stone beauty created by one of America's greatest architectural innovator.

Fallingwater was like something out of a storybook as it lay snuggled against the snow-covered slopes. For a hundred years it had been a Mecca for architects and the general public. Until 2030 it had been maintained by a local Pittsburgh conservancy. The State of Pennsylvania took over its care for a few years until it was unable to maintain historical and cultural sites in the state. Fallingwater, like all of the national monuments or tourist attractions of the U.S. was left to fend for itself.

They stood silently looking at the beauty and then Elizabeth said, "I remember one of my neighbors telling me that locals had volunteered to maintain the premises but had to give up a couple of years ago. It's been untended since then."

Again they were quiet and Elizabeth added, "My God, look at it. It's almost invisible with the snow and all the growth. It's so sad, Kurt, so sad. When was it finished?" she asked.

"It was built during the nineteen thirties. I think it was commissioned in 1936 and finished in 1938 or 1939 when they added the guest quarters above it. You know the story, I guess."

"Oh, a little bit. Frank Lloyd Wright was an eccentric genius, and all that. If he could see it now!"

"Well, you're right. It was built for Edgar Kaufmann, owner of a Pittsburgh department store. They collaborated on what became to be called the greatest American architectural structure of the last century. This morning it's hard to see with the snow falling, but he built this stone house within the confines of a gorge formed by Bear Run. It comes out of the woods and flows under the house. It's absolutely incredible.

"Look at it, Kurt. It's like a disguise of sort. Underneath that shabby exterior is a beautiful lady, awaiting birth. It's a Greek tragedy. It just lies there, overgrown, unattended. Let's see if we can get in," she said.

Fallingwater lay silent, guarded by dilapidated wooden barricades in front of the narrow, stone-enclosed passageway that led to the front door. Hanging, naked limbs of oaks, pines, and assorted vegetation all blended into a protective cocoon that curled around the layered structure. It was as if nature had become the protector of this human endeavor, now being governed by the woods and the stream, not guardians, who'd pampered its every need over the years. It had passed the test of the years. It was solid and hadn't caved in or fallen into the stream as predicted when first designed. In a symbolic way, this was the legacy of an American way, since vanished. If in another five hundred years, Fallingwater was discovered by a wanderer, what would that person think of those who had built it?

Elizabeth saw an aluminum container in a drop box by the wall. She opened it and inside was a journal written by John Fitzgibbons from the Western Pennsylvania Conservancy. Mr. Fitzgibbons signed the journal as VOLUNTEER CHAIRPERSON, FALLINGWATER. It was an epitaph for a nation as well as a monument.

Fitzgibbons wrote a brief history of Fallingwater and described how he was going back to his native Scotland, because there was no longer anyone to fund the maintenance of the structure. He left this letter for whoever came to Fallingwater. He wrote about how difficult it had been for him and many older volunteers to try and keep the "beautiful lady" alive. It eventually became impossible. Elizabeth read the letter and when finished, refolded it tightly and returned it to the aluminum container which she dropped into the mailbox. "Hopefully someone coming to rescue 'the lady' will take note of Mr. Fitzgibbon's letter," she said.

Kurt looked at her and said, "Well, let's get on with it. We have to see if we can be inside before noon. The contact may be zeroed in to exact coordinates on the building, whether that's electronic or even a possible physical drop. I just don't know. We have today and tomorrow to make contact. At this point we can't take any chances."

"How are we going to do this, Kurt?"

He studied the barrier and noticed logs that had shifted exposing a small opening. He and Elizabeth were able to move them aside and climbed over to the entranceway leading to the front door.

Kurt checked the door which was padlocked. There were several signs in faded letters stating Atlas Security, and he could see the security wiring system. It was solar powered and probably out of commission. Kurt backed out through the small opening to search for another entranceway. Tree trunks probably struck by lightning were lying along the side of the house. He laid one against the wall and used it to climb onto the second-floor terrace. An unlocked window provided him access into the second floor. Elizabeth waited outside as morning light penetrated the overhanging trees.

She heard Kurt yell from inside the house, "We would need a wire cutter or crowbar—something to snap the locks. You will have to use the tree trunk propped against the wall, and I will help you up."

For the next hour they walked around. The interior was nearly empty. All that remained was the built-in furniture, protected by heavy canvas coverings. Gone were the paintings, pictures, and sculptures of the Kaufmann family. He recalled the glossy waxed gray stone floors that today were dull, dingy, and covered with leaves and branches.

The famous glass windows that opened the rooms to nature were dirty from years of driving rain and wind-blown dirt. Kurt looked out the grimy windows recalling the forest fires of two years ago. Lightning caused fires to rage in the dry woods for days until a torrential downpour finally extinguished the spreading flames. Looking about, he noticed no apparent damage to the house. Possibly the stream had protected Fallingwater or the rains arrived in time. The structure probably wouldn't have suffered any damage anyway because of its stone construction.

"It's from those fires two years ago," he said as he rubbed the black-smudged window.

"Bet you're right. I was afraid down at Morgan's Creek that

we might have fire. Didn't happen, but we sure had strange weather," Elizabeth replied as she looked around the desolate home. She thought of Mr. Fitzgibbon's letter and said, "I can't believe how quiet and sort of spooky this place is. What do you want to do while we wait?" she said to Kurt who was still staring out of the window.

They stood silent, looking at the most magnificent structure designed by an American in the America of the past, now empty, but with a strength personified by the light that radiated through the dirty but classic windows. The two of them looked around wide-eyed as if they had seen a ghost.

Elizabeth looked out through the same windows that Kurt was staring at and said, "You know, I think we should take a break. Let's have our snacks and take a rest. Let's see if the contact is made at noon. The snow has stopped and the sun has come out. It looks like it's going to be a cold but beautiful, clear day. You can check the weather for today and tomorrow. That will be critical." She stood next to him, draping her hand over his shoulder as they looked out into the sun hitting the snow-covered branches below Fallingwater.

"As far as the weather is concerned, the prediction is for clearing today with a cold front and possible heavy snow accumulation tonight or early tomorrow morning. Thanks for that dose of reality. You're right." Looking at the famous staircase that led to the stream below, he said, "I'm going down there to fill our canteens.

"Yesterday, I had a message stating the contact would be made at noon, which would have been either yesterday, today, or tomorrow. If nothing happens at noon, I'll make another call. If nothing happens by tomorrow, we will retrace our steps down Three eighty-one and head for Cumberland. It all depends on Dr. Alexander's contact," Kurt finished.

"Who is this contact? Do you know?"

"I don't. The code name is Cobra, I know that much. All I know is that the good doctor has been in communication with UN officials. We have to be prepared for anything, that's for sure," Kurt said. "We'll keep packed in case we have to leave in a hurry. We have less than an hour, so let's take a break and have something to eat."

They walked over to steps that led down to the stream. They sat on the steps, close to each other and watched the water fiercely cascade on the way to the ocean.

chapter thirty-four

A t daybreak, the same boy who alerted them the night before came into their room to awaken them. As they were leaving, Warlock gave him a couple of coins. He smiled in gratitude and handed them large cups of coffee and a bag of breakfast bars. Security accompanied them to the Skimmer with the two women both with plastic cuffs around their hands. By the time they got settled in the Skimmer and ready for lift off, the early fog began to lift. A bit of sunlight forced its way through thick, dark morning clouds.

The Skimmer was crowded with the two ladies in the jump seats. Warlock was in the pilot's seat and Martin next to him. For the next three hours, they flew up and down the Youghiogheny, between Bruner Run and Ohiopyle. Once Warlock thought he had picked up activity near an old fire tower at the nineteen-hundred-foot elevation. He took the Skimmer down. They walked around, but found nothing. While they were on the ground, the weather changed and light rain began falling. According to their GPS map, they were over Morgan's Run and were swinging around back toward Ohiopyle when Warlock noticed something on the ground. He swooped down onto an abandoned farm about a half mile off the river and the trail. They disembarked in a lightly snow-covered field next to an old stone farmhouse. After securing the two women on the front porch, Martin and Warlock spent almost an hour scouring around the barn and the sprawling main house.

"This place is probably two hundred years old," Warlock said, as he tried the front door.

"Guess so," Martin responded.

Warlock finally forced the lock and the door swung open. The two of them walked around the house, checking the cupboards and looking into closets.

"Someone's lived here," Warlock said, as he stirred the still-red embers in the fireplace.

"It's been lived in, all right. It's very neat, not a mess, but it looks like they left in a hurry. There's a lot of stuff here."

"Maybe they are coming back," Martin offered.

"Don't think so. Looks like all that is left is furniture. I don't see any personal things. Anyway, we can check with Central on ownership of this place. You're right, maybe someone's still here, but I think they took off. Nothing here for us. I don't see any evidence of your friend Sloan, so let's get going."

After releasing the two women on the porch, they all returned to the Skimmer. Warlock said he wanted to inspect the landing gear. The two women and Martin sat in the Skimmer as the sky above them darkened. Isabelle spoke up, "What are you two doing anyway?" she asked.

Martin didn't answer right away, then turned and said, "We're on a search mission."

"What are you searching for?"

"A man, an Anglo deserter. A man who is very dangerous to our new country."

"Are you with Security?"

"Me, no, I'm just a patriot, but the Major is a veteran Security man."

"You said the man, the Anglo, is dangerous to your country. In what way?" Elena piped up.

"We believe he stole information about our Aquifer System. Do you know about it?"

"It's the largest water system in the hemisphere, and it gets a lot of media attention. Apparently, other counties may not have access to that water," Isabelle said.

"Well, that may be. It's up to our country to determine how the water is allocated. It is our system and we will decide, not America, Columbia, or the UN, for that matter."

"Isn't that..."

"It isn't anything and we've talked enough about it. Just know that we will have another passenger going back to Pittsburgh. If we pick him up today, he'll have to be stored in the rear compartment, and you will all be turned over to Security tonight. Any more questions?" he asked tersely. There were none from Isabelle and Elena.

Warlock climbed back into the Skimmer and started the engines. As they took off and swung east, Martin began to concentrate on a section of the topographical map in the Skimmer's front panel screen. The river always returned to the screen as he drifted about the landscape.

"I asked you before about Fallingwater. What is it?" Martin spoke into the mouthpiece to a deeply engrossed Warlock who was studying the weather screen. "Warlock, what's Fallingwater again?" he shouted.

"I heard you the first time, for Christ's sake. Fallingwater was a house built by an American architect, Frank Lloyd Wright, back in the middle of the twentieth century. It's built right over a stream, Bear Run to be exact. As far as I know, it's been empty for a long time, maybe ten years. A long time ago it used to be a big tourist attraction in the U.S. I'll bet Mother Nature has sucked it right up. It's not too far from here. Fact we were right near it yesterday afternoon," he responded and went back to his task of flying as close to the curling and disappearing river as possible.

"We okay with fuel?" Martin said.

"Good shape, our cylinder has about twenty percent left. If you want, we could make a whole sweep to Cumberland and back. The real problem is the incoming weather front, looks bad, real bad."

"Well, maybe we should get back to Pittsburgh by midday. Sludge left a message wanting an update on our search. I'm sure he's having some pressure put on him. So let's keep trolling as long as we can, then head back to Pittsburgh. Maybe we'll ask him for some help like some troopers with cycles that can travel the trail. I can't believe that he's gotten that far, so fast," Martin said, rather disgusted.

"What's the matter? Think he slipped through? You know, man, you're doing something no one cares about. I just checked the online security reports, and there have been no more sightings of anyone on the trail. I mean Sloan may or may not have what you think. Secondly, so what? Security can probably counter anyone trying to screw up the system. But I got my orders, so we'll give it one last shot. After that I'll get you and your two guests back to base. You can do whatever you want then," he said banking the skimmer.

"Okay, let's do it," Martin shouted. He turned and looked out through the portals. Down below, the density of the woods was amazing. Occasionally an old road or a shiny roof would appear reflecting sunlight, but for the most part, it was desolate.

The two women were quiet behind Martin and Warlock. Isabelle was peering out of the small window. She looked at the back of Martin's head, leaned forward and said, "Mr. McDonald?"

"I didn't give you my name, lady."

"I know you didn't, but your friend, the Major, called you

that, so I assume that is your name."

"Don't get smart, lady. What do you want?"

"That place you mentioned before, Fallingwater is quite a spot, world famous. I taught a lot of history and Fallingwater was always part of the section on American landmarks. It was right up there with the White House and Lincoln Memorial. It's a historical icon. It seems strange we are flying right over it."

"What's strange about it? It's another relic of a bygone era. As the Major said, it's probably covered by the woods by now."

"Quite a shame, I'd say. It's the most historic place around here," Isabelle responded loudly.

Martin heard her and then looked at the GPS map. Suddenly, a thought hit him as he looked back out the side window of the skimmer. "Listen, Warlock, I have an idea. Can you land near Fallingwater? If the map is correct, it's back there a way. I got a hunch, a hunch that our historical genius couldn't pass up a last opportunity to see that place, especially since I remembered he brought it up on his library research scan. Can you find a spot to land? I'll look around a bit, and then we can take off for a sweep to Cumberland before heading back."

"Sure, if that's what you want. I'll bring it up on the screen."

Martin looked over at Warlock who was directing a laser-pointed light on the colored map and began to magnify to a specific degree setting. "That's the right coordinate. It will take a second. You watch while I buzz around again."

The two women were silent in the backseat. Then Isabelle leaned over and talked into Elena's ear. After a few seconds, she came away and looked outside. She sat back and closed her eyes as if trying to catch a nap as the Skimmer zoomed over the river visible below. Martin had been watching her and turned to the black lady sitting squarely in the tiny seat.

"No secrets, teach. By the way, since you're a professor, you're going on a field trip. You've read about it and taught it, now, lady, you're going to visit it. We are going to drop in on that historical place from the good old USA, Fallingwater," Martin said.

"I can't believe that we are actually going there. I've always wanted to see it. Such a miracle," Isabelle said smiling and looking over at Elena.

"I think that Anglo, who is a history nut, might have taken a detour. If not, no harm done, we'll be in Pittsburgh late today. So, ladies, we're heading down to this 'masterpiece,' as you call it. Hopefully our quarry thinks it's a 'masterpiece.' We'll be there in a few minutes." He turned to Warlock, "How's it looking? Can we go in?"

"There is an open field where we can land," Warlock replied. "I'll land there."

"That looks perfect, but can you cut the power a bit? We should try and come down as quietly as possible, just in case he's here."

"No problem." Warlock turned to the two women in the backseat. "Ladies, we're going to land in a minute." Both straightened up in unison, looking outside as the craft dipped lower over the trees.

Suddenly the Skimmer slowed, quieted, swept even lower over the trees, circling once again, before slowly descending into the open field. It was a quiet and delicate landing. Warlock looked out his window to the site where they had landed. "Looks like we walk up that pathway," he shouted. Martin was out first, then turned to help the two women exit.

"You coming now, Major?" he yelled up to Warlock, who was fiddling with the weather station.

"I'll be along. I am trying to get an idea of the weather for the next couple of hours. That cloud bank last night was a teaser, nothing happened, but apparently the real thing is coming in later today, a cold front with some big-time snow. I'll catch up with you in a few minutes."

"Okay, let's go, you two."

Martin reached under his jacket and rearranged his laser gun. Warlock was the Security guy, but he was glad he had picked up the weapon especially since he had the women under his watch. For some reason, which he hadn't figured out, he was suspicious of them. Their story made little sense to him. He had made a point to himself to talk to Warlock about his concerns as soon as possible. Meanwhile, he would keep close tabs on them with his laser gun ready just in case.

"This place looks desolate," said Martin. The women, hooked together, walked behind him as they moved cautiously up the walkway. The noise from the roaring water could be heard, and Isabelle looked at Elena, smiled, and gave the wrist cuffs a slight jerk. At the top of the rise, they could see Fallingwater through the trees.

chapter thirty-five

t was close to noon. Kurt and Elizabeth sat listening to the forceful flow of the mountain stream roaring under the rock-borne home. The light snow had melted on the ground, but according to this morning's weather scan, a new and much larger storm was on the way. Kurt had thought about starting a fire in the stone fireplace, but he was afraid the smoke might draw unwanted attention. They were both quiet, watching the stream below. Kurt glanced at his watch. It was now a few minutes before noon.

Kurt and Elizabeth walked to the outside terrace, entered his numbers and looked at the video screen. All that came up were three words, ON SCHEDULE—TODAY. It was noon and contact had yet to be made. He walked inside and said, "Well, there was a new message."

"What was it?" Elizabeth quickly asked.

"'On schedule—today' is all it said," Kurt replied.

"What do you think that means?"

"We wait. If nothing happens today, we stay until noon tomorrow. That's the way I read it. By this time tomorrow, we will be on our way, either to Columbia on our own or somewhere with our UN contacts. I say we take some time to enjoy Fallingwater, and later, if necessary, we can plan our trip to Columbia."

"Sounds like a plan to me," Elizabeth replied.

As if on cue, they heard muffled sounds coming from the walkway. Kurt looked over the terrace wall and muttered in disbelief. "Oh, my God, I don't believe it." It was like a slow motion sequence in a movie. Coming down the walkway was Martin McDonald, followed by two black women in blue uniforms with their wrists tied in front of them. Behind them was a large, square man in a Security uniform. Kurt was instantly in a panic state as his body tightened.

They quickly moved inside. "It's McDonald, the guy from my house. The one I told you about. My God, this is a nightmare. What in the hell is he doing here?" he shouted.

"Kurt, what's wrong? What's going on?" she said.

"This is incredible. He's the one who was snooping around my room. The guy I had the arguments about patriotism, Martin McDonald, that's him, coming down the walkway. Why the hell is he here, of all places? And it looks like those women are his prisoners. Elizabeth, this looks bad. Must have something to do with that Skimmer we saw yesterday. He must be searching for me. For me, not you. We have to get you out of here."

He looked out through the window of the living area. He could see the group had stopped and Martin was talking to the other man. "They've stopped. This may give us some extra time."

Kurt turned to Elizabeth who was packing her backpack. "You can get out now. You know the trails and you can be home by tonight," he said anxiously.

"Sloan, I made a commitment. We're in this together. Who knows what he's up to, but whatever it is let's deal with it."

"Okay, but let's see if there's enough time to find a way out of here. Maybe we can get up to the guest quarters and into the woods." He hurriedly grabbed his backpack and slung it over his shoulders. "Somehow he's followed me," he shouted over to Elizabeth, who was dressing in her hiking outfit.

"Hey, calm down. So what if he finds us here. We're old friends. What can he do, anyway?" she said.

"The file I made. The data I told you about, the chip. For all I know he works for the Administration. That would explain his paranoia about me. Maybe he found out what I was researching. I don't know. I do know the guy doesn't like me. Maybe he found out about the data and also figured out that I was trying to leave the country. That would be easy by just checking my workstation. He already knew I wanted to leave from the last time we argued. Elizabeth, this guy is a fanatic patriot of Atlantica. He hates everything about our Anglo heritage. His being here is no coincidence. The man is on a mission, and I'm the object of that mission. Let's get out before he comes back."

"You told me the file wouldn't hurt the country?" she said warily, as she put her pack over her shoulders and adjusted the straps.

"I don't think it will, but I am sure it will help the UN stop whatever Atlantica is trying to do. The data is in a capsule in my sleeve pocket," he replied tapping his right arm. "If he finds this, I'm history and not the kind I enjoy."

"Can it be that important, Kurt?" she asked.

"It certainly could be. It's critical to the discussion of sharing the Aquifer resources." He tightened the straps and zipped closed loose pockets.

Kurt said, "Okay, everything is packed." Elizabeth followed Kurt through the open living space onto the outside terrace.

Voices could be heard again coming from the front door. It was hard to hear what was being said because of the water roaring from below.

"Damn it," Kurt said, "we're stuck. The only way out of here is through the stairwell, into the water, and that won't work. Okay, let's just play it by ear. Let me talk. I know this guy."

"I say we go back in and drop our backpacks, so they don't think we were trying to run," Elizabeth said. Together they returned to the living area.

He unzipped his right-arm jacket pocket, pulling out the silver capsule. He looked closely at the tiny object held in his hand amazed at the power it contained. "It's all in here, Elizabeth," he said.

"Kurt, let me have it," she suddenly demanded.

"What would you do with it?" he asked. The voices from outside were becoming louder.

"They won't search me as they will you. Hurry, give it to me," she said quickly.

"I can't do that," he said.

"Kurt, we're in this together. Let me have it," she said, holding out her right hand.

He looked at her, pulled out the silver capsule, and handed it to Elizabeth.

"Now, go see them. Act very surprised. Think of something. Go ahead, I'll hide this. Hurry. Act normal, whatever that is," Elizabeth said as she began to adjust the belt on her tan pants.

Kurt went to the front door and could hear them talking. "They don't know anyone is here, that's obvious. That son of bitch, McDonald. What's he trying to do?"

"Listen, the capsule is hidden. Go up to the terrace and shout at them so they know we are here. Act surprised, but normal."

Kurt could see the security man coming down the path carrying what appeared to be a laser weapon. Kurt yelled, "Who are you and what are you doing here?"

Warlock raised his laser gun and pointed it at Kurt and

shouted, "That's more of a question I should be asking you. Who in the hell are you and what are you doing here?"

"I'm a tourist," Kurt quickly replied.

Warlock suddenly laughed and said, "That's a good one, all right." Then the smile vanished, and he yelled again, "Who the fuck are you, Mister?"

"I might ask you the same thing, except that I can tell you're probably with Security," Kurt answered.

"You got that right. Is your name Sloan, by any chance?"

Kurt looked down at him and answered firmly, "Sure is. How'd you know that?" he replied.

"I can't believe it. McDonald was right all along. He had a hunch about you and needs very much to talk to you. Come around to the front. I'm going to use this lock buster, and you can greet your old friend." Warlock walked along the path toward the front door.

Kurt went back to the door where Elizabeth was already waiting.

"When the door opens, you greet him and the others. Introduce me and tell them you and I are family friends from the old days. You came to my farm and we decided to visit Fallingwater since it has always been a favorite place of ours." As she finished, there was a smashing sound from the entrance area. Male voices could now be heard.

The wooden door was slowly pushed open and McDonald entered and looked right into the Kurt's face. He had the same smirk on his face that Kurt remembered so vividly from their past encounters. Martin turned to see where Warlock and the two ladies were. He motioned to Warlock. "He's here. I sure nailed this one," he said defiantly.

Kurt took a step toward Martin and said, "McDonald. What the hell are you doing here?"

Martin didn't budge, but looked over at Elizabeth, who

stood straight up like a soldier at attention. He turned back to Kurt, as the expression on his face changed quickly from a smirk to a tight grimace.

"Well, that's a good question, Sloan. One that I don't have to ask you because, oddly enough, I know what you are doing here. Not here, in this pile of crap, but in the mountains. It's a long way from Greenfield and the Castro Library, Sloan. Doing research?" he laughed. As he said that, Isabelle and Elena came through the front door still handcuffed with Warlock right behind them. They walked up to Kurt and Elizabeth and nodded.

"Couple of fellow travelers, Sloan. Don't know what their story is yet, but of course I know what yours is," he said.

"What the hell does that mean?" Kurt countered.

"My Security man, Major Craft, is with me, and we're taking you back to where you came from. These two ladies are going with you. There are some very important people that want to talk to you. In case you get any ideas, we are both armed, so don't think of getting away from us. He pulled out a small laser gun from his belt as he turned to Elizabeth. "Who's your friend, Sloan?" he said to Kurt.

Kurt, who had been trying to keep cool, snapped, "Elizabeth Morgan, an old friend of my family, who lives near here. She showed me a route to get here and now is going back to her home."

"No one is going anywhere, Sloan, especially you. We didn't make a special trip to see this house of rocks."

Kurt looked at Martin and said, "You mean to tell me you came here looking for me, to take me back to Pittsburgh. Why, for God's sake. I'm a historian, visiting a place that is one of the great treasures of architecture. That's all, McDonald. You're standing there holding a gun on me like someone out of an old movie. You came all the way here with Security to take me back to Pittsburgh. I appreciate the concern and the offer, but McDonald, that is my home, for Christ's sake, and it has been a hell of a lot longer than yours."

"That's the first bit of truth you've come up with. It is your home, and that's where you're going back to," Martin responded. "But Sloan, I don't think you had any intention of going back."

Warlock walked up to them, and Martin said to him, "See what I found. Do you believe it? My hunch was right. He's here, bigger than shit."

At that moment, Isabelle and Elena moved forward to where Martin, Warlock, Kurt, and Elizabeth stood. The women reached out to Elizabeth in greeting and they shook hands. Then the two of them went to Kurt and did the same thing. "I'm Isabella Dupree," she exclaimed in her usual enthusiasm. "This is my associate, Elena Carver."

At that point Martin interjected, "Warlock, this is my man. The one we've been flying all over these mountains for the last couple of days to find. The one that's going back to Pittsburgh with us. The other one is supposedly a friend."

Warlock looked at Kurt and said, "So you're why I've been zooming all over this countryside. McDonald, your hunch worked out. I'll bet this is the guy the Security squad chased along the river day before yesterday. Right near the walkway. It was on the Security alert report."

"No doubt that would have been Sloan. I remembered a photo he had in his room. It wasn't there the other night. It was a large color shot of this place. I didn't put it together until I saw Fallingwater on the map. Anyway, it paid off. So, Sloan, what are you really doing here?"

"I'm a tourist. The first one in a long time, the way this place looks."

"People have got more important things to do these days

than look at some relic of the old United States of America," Martin said mockingly.

"Well genius comes in all colors, McDonald. Maybe someday you will recognize that; meanwhile Elizabeth and I are about done here. I don't know why you're here, but we'll be off. I can't say it was nice seeing you, McDonald. Ladies, and gentleman," he said looking first at Isabelle and Elena, and then Warlock. He reached for Elizabeth's hand and started walking back to their equipment.

"Nice try, Sloan. Let me explain something to you, slowly. Maybe then you'll get the message. You are employed, still, by the Administration of Alleghenia in Pittsburgh for the Atlantica Republic. You get paid, each month by a credit to your national account from our Treasury in Nuevo York. For that you do research and data gathering for the Historical Division, more specifically and recently researching the development of the infrastructure of early Pittsburgh and Pennsylvania. Your topic lately seems to have been the development of the subterranean water system according to your log-ins. Funny thing is your superiors never authorized you to be researching the water system. Why would you be researching subjects not in your work classification, Sloan?" he asked angrily, looking right at Kurt.

"I'm not going to answer you, McDonald. We're leaving now. Elizabeth needs to get back to her farm. So unless you've got more questions, we'll be on our way."

"Warlock, I may need your assistance. All depends on bright boy here." Martin said bringing up his gun again.

"Put that away, McDonald. War is my game. I know how to use that buzzer. You just decide what you want to do with him."

Warlock took the gun from McDonald, waving it at Kurt.

Elizabeth watched McDonald and then turned to the two black women who were standing back by the fireplace. The tall one looked at Elizabeth, a slow smile taking over her broad face. Elizabeth smiled back as if she had received a silent message.

arlock held the laser gun pointed at Kurt and said, "How about heading into the dining area. Up against that wall there, sit down, and we can talk about this situation. I don't know you, either of you, actually. I got my orders, and they are to assist McDonald in the apprehension and return of you, Mr. Kurt Sloan, employee of the Alleghenia Administrative System, to Pittsburgh. That's what my warrant reads and that's what I'm going to do unless I get orders otherwise."

"Warrant?" Kurt replied.

"Issued by Judge Julio Cintron of the Sixth District Court of the Atlantica Republic. It goes on and on, then says"—Warlock looked closely at the 4 x 6 screen in his handheld scanner—'to enable the Security Division of the Atlantica Republic, Alleghenia District, to apprehend, return, and interrogate Mr. Kurt Sloan as to breaking his security code, leaving his workstation, and resigning his position without notice.' That's all. Nothing too complicated. Course we have to frisk you, and that should be done now by McDonald."

"Right, Sloan. Stand up and take off your clothes. Warlock, you check him out while I go through his backpack. Ladies, you go down that hall while this is going on," Martin said. "I'll figure out a way to check you three, but right now, I need to check my friend, Mr. Sloan."

The two women and Elizabeth left the area. Kurt slipped off his jacket and pants, while McDonald began to rummage through his backpack.

"Toss your clothes over to me," Warlock said.

It was an odd scene. A tall white man stood in his underwear, while an older, bulky, tanned Latino man held a gun. Against the wall of this classic home, a young black man fingered through a leather notebook, as he stood over the opened backpack. There was no noise in the living area, except the sound of rushing water coming from the stairwell. After a few minutes, Martin put down the backpack and looked over at Warlock.

"We gotta talk," Warlock said as he walked over to Martin. "There's a problem. Let's go over there," he said gruffly looking over to the fireplace with the sloping and deeply imbedded boulders in the stone floor.

"Did you find anything?" Warlock asked with his foot on the threshold.

"No, not on the first go-around. But we will. I know it," he quickly answered.

"What did you find?"

"The usual items that a man would use in hiking a long distance," Warlock replied matter-of-factly.

McDonald was fuming. Warlock turned away and looked over at Kurt. He had a puzzled look on his face.

"McDonald, this guy does not look like the usual enemy combatant that I've faced in my military career over the years. He looks like what he is, a historian taking a hike, who met an old female friend. Who, by the way, is quite a good-looking female friend. If I were him, I would not be happy having us intrude on this rendezvous," he ended looking back at Sloan, who was now sitting up against the wall. He turned back to McDonald, "Now what?"

"That was preliminary, Warlock. There will be a more extensive search and interrogation when we get back to Pittsburgh. Our warrant states that we must bring him back for interrogation. That's what we're going to do. He may have hidden things along the way, stashed it for future pickup. Who knows, but we will find out. Yank his scanner and any other Telcom piece he may have. We'll see who he has contacted or vice versa. But I think his data is still with him or even here. He needs that when he gets to Columbia. That's where he was going, and he needed something of value when he reached their border, so I'm betting he still has it with him," Martin said.

"You're getting a bit far-fetched, aren't you. You need a specific warrant for Telcom units. You should know that. Your warrant doesn't cover that, besides this guy doesn't seem like a traitor, a saboteur, if you know what I mean."

"I know what you mean, and it means nothing. I know he has something, and I also know he's trying to get overseas. He didn't have any plans to go back to Pittsburgh. I even figured that out from some of the people I talked to. We're taking Sloan back to Pittsburgh. So go over the place one more time and also ask him for his Telcom devices. Then, we'll figure out a way to check out his lady friend. Maybe I'll use the ladies. Promise them leniency with Security or something. By the way if he refuses to give up his Telcom devices that will prove my point. Once we know there is nothing here, then we'll leave." he said. "Sloan, stay just where you are," Martin barked.

He and Warlock walked toward the kitchen where the three women were standing in a circle. They stopped talking when Martin and Warlock approached.

"You two, you say you want to make a new life in Atlantica, right?"

Both Isabelle and Elena nodded their heads.

"As I said to you when we picked you up, you're going to

Pittsburgh to be turned over to Security for interrogation. I need you to prove your loyalty to this new country you say you want to be part of by checking her for any suspicious possessions, either in her backpack or on her person. Will you do that?"

Isabelle looked at Elena, then turned to Martin and said, "If it will get us out of these bracelets and you put in a good word for us, we'll be glad to do it, right, girl?"

"Okay. Warlock will be right at the open door while you do the search. He won't watch, but he will listen. You understand?"

"We do, sir," Isabelle said to McDonald. In a few seconds he had undone the wrist cuffs. They both rubbed their wrists.

"Warlock, come here," Martin shouted.

Warlock, who had stepped back to check on Kurt, returned.

"The ladies are going to search this Anglo woman here in the kitchen. You stay by the open door while they check her and her backpack," Martin said forcefully. "Okay, ladies, get it done."

Martin walked back into the living room where Kurt was still hunched against the wall.

"You know, you could save us all a lot of time and yourself a lot of discomfort, Sloan, if you would just tell me what you have done since you left Pittsburgh."

"McDonald, my father brought me to Fallingwater when I was a kid. It is probably the best memory of my father. I needed to get away. Things were piling up in my brain. I couldn't decide what I was going to do with my life, so I just left," he said quietly without looking up at McDonald.

"Sloan, I did some checking on you, man. You have been a busy Anglo the past few weeks, very busy. Looking up stuff you shouldn't be looking up. Then just taking off without informing your personnel officer or even your supervisor, Dr. Alexander. He was really upset that you left him after all he had done for you. What you have done by leaving without permission is by itself a punishable crime. When we find the data, you will be spending more time in your homeland than you ever wanted, but in a detention center. So, you'd be better off if you just told me what you're doing here."

"No matter what I told you, I'm guessing, you wouldn't believe me, McDonald. For some reason, you're after my ass, come hell or high water. Just let the lady go, and I'll go with you. If it's Security that you're taking me to, I'll wait until we get there. Meantime, she didn't do anything but show me how to get to Fallingwater. So let her go, McDonald."

Suddenly, the look on Martin's face turned to a scowl and anger spread over his face. "Sloan, I'll see you in that brand-new jail on your beloved Monongahela River for the rest of your life. I can do it because I'm going to prove you are a goddamn Anglo spy who's taken valuable documents about our Aquifer System. I will find that data either on you or on that babe down the hall. All I know is that you are going down. Suit yourself. Either you tell me what you have done with the data or I'll turn my Security accomplice, Major Ramos Craft, on your body. Security couldn't care less if you're a bit bumped and bruised when they get you. Do you hear me, you Anglo son of a bitch?" he yelled right into Kurt's face.

For a second it was quiet then the silence was broken by voices coming down the hall. Elizabeth was walking toward them, followed by Isabelle and Elena who in turn was followed by Warlock.

They gathered around Martin and Isabelle spoke up, "Nothing on her or in her backpack, Mr. McDonald. Empty. *Nada*," she said forcefully.

Martin's scowl remained. "Okay, for now we're going to

search every corner in this place. Pull every loose stone in the wall. Check in that chimney. Every place something could be hidden. When we finish that, we'll head back to Pittsburgh with or without the information. I'll let Security take it from there."

"You two," he snapped at Kurt and Elizabeth, "sit over there by the fireplace." Pointing to Isabelle and Elena, he said, "You two, sit on the covered sofa. Warlock, you watch them. I'm going to look around to see if Sloan hid anything. He didn't know we were coming, so maybe it's something I can quickly find."

Martin began looking, for the first time at this old stone home. Water could be heard cascading underneath. "Man, sounds like we're inside a waterfall. Some strange place. It's so small. Can't see why this is so special. So goddamn small," Martin said muttering to himself as he walked off.

Now what's going on? Martin thought as a thundering sound was heard.

Warlock came after him and said, "Did you hear that? There's a bomber of a storm coming. I forgot to tell you before that the storm is predicted to come in much earlier than forecasted. Sounds like it's already here. Strong wind, rain, then snow after dark. Potential for a lot of snow. I monitored the Weather Central. You could see the stuff coming down over the Point in Pittsburgh. Couldn't even see the rivers. It came off the Euro satellite."

"I can hear the damn wind and see those trees bending over. How much time do we have?" asked Martin.

"This one is early. It's a northeaster that was supposed to head out over Nova Scotia, but it ran into a front coming down from Canada and is circling over Atlantica. It's a gigantic swirling pattern. It's picking up more moisture over Lake Erie. When it reaches here, it will all be snow."

"It's only rain now, Warlock. Surely we can fly in a heavy rain, just put the Skimmer on autopilot, right?"

"Wrong. Okay in rain. I told you, McDonald. By the time it reaches here, it will be colder, well below thirty-two. It's a bit rare, but in an hour or so, it's going to be a bitch. My point is we can't leave. We better get some wood in here fast. I'll go back to the Skimmer and get the provisions I've stored in the emergency compartment. But there's no way we can get off the ground in time, and I think we're going to be stranded here."

"I don't believe this. Why can't we just leave now?" Martin said disgustedly.

"No time. Even if we get up, we're going to get hammered in the air. As soon as we're airborne, we'll be heading right into it. That snow will be absolutely blinding. I can't take that chance. In fact, while we're bullshitting, our time for survival is ticking away. I'm serious. We gotta move."

"Okay. Let's go. Let me handle this. You go get the stuff from the Skimmer. I'll send the big woman with you, and I'll handle the rest of them here. Just be careful and watch. There's something about that woman that I don't trust. Let's see what is in this place we can use, and we'll get as much wood from the outside as possible."

They went quickly back to the group, who were now looking outside at the swaying trees and slashing rain.

"I'm going to have the Major give you a breakdown of what is happening," Martin said.

"Listen closely, all of you. We have a rough storm coming in within the hour. When it's over, probably tomorrow, we're flying to Pittsburgh and you'll be turned over to Security. For now, we have a problem. This storm is coming out of Canada off Lake Erie. First, we'll have heavy rain, then it will turn to snow. By tonight, it's going to get much colder. We have to get all the wood we can find outside and bring it in here, so we can get a fire. We're going to have to keep it going because the temps are supposed to drop drastically in the next couple of hours. If you don't want to freeze to death in here, you can help get ready for this storm. Is that clear?" he loudly asked.

All four nodded.

"Okay, here's what we're going to do. You"—Warlock pointed at Isabelle—"you come with me. We're going to the Skimmer and see what we can bring back. McDonald will have the rest of you get the wood. Move. We have about thirty minutes before the rain comes and soaks everything."

Warlock was out the door and heading up the walkway with Isabelle behind him. McDonald told Kurt to search the basement for any usable wood and Elena to go outside and see what she could gather.

Martin and Elizabeth began a search of Fallingwater. Except for the built-in furniture, the stone structure looked barren. In a few minutes Kurt came back with his arm full of logs, followed closely by Elena with a load of branches. They dropped their armfuls by the fireplace, as Elizabeth came down from upstairs.

"We found some old logs on the third level," Elizabeth said coming into the main living area with her arms filled with slender curved logs. "Someone stored logs in the guest room. This stuff is so dry and light. Probably been there for years," she said, dropping her load of logs by the pile Kurt had built next to the fireplace.

Elena headed back out the door as Kurt took Elizabeth's arm and squeezed it. "How are you holding up?" he said quietly looking at her. "How did the search go?" he asked as he scanned about the room looking for McDonald.

"Fine," she answered in a whisper. "Listen to me"—she also looked about—"Your contact has been made."

"What do you mean?" Kurt whispered incredulously.

"The ladies. They were on their way here when they saw the Skimmer at Ohiopyle last night. They gave me the code name, Cobra."

"That's right. Who are they?" Kurt asked in a whisper.

"They said they're agents from UNIA in Paris. They are stationed in Montreal and were dropped at Ohiopyle. The South Carolina stuff was a cover. They were ordered to pick you up here at noon either yesterday, today, or no later than tomorrow," she said into his ear. As Elizabeth spoke in a whisper, Kurt could see her body stiffen. She suddenly reached over, grabbed one of the logs and said loudly, "We need to get more of this type, Kurt," as Martin burst into the room.

chapter thirty-seven

"Why are you together?" he yelled at them. "You're supposed to be split up."

"This stuff is too brittle. I'll help get a fire started, but we need more hard wood. I'll go out," Kurt said as he walked quickly outside.

"Make it fast, Anglo. We haven't much time left before the wood out there will be soaking wet." The wind and rain mixed with snow, accentuated the harsh change in temperature.

Sloan brushed past Martin, with another load of now wet wood and dropped it by the fireplace.

"Let's go, Morgan, get the rest of the wood inside."

"Glad you finally knew I had a name," Elizabeth yelled at McDonald, who looked back surprised at the strength and sarcasm in her voice.

"All I know is that you're a friend of the Anglo, so you're not a friend of mine," Martin quickly replied. "Just get your job done." He held the door for Warlock and Isabelle who came in with water dripping off their clothes and faces. Warlock entered carrying the large box of provisions. It was becoming bitter cold outside.

"Sloan, get a fire going," Martin yelled at Kurt.

"I'm going to need a flashlight to check out the chimney," he replied.

Martin walked over and handed him a narrow black flashlight. "Here, take this for now. We'll pick it up when you're done. Just clear it out and get the fire going."

Kurt went up to the wide opening of the fireplace and looked up the chimney. He found a handle to the side, pulled it, and heard a scraping sound. An avalanche of leaves, dirt, and parts of birds' nests fell to the floor. He leaned under the opening and looked up the dark channel and could see a bit of light. He pushed an assortment of debris on to the hearth. His mind began to drift to the two women. It was incredible how they came on the scene. They would have been the last people he would have suspected of being his UN contacts. He realized he had to act like he knew nothing, but he was experiencing a combination of excitement, anxiety, and a bit of fear. *Who are these ladies, anyway?* he thought.

"We can use some of this stuff as kindling," Kurt said to the others. "I want to find out exactly what you're up to, McDonald, because I promised Elizabeth she would get back to her farm."

"No one is going to any farm, Sloan. I've said this once before. Listen to me. You're both going back to Pittsburgh. Why do you think I've taken my time and that of the Major? This is serious trouble you and your lady friend are in. You have got some explaining to do. Get it? For your information and hers, too, I think we've already been to the farm. We searched it pretty good. Nice old place, but I don't think either one of you is going to be seeing it again for quite a while. By the way, don't give me any more of your holier-than-thou attitude you always used back at the house. One day you're working for Alleghenia and the next day you take off for the land of your dreams with government secrets. That's treason, plain and simple. So, for now, just do as you're told. Get that fire started, and yes, we do need to talk, but I'll be asking questions and you'll be answering them. Any more wood coming?" he shouted.

Kurt, who was on his knees collecting the kindling while Martin had been ranting, just kept working the woodpile. He didn't acknowledge Martin.

"Do you now understand, Sloan?" he said leaning over toward him.

"Loud and clear, McDonald," Kurt responded in a monotone.

Martin leaned down and picked up the black flashlight he'd given Kurt. The living area was silent as Martin stepped away from Kurt.

"Sloan, just get that fire going. We're going to need heat in here," and turned away from Kurt.

Elizabeth joined him and pulled a long wooden match from a narrow box in her backpack and lit the pile of wooden debris. "What was that all about?" she asked.

"It took all I had to keep quiet. Knowing those UN ladies were here made me keep my mouth shut."

"Good move. Okay, let's get this fire going. No matter how this works out, it's going to be a cold night in here."

The wood slowly caught fire, and Elizabeth began to wave at it with her hands. The fire began to crackle, then roared with red-orange flames reaching up into the bowels of the stone chimney. Kurt laid more wood in a triangular pattern to allow air to move into the building fire. He was amazed at the heat that filled the living area.

Outside the waves of wind and rain became mixed with heavy-flaked snow. It was quickly becoming more snow than rain as the swirl of flakes began to cover everything in a brilliant white. Warlock's prediction was right on schedule. It was a blinding storm. Tree limbs could be heard creaking and sighing from the barrage of wind and snow. It was incredible that in such a short time the weather could become so devastating.

Inside Fallingwater, the fireplace was now blazing. The last of the wood was added to a pile of assorted logs and limbs beside the fireplace on the stone floor. Since the loss of light outside, it had become like a medieval castle.

"Okay. Anyone see candles anywhere?" Martin said to the group gathered around the fire.

Warlock answered Martin's question, "I didn't find any candles, but we have some emergency lights from the Skimmer. I'll make one more run to see what is left. Gotta go now before it gets much worse," said Warlock, zipping up his jacket. "There's more food rations, plus some lighting materials in the tail section."

"No, I'll go," Martin said. "You keep this place organized. Just tell me where the stuff is you need."

"Behind the left rear seat there is a storage compartment. Bring in what is left."

"Okay. I'm off. I'll be back in a few minutes. Make sure the historian and the others don't do anything funny, like throw a disc in the fire."

"It's covered," Warlock said as he took off his coat.

Martin went to the front door and opened it slowly. A rush of snow and cold air poured across the living area making the flames wave. Martin quickly left and the door slammed shut.

"You heard him, Sloan, stay where I can keep an eye on you. We've got to organize what we have."

Elizabeth spoke up, "There are boxes upstairs in a bedroom on the second floor. I found some folding chairs, blankets, and a couple of old mattresses. There's more stuff, but I didn't check it all out."

"We'll go see," Isabelle said. "Come on, Elena, come with me." she said.

"No, you go one at a time. When one gets back, the other can go, assuming you find something. Go ahead, big one,"

Warlock said, waving his weapon at Isabelle.

"Big one, you say, big one. I take that as a compliment," Isabelle came back at Warlock. For the first time, there was broad smile on his face.

"Whatever, go ahead," he said. Isabelle hurried toward the entry area. Her steps could be heard echoing off the stone walls as she hustled up the stairs.

"Well, we're getting somewhere," Warlock said to the others. He looked at Kurt and Elizabeth and said, "Listen, you two, I don't know exactly what this all about, but I do know what the warrant states and what McDonald is saying. My orders were to fly McDonald wherever he wanted to go and follow his instructions. My job was to find you and get you back to Alleghenia Security. The first part is done, and now we have to wait out this storm before the mission is completed. Sloan, I suggest you cooperate because if you cause any trouble for us, I have my orders and I will carry them out. My mind works simply. We found nothing in our first check, so I want you both to get your backpacks and bring them back here." Kurt and Elizabeth brought them back to where Warlock was standing.

"Empty your backpacks on the floor. We need to see every pocket opened."

Sloan and Elizabeth emptied their contents in front of a large boulder on the floor.

He scattered his items on the floor. "Some rations, coffee, my notebook, underwear, two changes of clothes, shaving kit, and some other stuff. Maybe a few things we can use tonight," said Kurt.

Elizabeth added, "Here's all I got. Some women stuff, too, which won't help. There's some peanut butter, muffins, and fruit, which will help."

Warlock poked at their belongings with his hand. He came

to a bag that was wrapped tightly. He poked at it and said suspiciously, "Okay, what's this?"

Elizabeth laughed and said, "Oh, that's just some old scotch whiskey. We'll not suffer from lack of libation, if anyone cares to indulge."

Warlock looked up and at her saying, "Scotch, Jesus, I haven't seen that lovely liquor in a couple of years. Let me see that." He leaned over and grabbed the bag carefully. He unwrapped two bottles and looked closely at the labels on their cardboard containers. A smile slowly spread over his face, one of the rare smiles for this professional military man. "I'll be in charge of this. When McDonald gets back, we'll put all our goods together. See what we have, then we'll wait out this storm, but I'll take special care of this. Where the hell did this all come from?" Warlock asked as he flopped one of the containers over in his large hands. He put it on the floor and began to rip it apart. He pulled loose the bottle with a white label and looked closely at it. "Jesus Christ, this won't be so bad after all. You drink this stuff, Miss Morgan? If you do, I gotta think twice before helping turn in a woman carrying this stuff around," he said half laughing. "It must be over thirty years old by now. Think it's still good?"

"It is," she said emphatically. "I've had a taste or two over the last year. It's a rare single malt from the Hebrides. My father's favorite. Go ahead, have some. I'll join you whenever you crack it open."

"Can't now. We need to get things orderly here first. Don't want to get off track. Duty first, which reminds me. Sloan, I was just thinking, since we're looking through all your gear, why don't you just cough up that disc. If you have it, give it to me now. It will make your hearing much easier in Pittsburgh. I'll tell them you turned it in voluntarily. Okay, one more time, drop your drawers, and we'll get on with the search,"

Warlock said.

"I don't have any disc on me, I'm telling you," Kurt replied.

"Okay, the rest see if you can find any other supplies to help us get through the night. Sloan, drop them now," Warlock growled dropping his mild demeanor quickly.

Kurt slowly took off his clothes again, stepping slowly onto the hearthstone. He was standing in a set of tan underwear. "Now what, Major? You want me take these off, too?" he said.

"Stay that way, smart guy. Keep that up, and you'll have me all over you. I want you to do an arm stretch, straight up." Warlock held the laser gun while he patted Kurt's body. "I have all your telecommunication devices. Now put that watch and jewelry in this pouch."

Kurt tried to keep calm as he removed his wrist unit and two rings. He dropped them into a clear pouch that Warlock held in front of him. "Okay, that's all for now. I'll check them later and Security will do a further search plus a skin and internal scan. If you have it, we'll find it, but it would be better if you just gave it to me."

"I don't have it, Major. Can I get dressed now?"

"Go ahead; that's your story. Grab a seat over there on the floor. We need to settle in for a while." Elizabeth came back with her arms full of blankets and put them down where Kurt was sitting. At the same time, Isabelle came back carrying an old mattress and more blankets.

"Anything left up there?" Warlock asked.

"No, just a couple more blankets and a few cushions that we can use as pillows," Elizabeth answered.

Warlock ordered everyone to sit down. "We'll wait for McDonald to return from the Skimmer." They were all sitting back from the fire. Through the dark-framed windows, the snow could be seen by light from the fire. The stream could be heard roaring a bit higher from the step area below. Another winter at Fallingwater, which had weathered everything a winter could muster over its long history. Once again, early this year, winter had arrived, and it still echoed with the integrated sound and sway of nature ricocheting off its still stylistic stone, cement, and glass.

chapter thirty-eight

artin returned covered in snow, dragging a collection of survival materials, including food packs. "We can use some of this," Martin said as he placed the items on the floor. "Looks like it's dinnertime."

Isabelle and Elena began eating the food Elizabeth and Kurt had carried in their backpacks.

Between the flickering flames and several emergency lights from the Skimmer, the living area became an eerie combination of light and shadows.

Warlock pulled McDonald aside, "Got the toilet working. It should work for a while. We have to keep putting snow into the cabinet. We have the fire going, mucho water, and with what you just brought in, enough rations for at least two nights. Hopefully, we won't be here after tonight."

"Let them know you are the authority figure. I think it's better if you act like you're in charge," Martin said to Warlock.

Warlock laughed and quietly replied, "You know, you sure have a way with pissing people off, even me. I'll play your game," he said sourly.

"Listen up, everyone. We're set, at least for tonight. Ladies, the toilet works, for now. Men, we'll go outside, if need be. We have plenty of water and food. We just have to keep that fire going all night. We'll take shifts," Warlock said firmly.

"Home sweet home," said Isabelle.

Over the next few minutes, this odd group sat in a circle around the fire like a scene from an old western movie when cowboys sat watching the flames lick into a dark and foreboding coyote-sounding night. No one was talking. It was warm near this fire tonight at Fallingwater in the year 2050. Each had warmth and sufficient food. The fire crackled. Warlock put on more logs, and they sizzled because they were a bit damp. No one moved or talked; they seemed mesmerized by the roaring flames. It was if they were all were mulling over their reasons for being here, at this particular moment and trying to figure the outcome after this night was over. Martin made the first overture.

"Listen. I want to say something and only want to say this once. This is for you three ladies. The Major and I are holding Kurt Sloan on suspicion of taking important data that belongs to the country of Atlantica. That's called treason. This is not my work. My life is as a student. Study is all that I know. Soon I will be sent to Paris to continue these studies, so I can come back and help my people and this country succeed. Over the last few weeks I believe that man over there downloaded the development plans of the Pittsburgh Aquifer System. That's treason in my way of thinking. That is why the Major and I are here and why he is going back to Pittsburgh, his old homeland, for interrogation. You others may be different. I don't know how involved you may be in this plot. I don't know if you"—he looked at Elizabeth—"are an old friend or just an accomplice. As far as you two are concerned," he said looking at Isabelle and Elena, "I certainly don't know why two attractive, intelligent women in uniform with weapons are snooping around our craft in the middle of the night. Your story is pretty good, but your accent is not quite South Carolinian. You all are suspects.

Don't think about not cooperating with me or the Major. This is the way it is," he said sternly. "Is that understood?" he ended looking directly at Kurt and then slowly to all gathered about the fire.

No one replied. After a minute, Kurt got up and went to the window panels in the living area next to the fireplace. He stood in shadows, but light flickered from the changing, soaring flames coming from the fireplace. He looked out through the windows. He said wistfully as if he was by himself, "That's some storm out there, some storm. It reminds me of so many that I have seen, felt, and even played in over the years. When we were young, we loved to play in the snow." His tone was dreamlike as he continued quietly, "Everything has changed since those days, everything," Kurt finished still looking out through the windows. Then he looked back to the group realizing that he had been reminiscing out loud and said, "It's like what we're getting tonight, weather off of Lake Erie," he finished quietly without acknowledging Martin who stared at him with contempt.

"You almost had me in tears, Sloan. Here you are accused of treason and you talk about your perfect, yet, sordid past. That doesn't get you off the hook in this day and age. Back to my point, Sloan. Did you take the data? Did you create a chip of that data?" Martin said, his voice rising. Kurt did not respond.

"I'm tired of waiting for him to turn over that data, Warlock. The data is somewhere, either here or at the farm. If we can't find it, we may have to go back in a couple of days and tear the farm apart."

Kurt could tell this comment brought fear into Elizabeth's face. "McDonald, you mentioned the Aquifer System a while ago. Do you have a clue why I would be interested in this system? Do you know who built the water system?" he quietly asked Martin.

"All I know and all I care to know is that it belongs to Alleghenia and it will be fully operational in a few months." Martin said, glaring at Kurt.

Kurt calmly looked at Martin and said, "McDonald, my father spent twenty years of his life designing that system to be the world's largest, and most importantly, the greatest distributor of water to the entire population. He built it for all people, rich or poor. Did you hear what I said, McDonald? All people! Now your great country doesn't want to share this system with all people. Atlantica is going to blackmail millions of people in this hemisphere for its own gain which is not what my father or the U.S. intended for this great water system. Maybe that's why I was looking at my father's legacy, McDonald," Kurt said angrily.

"You never give up, do you? You come up with one fantasy after another. Our country would never do that, never. Am I supposed to be impressed by your father having something to do with the System? I'm not, believe me. Sloan, you're incredible. Hooray for your father."

"That's right, McDonald. Three cheers for my old-line Anglo dad, who made sure the system was made accessible to all. It looks like your great democracy is not going to abide by its original intent or the UN Charter."

Martin looked back at Kurt without any expression. The living room was silent; none of the six moved. Finally, Martin pounded his fist and turned abruptly toward Kurt.

"You are amazing. You're quite a storyteller, Sloan, but I don't believe you. But I do know our country will do whatever is necessary to protect our future. But the bit about your father was touching. It's commendable that your father is a hero in your eyes. That has nothing to do with you stealing valuable information from my government.

"Warlock, it's getting late. Tie up Sloan and his friend for the night. As soon as this storm breaks, we'll be out of here. You two," he said to Isabelle and Elena, "sit over there by the others." Martin walked over to them, took out the plastic wrist bands, and strapped them on the women.

Warlock finished tying Kurt's and Elizabeth's hands, and then knelt down by the fireplace. "I'll work on this fire during the night. We're going to have to take turns, McDonald, if you want to keep an eye on them," he said as he began stirring the burning coals.

"It's near ten. You watch them until midnight, and then I'll take over until three. If I'm tired, I'll wake you, if not, I'll stay until dawn. I don't ever sleep much. No one is going anywhere in this weather. I want to make sure everything is tied down here, so that when we leave in the morning, we can go right to the Skimmer and get to Pittsburgh. That's my mission. Security will be pleased with the work we've done, Warlock, believe me. This will do us both a lot of good," Martin said.

"I don't know about that, nor do I care. I know the folks in Security. If that guy has any information, they'll get it, one way or the other. I was listening carefully when you two were talking about the Aquifer, because that's where I'm going for permanent assignment next month. I'll be in charge of airborne security based in Johnstown. If that guy is jeopardizing that facility, I'm glad I was asked to help you. In fact, I'm going to contact them right now. Give them an update, so they can be ready for us when we arrive. Since you're the leader of this search, I'll let you talk to the supervisor; then I'll get on and talk to the investigators," Warlock said. He went near the outside windows in the dark and could be heard talking to his superiors. Martin noticed the fire going down and added some of the large, dry limbs to the receding fire. It blazed again. He noticed all four of them had their eyes closed.

Out of the darkness came Warlock holding a tiny, compact phone in the palm of his hand. He gave it to Martin. "It's Sludge, for you, McDonald," Warlock said impressed.

chapter thirty-nine

allingwater was submerged in heavy snow. Like a lantern in a lonely house on the beach, the flickering orange to yellow light that seemed to flow with the updraft in the wind gave this solid sanctuary the look of a jack-o'-lantern. Tonight it was a temporary home to six people, all with different life stories and reasons for being there. In an odd way, it was an accidental retreat for them to be here, but when they left Fallingwater, their lives would be different because of this early winter night in this historic mountain retreat. Fallingwater was for one night a sanctuary that would affect their lives, forever.

The night at Fallingwater had gone as Martin anticipated. He stayed up most of the night after relieving Warlock at midnight. The four prisoners had fallen asleep, the Africano ladies lying across the floor on mattresses in front of the fire and the Anglos lying next to each other. Warlock slept facedown on a mattress with several heavy, brown military blankets pulled over his prostrate body. He snored loudly throughout the night.

After everyone was asleep, Martin walked through the house with his flashlight. He could make out little in the darkness, but tried to assimilate what was so unique about this supposed classic structure. He looked for any loose stones or crevices where Sloan may have hidden a disc. He found absolutely nothing. The structure was small, uncomfortable, and obviously designed for a small family, either in size or numbers. He realized how tired he was. His body ached from the days of uncomfortable positions in the Skimmer and the various places he'd tried to sleep. Strangely, as he watched light overtake the darkness outside, he felt extreme physical tiredness as well as emotional exhilaration in what he had accomplished. He also realized that not finding the data was actually a good thing because it would get Security actively involved with Sloan. His mind wandered as he looked around the scene in front of him. He had come a long way since his days playing soccer amongst the burnt-out cars on the field beside the empty Catholic Church. None of those here had any clue as to what he had gone through to get where he was. After this day, his future would be secured. The fire had dwindled down to a gentle crackling. *We can get out of here,* he thought as he dozed off from exhaustion.

Dawn came suddenly for Martin in the form of brilliant light poking through the snow-laden limbs of the myriad of trees that surrounded the mountain home. As he awoke and turned toward the group he froze. Isabelle, the tall lady from South Carolina was on her feet, pointing a large pistol at him. He straightened up, scared by the angry look in her broad black face. Her white eyes glowered at him. Beside her, Elena stood with a weapon pointed at Warlock, who was still asleep. What really tightened Martin's stomach and actually brought a slight gasp was looking at Sloan and Morgan get up and walk toward him.

Martin noticed they were fully dressed in outdoor gear. No one spoke as the three came up to him. Finally, Isabelle said, "Mr. McDonald, we are taking control of this situation. You and the Major will be treated with respect, but you are now prisoners of the UNIS. We have an international warrant for the apprehension of Mr. Kurt Sloan and Miss Elizabeth Morgan of the State of Alleghenia of the Republic of Atlantica."

McDonald was, for the first time, speechless. He could not believe what was happening. He looked over at Warlock who still had not moved.

"Our mission is to escort Mr. Sloan and Miss Morgan from here. We will not harm either of you, but we will stun you into unconsciousness if you attempt to either escape or stop Lieutenant Carver and me. Do you understand?"

Martin looked at her, recovered from the shock and said, "I don't understand anything. You are in Atlantica. You are interfering with an internal legal apprehension of a traitor. When my government understands what you are attempting to do, it will bring their full wrath on you personally and who you represent," Martin said, getting more strength as he talked.

"That's quite understandable, Mr. McDonald. Well said, actually, but that has nothing to do with our mission which will end in two hours. From that time on, when you're able, you and the Major will be able to leave freely. We wish you no harm."

At that moment Warlock rolled over and looked up to see Elena holding a weapon pointed at him. He jumped up, but she pushed him back against the wall with great strength and agility which completely surprised the large man. "What the fuck are you doing?" he screamed.

"We are taking over this operation, Major," Elena countered.

"Taking what over? This is a Security operation of Atlantica. Who the hell are you and what are you doing pointing that thing at me?" he said as he looked over at Elena. "You don't know what you are doing, ladies. This will get you killed. Our country seeks passive solutions, but not when it comes to holding two of their own at gunpoint."

Isabelle said, "Makes sense. That is our code also, Major. We just work for different powers with different agendas. Ours is based in Paris, and we are to bring these two back to our headquarters, today," she firmly said.

"You are with the UN?" Warlock asked.

"We are, UNIS, to be specific. You two will be allowed to fly out of here in three hours for wherever you want to go, Pittsburgh, I presume. We will be leaving in two hours. In the meantime, we'll pack our belongings and place yours in the guest quarters. We'll also clean up Fallingwater for the next visitors. Right now, I want you to go over by the fireplace where you can use your own wrist cuffs plus our locking device. Go now, please," Isabelle said. Neither man moved. Isabelle kicked Martin in his rear and yelled, "Now, Mr. McDonald, move. I can be a very impatient person." Martin looked at her and then slowly walked over to the fireplace and slid down against the wall. Warlock looked with angry eyes at the gun pointed at him by Elena. She waved the weapon at him without saying a word, and he slowly got up, walked over to Martin, and moved down the stone ledge. They both had expressions of disbelief on their faces.

Martin and Warlock put the cuffs on and snapped the clips shut. Elena went over and checked both wrist locks.

"There, good," she said, stepping back.

"Now loop that wire connection over both your wrists and push in the timer," Isabelle instructed. Both men hooked the wire through their wrist cuffs. The wire had a small black box attached with a red light blinking. Elena checked the wire and the box.

"Good," she said, stepping back again.

"Okay, relax men. You have a wait ahead."

"Elena, get all the items they collected from Sloan and Elizabeth, Telcoms and anything else you find. We don't want any of it left for them to take," Isabelle said. She looked at Kurt and continued, "Mr. Sloan. I would like you and Elena to go outside and see if you can get up the walkway. I need you to get to their Skimmer in the parking area. We'll use that for the location for our pickup. Check it out and come right back. I have to call our contact who's waiting for my signal to land. Once the contact is made, it will take twenty minutes to reach us, but with all that snow we don't know the condition of the lot. Elizabeth, you pack our bags and put everything in the kitchen area. I'll stay here with them. You two better get going. The sooner you get back, the sooner I can call our people."

Kurt and Elena grabbed their outer jackets and left. Elizabeth began to collect the loose items around the living room, putting them into piles for each person. Martin and Warlock watched from their places against the wall. When Elizabeth went into the hallway, Isabelle remained.

Martin looked up at Isabelle and said to her, "How can an Africano be doing this to me and our country. You are a traitor just like Sloan. No different, except you're a traitor to your parents and to your African heritage."

Isabelle didn't respond right away but looked at Martin. She walked over to him and said, "McDonald, you have no clue what I'm all about. You don't know what I've gone through in my life. Here's what I do know, McDonald. I know that I am working to bring peace to this world for all people and in this case, life through its basic source, water. Listen to what I say, McDonald. All people, black, white, yellow, tan, and combinations thereof, need water to survive. My job with UNIS is to secure solutions when there are people or countries trying to control others and create conditions that might bring countries to the brink of war. If our information is correct, this is a perfect example of why we are here, to help alleviate a problem that's about to break loose. It's that simple,

McDonald."

"Sounds good, but I'm trying to help this new country of Latino and Africano people be in control of their future. This Aquifer is our water system. I am sure our government will work out some allocation program, but in the meantime, let the Major and me take this Anglo traitor to Pittsburgh. Maybe by getting the data he stole, our government will take that as an overture from the UN, that you are acting in good faith."

"I'm not here to debate with you or anyone, McDonald. Those are not my orders. The Major will understand what that means. The UN is the only legitimate arbiter. This information will put everyone at the same level. So, just sit back. You will be allowed to leave in less than three hours, and you can explain all this to your superiors in Alleghenia. This is bigger than you, me, or the Major. You two will go to Pittsburgh shortly, but without Sloan or Elizabeth."

"You're Africano. You have forgotten your roots," Martin said angrily.

Isabelle responded slowly, "McDonald, I was born in Ghana and educated in France by a UN service organization. My childhood was spent living five feet off the ground in a shack until my father could build a hut. We lived on what we grew or what we got from UN food deliveries. That's why I work for them." Then she cocked her head toward McDonald and smiled, saying, "Ghana is my home, there is where my heart is, and it has tremendous water problems. I know the importance of fresh, clean water. This mission I am on is important to the UN and to me."

Warlock, who had been listening, spoke, "A couple of questions."

"Sure, go ahead," Isabelle quickly answered.

"How did you get to Ohiopyle and where did you get those weapons? As a Security person myself, I need to know."

"We were dropped by chutes outside Ohiopyle because of the landing field near our destination, Fallingwater. We had to get here by noon yesterday and we had to leave by noon tomorrow. It was a three-day window. Ironically, you just got us here sooner than expected. When we saw your Security Skimmer, we were surprised because your presence had not been monitored. We were prepared to neutralize anyone who tried to interfere with our mission. But you interrupted our plan. That caused us to rethink our plan," she said.

"Okay, but we disarmed you."

"You did, but not completely. On our person we had these weapons. Note how thin they are. We had them inside our thighs, which we hoped you wouldn't inspect and you didn't. Last night we disengaged and put them together. Does that answer your questions, Major?"

"Unfortunately, it does. It's my fault for not doing a thorough body search. Clever, I must say," he replied.

"But we had you captured. What were you going to do if we hadn't stopped here," McDonald asked.

"The fallback was Elena's slide gun, a slim, blue laser gun hidden in her hiking boot. Our plan was to immobilize McDonald and force you to take the Skimmer down, but fortunately, that was unnecessary," she said.

"My God, we really screwed up," Warlock said.

At that moment Elizabeth came back into the living area.

"All of their things are set aside for Kurt to take to the guest quarters," she said. "I need to finish packing our stuff."

Kurt and Elena returned from the Skimmer. His face was flushed. He looked at Martin and Warlock, then over at Isabelle, "The pathway is deep with snow, but it's melting fast. The sun is already working on the drifts. We cleared a space about the size of the Skimmer. Is that enough?"

"That's good," Isabelle answered. "Elizabeth, give everyone

some food packs. Kurt, would you take their gear to the guest quarters while Elizabeth and Elena finish packing."

In the next hour the gear was packed ready for their departure. Fallingwater was thoroughly cleaned of debris from their stay. Isabelle went outside and made her contact call. The temperature inside had risen as the sun beamed in through the windows.

"Okay, your backpacks and personal items are in the guest quarters. Once we have entered a safety zone, we will release the locks and you can retrieve your items. I want to say to you, as a representative of the UN, I understand what you were trying to do. Actually, Mr. McDonald, I admire you for your determination to protect your country, and Major, I certainly admire your dedication to your profession. Having said that gentlemen, we leave you in peace and in safety. Please convey how you were treated to your superiors. We are leaving."

Kurt was standing in the living area, backpack tightly fixed over his shoulders. He walked over and looked down at Martin. "McDonald, I must tell you, you were right all along. I did take data at first for my father's legacy, but then I realized I needed something to convince the authorities at Columbia to give me passage. The Aquifer data provided me with both. When I learned of Atlantica's plan to blackmail other countries for water, I was incensed. Fortunately, through contact with the UN, I will be able to supply them information that will help them mediate this problem. Everything miraculously fell into place. McDonald, only trouble can result when water is used as a weapon. You still have your country. What the UN will accomplish will be used to benefit all people," he ended. He looked at McDonald and added, "I guess you'll come out of this okay. For me, I'm leaving the land I love. I hope that somehow you and your country can get over your insecurities. If I had one piece of advice, it would be to accept Anglos who want to come back and be part of this county. Welcome them back and value their expertise. If you do, you will achieve a truly democratic society. Good luck, McDonald. I hope you find what you want."

Martin replied, "To the end, a philosopher. Go, Sloan, to your land. Maybe we'll bump into each other again. I'll be in Paris soon. Come on over and maybe we can have a beer some night, like the good old days," he said smugly. "Our country is better off with you leaving. At least I know that much. If I had anything to do with that, I'm happy. But you know, Sloan, you're still a traitor, no matter what you may think you've done. That's who you are," he said.

The man didn't learn a thing, Kurt thought.

Martin asked, "Who helped you, Sloan? That Puerto Rican friend? The good Dr. Alexander? Who gave you the UN connection?"

Kurt was surprised by the question, forgetting it was a loose end. He didn't answer right away, but then said, "Martin, you know they're both my friends. As a matter of fact, Dr. Alexander encouraged me to stay because he felt I could record the history of Atlantica. Raoul didn't want me to leave. I left them both as good friends. As far as the UN contact, I'll let that question go unanswered. I'm just glad it was made, and frankly, you should be to."

Isabelle interjected herself in the debate that was going nowhere and said, "Okay, enough of that, we have to get moving,"

"You two, your locks are on timers which will be released by Elena over the Atlantic. So, *adieu*," she said and the four of them went out the front door.

It was like a death knell in the mountain home with the stream noise cutting through the silence. McDonald looked over at Warlock who whose face was tight.

"Well, I was right, but this is not the way it was supposed to end," Martin said quietly, looking straight ahead to the empty living area.

"No, this is not the way any mission of mine has ever ended. I am Security. It was my fault for not frisking the ladies when we first found them. I got their obvious weapons, and they conned me, plain and simple."

"They conned *us*, Warlock. I hadn't a clue that this whole thing was such an international affair. Do you think Atlantica would use the Pittsburgh Aquifer for gaining trading concessions?"

"Of course, they would. I knew about that when I took the assignment. My superior is in Nuevo York, not Pittsburgh. He told me six months ago that the Natural Resources Administration will be operating the Aquifer and that it would become the key to Atlantica's power. What we didn't know is that your search had become an international affair. No one had a clue. It's amazing what you turned up, McDonald. The result is that they're going to screw up our government's leverage. At least we can warn them of what we know. That may help a bit."

"I don't know what I'm going to tell the Administration when we explain what happened. What do you think?"

"The truth, goddamn it, the fucking truth. They will understand when we tell them that UNIS agents, posing as refugees, surprised us and took our prisoners. As I said, it will alert them as to what the UN will be doing in the coming months. Don't forget the Administration was blindsided on this one. We have no choice, McDonald. We'll just have to wait, because there's no way we can get out of this fucking lock mechanism. I really screwed up," Warlock exclaimed. "Before you know it, you'll be going to Paris. But for what you did, you'll still get points. So buck up, I'll have you home by noon."

"Home, my home is in Jamaica, man. My life is in Alleghenia, then Paris, and hopefully Nuevo York. Someday, I'll get back to my home. Someday, I'll be sitting on my favorite beach, sipping a *cerveza*. But not yet, I have a lot to accomplish. I have big plans, Major, and who knows, maybe I'll see that guy Sloan again, somewhere, sometime."

chapter forty

he four were standing beside the Skimmer in the parking lot. The open area that Kurt and Elena had cleared off earlier was wet from water running in rivulets from the quickly warming drifts.

Isabelle was holding her GPS unit. She pushed a series of numbers on the screen. Immediately the crosshairs picked out Fallingwater. She reached in a pocket on her sleeve and pulled out a thin, silver-colored card and depressed the edge with her thumb. A window appeared exposing a keypad, which she tapped and instantly heard a voice.

"Chief, it's Magnus. Glad your safe and coming in. I see your location. Can I come down?"

"Yes, come get us. We have them," Isabelle answered.

"That's good. We came in early this morning and have been hovering, so my ETA should be just shy of five minutes. Will that work for you?" he asked.

"It will. There are four of us. Is that a problem?"

"No, we're good."

"Zoom in on Fallingwater," she said.

"Done."

Isabelle watched the screen and said, "About two hundred yards up from the house, you should see an open area where a Skimmer is located."

"I see it."

"We cleared space beside the Skimmer, so land there. We're ready as soon as you land," she said.

"You having any problem with your captives, Captain?" Magnus asked.

"No, they have been neutralized. I'll fill you in later," Isabelle responded.

"By the way, the boss has a question," Magnus said.

"Do you have the material?"

"I do. Our sources gave it to me last night. It's secured on my person."

"Great job, I'll have that sent back to Paris immediately. Okay, we'll see you shortly. Glad you're coming in. You should be back in Paris in a few hours after our stop in London, as ordered."

"Roger," Isabelle said and closed the unit.

They silently awaited their departure. Kurt looked around this familiar location. His life seemed to be replaying as he stood in the brilliant sun in this tranquil setting. So much had changed. Where once he wavered about leaving, he now was sure this was the right move, especially with Elizabeth Morgan at his side. This woman, in such a short time, had become a powerful influence in his life. Why had he stopped at that particular farm on his journey? Never much a believer in fate, he certainly couldn't rationalize that move. Her mind, persona, attitude, gentle but forceful way, intrigued and then captivated him. They seemed to blend in so many ways, and he knew for certain he didn't want it to end. He knew that she was a sudden, but important new factor in his life. Whatever he did, he wanted her to be with him. Kurt knew that this was a critical time in his life. Above them he heard the craft coming in from the direction of the river.

It came in fast and stopped right over them. It took another minute for it to land in the center of the cleared area. As soon as it settled, the side door opened and a small, narrow-shouldered man in a blue UN uniform stepped down a ladder as it hovered a few feet off the ground.

"Right on time, Captain," he offered.

"No time to waste, Magnus," Isabelle said turning to her three companions. "All aboard, our next stop is a mid-flight rendezvous."

Kurt looked around at the trees, bushes, and fading colors around Fallingwater. He might never be here again. The pilot walked around the perimeter of the landing area, checking the craft as it remained hovering in place. Elizabeth and Elena were the first on board and Kurt followed up the three steps into the craft. Isabelle climbed in behind him into the oblong shaped cabin and took her seat behind the pilot's deck. The pilot looked around the landing spot and came up the steps, slamming shut the door. They all tightened their seat belts, and the pilot asked Isabelle if he could leave. She looked over at Kurt and Elizabeth who were across the aisle. They were looking out the port windows to the trail that led to Fallingwater.

"Take it up, Magnus, and then hover over Fallingwater and hold for a minute. Let them take a last look. This place is important to them," she said.

She glanced over at Kurt and Elizabeth who probably had no idea how critical their work had been. They were smiling at the sight below.

"Thanks for circling over. It's gorgeous, Isabelle," Kurt shouted as he looked below. "This is the way I will remember Fallingwater, proud and beautiful. Elizabeth took some video, so we're okay about leaving," he said.

Then he looked down to the rooftop below and said, "It's all in their hands now to make this great land what they want it to be. For me, it's a whole new ball game, as my dad would always say when change was an absolute."

"You're right," Elizabeth said turning toward Kurt. "For you and for me, the hard part starts. This has been great adventure, but living in a totally new country without the comfort zone of familiarity, that is going to be a test, I think, for both of us," she added.

Isabelle talked into her mouthpiece and almost immediately they flew away from Fallingwater. Kurt looked back down again, and he caught a brief glimpse of the layered home over the stream at a faraway angle. He realized that from any spot, it was a classic. He wondered what Martin McDonald was doing and thinking about at that moment. He was a strange man, but Kurt knew he was driven, goal oriented and that this setback would not deter him from his life objectives. What was unbelievable was that recovering his family history had turned into a confrontation between the UN and Atlantica over water rights.

"There's the Yough down there," Kurt said. "It curves so much, you don't realize that when you're walking alongside it."

At that moment, Elizabeth shouted over the hum inside the cabin, for everyone to look down off to the left of the riverbank. "Can you have him slow down, Isabelle?" she asked.

As the craft slowed to a hover, Elizabeth leaned over Kurt and looked out of the window. Outlined below, surrounded by a rectangle of trees, was her stone farmhouse. The sun broke for a moment in the fast-moving cloud bank. It sparkled off the water. The house sat squat in the middle of a forested area with the outline of a path going down to river. The pilot hovered over the farm, and Elizabeth took in the view as tears slowly ran over her cheeks. The craft stayed aloft over the farmhouse for a minute and then Elizabeth said to Isabelle, "Thank you. That's what I needed, a bit of closure."

Isabelle talked into her mouthpiece, and they took off over the mountains. "I asked Magnus to take this short diversion, but we have to head north to meet our master craft, so hang on."

Kurt and Elizabeth looked at each other as the craft began to accelerate. They didn't talk for a short time after they left the farm, both deep in their own thoughts. Then Kurt said, "Your whole life was down there and from up here it look so peaceful."

"It was peaceful down there," she replied leaning into the small curved backrest. "That's what enchanted me, the absolute peacefulness. What have you got me into, Kurt Sloan? But everything looked about the way we left it. I was surprised that McDonald stopped there, but the man was certainly full of surprises, wasn't he."

"From the day I met him," Kurt answered.

"Looking at the farmhouse, I was thinking I hope they don't tear it down."

"I doubt it. That could be a very productive farm for the government," Kurt replied. "They need organic production sites and that is a perfect one."

They retreated to their thoughts again as the craft soared over the mountains.

Isabelle leaned over from her seat on the narrow aisle separating them and said, "The pilot is on a UN Universal flight pattern. He can deviate a bit before the Atlantica Air Control Service requests he call for a change of course. I realize you are leaving your country, maybe for the last time, so is there anywhere else around here that you would like to see?"

Kurt looked at Elizabeth then tugged at Isabelle's sleeve, who was talking with the pilot. She turned to him.

"Is it possible to fly over the Aquifer System?"

Isabelle looked at him and did not immediately respond.

She turned away and spoke quietly into her mouthpiece. In a few seconds, she looked back and said, "Well, you are in luck. Our master craft will meet us over Lake Erie. Magnus says he can make a slight deviation, but we need to be cautious since this is a high security location. This will be a quick flyover."

chapter forty-one

"This is your skipper, folks. Up ahead you'll be able to see two mountain ridges; Chestnut to your left and Laurel Ridge off to your right. We'll run between them which is near the beginning of the Pittsburgh Aquifer System. You'll also notice we are being approached by three Atlantica patrol craft. Don't be concerned. They monitor and escort all planes in Atlantica air space. We'll fly our adjusted flight pattern until we reach the master ship."

Kurt looked out the window and followed the ridges of the whitened mountain ranges. He remembered his father telling him when he was a young boy of his taking extensive flights over these very ranges when the Aquifer was in its initial development stages. From up here you would never know there was anything underneath these mountains. There were occasional towers, not unlike the abandoned cell phone towers that still covered much of the terrain over the land. He could see off to the northwest a body of water which must be the Cambria Lake Reservoir, one of six reservoirs built in conjunction with the Aquifer. It spread for miles in the distance between the mountain ranges. He was amazed as he looked below at the scope and ingeniousness of the Aquifer, which then took his thoughts to his father. *What a mind,* he thought.

Elizabeth put her hand on his knee and said, "Must be

quite a thrill to know your father's work is finally going to be utilized as it was designed, for all people, because of what you have done."

"Funny you should say that, because I was just thinking about him and what a visionary he was."

"Kurt, I don't know if you've taken time to think this way, but you are right in the middle of one of the most historical events of this century." Elizabeth looked at him and said, "Culture and water, that's it in a nutshell. Cultural differences have divided the world, but water, which is in short supply, may unite it. Water is required by all cultures, all people. Think about what the headline may read a month from now in *Le Monde*. Dateline Paris, A NEGOTIATED SETTLEMENT TO THE ACUTE WATER SHORTAGE FOR THE NORTHERN AMERICAN HEMISPHERE. Historically speaking, that is pretty big stuff. It's quite a tale and will make a great addition to that leather-bound portfolio you have with you. One more thing, as I was talking away just now, I realized that the irony of what you have done may be a blessing in disguise for Atlantica," she said to Kurt.

"Why would that be?"

"Because when they come to an agreement with the UN, they will have gained international recognition as an equal partner in world decisions. That's the way things work in history. Sometimes by accident or the misdirected will of others, a situation becomes beneficial when first thought to be a detriment. I've seen it happen so many times in the past," she said.

Over the intercom came the voice of the pilot. "The master ship is within sight. You'll be on board in five minutes. Your next stop is London. Thanks for flying with me today," he said.

Isabelle leaned over to Kurt and Elizabeth, "Two things I need to tell you as we get ready to leave here. Elena informs me that she has contacted Dr. Alexander and informed him that you gave us the data and that we have another passenger. Ironically, when she told him the passenger's name, he asked me where she was picked up. Elena explained what had happened, and that we had just flown over her farm, he was astounded. It seems he knew Elizabeth's parents and had actually visited the farm many years ago. Anyway, I have been in touch with Paris and we will deliver the data as soon as we arrive."

"The second thing is that Elena will be releasing McDonald and the Major from their situation in approximately a half hour, as soon as we are well over the Atlantic. I think everything is ready for us to leave the Country. I must add that Dr. Alexander wanted me to make sure that you understand that the UN and he, personally, thank you for what you have done. That said, I want to add that you probably don't yet realize how critical your work will be in sorting out this potential conflict," she said as her wide black face opened into a broad smile.

Kurt looked at Elizabeth, reached out and gently clutched her hand, then looked over at Isabelle, "I think we do. In fact, we were just talking about how all the great changes in the world are now concentrated on two factors, culture and water. Down there it's all coming together," Kurt said, looking through the window at the mountain range which lay on top of the Aquifer. He slowly smiled, "There I go again, the idealist is alive and well. All I know at this moment, this present time, is that there will be water for all people and cultures at least in this hemisphere. My dad is a very happy man."

Isabelle said, "He should be, and I'm sure he is also a proud of you." She heard a beep in her earpiece and listened to the message. "We are over Lake Erie," she said, "and we will be connecting to the master ship." Up ahead in the brilliant blue, cloudless sky, the oval-shaped craft hovered in place awaiting their arrival.

"Will people a thousand, even a hundred years from now

remember anything about that bold experiment, the United States of America?" Kurt said.

Elizabeth answered, "Probably not. Oh, some leaders, some events, maybe the Declaration of Independence, the Civil War, the World Wars, the Terrorist War, and the Constitutional Convention of 2038, but that may be all they remember."

"You're probably right, so we have to be the catalyst for an accurate recording of all that has happened. That's what I've been doing, and it's what you and I can do together," Kurt said, patting the portfolio he had pulled from his backpack.

"Kurt, you have your theme. The story must be written of idealism at its best and worst of times. You must write this and I will help you. I want to help you. I insist on helping you."

Kurt responded, "I already have a title. An author wrote an article he called the prevalent attitude, the malaise of the country prior to its end, a cancer of complacency. I have never forgotten that line and that's my title, A CANCER OF COMPLACENCY."

THE END

addendum

In this novel there is one copyright reference and two American landmarks and treasures:

1) Reference is made to a classic work of T.S. Eliot, *Four Quartets* and a particular poem, "Burnt Norton." Harcourt, Inc.

2) Fallingwater, an American treasure, is a National Trust for Historic Preservation site. It is also a Commonwealth Treasure of the Commonwealth of Pennsylvania. It is entrusted to the Western Pennsylvania Conservancy, established 1932.

3) The Great Allegheny Passage is a newly opened trail that is one of the most spectacular hiking and biking trails in the country that covers 150 miles between Pittsburgh, PA, and Cumberland, MD, where it joins the C&O Tow Path 184.5 miles to Washington, DC.

David Borland
Author, 2050

GLOSSARY OF TERMS IN 2050

Africano—citizens of African descent
Alleghenia—western state of Atlantica
Anglo – citizens of Anglo/European descent
Atlantica—new country in northeast
Datafile—personal data unit
Heliocraft—small, solar-powered helicopter
InfoNetwork—citizen data network
Jet Craft—air-powered water craft
Latino—citizens of Latin American descent
Nuevo York—capital of Atlantica (old New York)
Palm phone—personal call unit
Publican—low-level security officer
Skimmer—air-propelled low-flying aircraft
Solarcom unit—personal portable solar generator
Telcom—phone/video transmitter
Topos—topographical scans of locations
Tram—overhead rail transit vehicle
Voicescan—voice security ID
World Net—world media network

CPSIA information can be obtained at www.ICGtesting.com
Printed in the USA
LVOW13*0946091113

360659LV00002B/111/A